IHIMAERA

HIS BEST STORIES

ALSO IN THE ANNIVERSARY COLLECTION

POUNAMU POUNAMU (NEW EDITION 2003)

THE WHALE RIDER (INTERNATIONAL EDITION 2003)

WHANAU II (2004)

TANGI (NEW EDITION FORTHCOMING)

ALSO BY WITI IHIMAERA, PUBLISHED BY REED

POUNAMU POUNAMU (1972)

TANGI (1973)

WHANAU (1974)

THE NEW NET GOES FISHING (1976)

INTO THE WORLD OF LIGHT (ED) (1984)

TE AO MARAMA (ED, VOLS 1–5) (1989–1995)

THE MATRIARCH (1986)

THE WHALE RIDER (1987, MADE INTO AN AWARD-WINNING FILM 2002)

LEGENDARY LAND (1994)

LAND SEA SKY (1994)

NIGHTS IN THE GARDENS OF SPAIN (1995)

KINGFISHER COME HOME (1995)

WHERE'S WAARI? (ED) (2000)

TE ATA: MAORI ART OF THE EAST COAST (ED) (2002)

IHIMAERA

HIS BEST STORIES

WITI IHIMAERA

REED

Reed Publishing
Te Karuhi tā tāpui o Reed (Aotearoa) (NZ) Ltd

Established in 1907, Reed is New Zealand's largest
book publisher, with over 300 titles in print.

For details on all these books visit our website:
www.reed.co.nz

THE ANNIVERSARY COLLECTION

Celebrating 30 years of publishing partnership between
Witi Ihimaera and Reed Publishing

Published by Reed Books, a division of Reed Publishing (NZ) Ltd, 39 Rawene Rd, Birkenhead, Auckland.
Associated companies, branches and representatives throughout the world.

ISBN 0 7900 0900 5

First published 2003
Reprinted 2003, 2004

Design by Christine Hansen

Printed in New Zealand

CONTENTS

A GAME OF CARDS 10

THE SEAHORSE AND THE REEF 18

THE HALCYON SUMMER 22

TENT ON THE HOME GROUND 51

MASQUES AND ROSES 58

THE BOY WITH THE CAMERA 63

A NEW YEAR'S STORY 70

BIG BROTHER, LITTLE SISTER 92

TRUTH OF THE MATTER 103

DUSTBINS 116

THIS LIFE IS WEARY 128

THE AFFECTIONATE KIDNAPPERS 138

THE WASHERWOMAN'S CHILDREN 143

WIWI 156

SHORT FEATURES 158

WHO ARE YOU TAKING TO THE SCHOOL DANCE, DARLING? 162

A HISTORY OF NEW ZEALAND THROUGH SELECTED TEXTS 167

LIFE AS IT REALLY IS 173

FALLING 181

A 60 SECOND STORY 186

LIFE AND DEATH IN CALCUTTA 187

SOMEONE IS LOOKING AT ME 191

BEGINNING OF THE TOURNAMENT 200

GOING TO THE HEIGHTS OF ABRAHAM 208

Whaia te iti kahurangi
Ki te tuohu koe, me tuohu
Ki te maunga teitei

E nga rangatira ma, tena koutou katoa.

Thirty years is a long career as a writer, especially since it was never something I thought of doing. In all respects my life has been a magnificent accident, and I often have the suspicion that it was supposed to happen to somebody else. However, this life did happen, and it happened to me, and in the process it turned me into a working artist.

My life has been devoted to the pursuit of excellence, equity and justice and I have tried to find these in every aspect — whether it be as a good son, brother, husband, lover, parent, friend or colleague — in all the careers I have had. Literature has become an extension of these pursuits, and it has given me the humbling opportunity to combine my passionate political beliefs as a Maori with my aesthetic aims as a man who always finishes what he starts and always does the best he can with what gifts he has. I like to think I articulate the concerns of the iwi and the times we live in. I constantly address the question, 'What really matters?', and I hope that I have been able to provide some of the answers not just for now, but for the ever-evolving future. This doesn't mean I'm always right. I'm partisan about being Maori and will continue to be so. If necessary, I will be the last man standing.

I owe so many people for this luminous journey. I thank all of you who have touched me and given me strength. This Anniversary Collection, which also celebrates 30 years with Reed Publishing, is my thank you to you all.

Na reira, ka nui te aroha ki a koutou.

Pursue the highest levels of attainment
If you must bow your head, let it be only
To the highest mountain.

A GAME OF CARDS

If ever I had a signature story, it would have to be 'A Game of Cards'. It is the opening story of my first book, *Pounamu Pounamu*, 1972, and, ever since, it's been my calling card.

Pounamu Pounamu is an alternative, indigenous text. It tells stories about Maori by a Maori within settings that are Maori and with characters who are central to that setting — heroes, heroines and villains — rather than supporting players or sidekick. In the book I began to privilege the Maori story and to write narratives that are driven from a Maori kaupapa.

'A Game of Cards' introduces characters who are representative of my fiction: a young male narrator, an iwi he belongs to and, above all, matriarchal women who represent the strength of the tribe and the means by which its values are passed from one generation to the next. In this case, the woman is Miro, based on my Nani Mini who was my Dad's beloved adoptive sister.

The story also introduces my main themes of aroha, whanaungatanga and manaakitanga — love, acknowledging kin and tribal relationships and supporting Maori identity. It further introduces Waituhi as the location for most of my fiction. William Faulkner had his Yoknapatawpha County; I have my Waituhi Valley.

I remember the agony I went through trying to figure out whether it was better to use a fictional name, like Faulkner did. It was the same Nani Mini who scolded me by saying, 'Are you ashamed of us? Are you ashamed of Waituhi?' I kept the name, Waituhi, but forgot to change Miro back to Nani Mini's name before the story was published. It didn't seem to matter: people from home immediately knew Miro was Nani Mini. Incidentally, Nani Mini's house is still standing. If you go to Takitimu marae and look down at the road, Nani's house is the one to the left of the lane.

A GAME OF CARDS

The train pulled into the station. For a moment there was confusion: a voice blaring over the loudspeaker system, people getting off the train, the bustling and shoving of the crowd on the platform.

Then, there was Dad, waiting for me. We hugged each other; we hadn't seen each other for a long time. But I could tell something was wrong.

'Your Nani Miro,' he said. 'She's very sick.'

Among all my kuia, Nani Miro was the one I loved most. It wasn't one way either: everybody used to say I was her favourite mokopuna, and that she loved me more than her own children who'd grown up and had kids of their own. She lived down the road from us next to Rongopai meeting house in the old homestead which everybody in Waituhi called 'Miro's Museum' because it housed the prized possessions of the whanau — the feather cloaks, greenstone ornaments, and the shields and trophies which Waituhi had won in sports and culture tournaments. As children we always used to think she was rich because she owned the most shares in what remained of our tribal land. We wondered why she didn't buy a newer, more modern house. But Nani wasn't thinking of moving.

'Anyway,' she used to say, 'what with all my haddit kids and their haddit kids and all this haddit whanau being broke all the time and asking me for money, what have I got left to buy a new house with?'

The truth was, that Nani liked her old homestead just as it was and didn't really care about money either.

'Who needs it?' she used to ask. 'What you think I had all my kids for, eh? What you think I have all my mokopuna for! To look after me, I'm not dumb!'

Then she would laugh to herself. But it wasn't true, really, because her family would send their kids to her place when they were broke and she looked after them!

She liked her mokopuna, but not for too long. She'd ring up their parents and say:

'When you coming to pick up your hoha kids! They're wrecking the place!'

I used to like going to Nani's place with the rest of my cousins. In particular, I looked forward to Saturdays because that's when all the women would take the day off, and turn up at Nani's place to play cards. Nani loved all card games — five hundred, poker, canasta, pontoon, whist, hearts, euchre — you name it, she could play it.

The sitting room would be crowded with the women. There they'd be, dressed in their best clothes, sitting at various tables among the sports trophies and photographs, the carvings and greenstone. In those days, Maori used to be heavy smokers, so the women would all be puffing clouds of smoke, laughing and joking and gossiping about who was pregnant — and relishing all the juicy bits too.

Nani Miro was always at what was called 'the top table', reserved for the best players. Both she and Mrs Heta were the unrivalled champions and when it came to cards Mrs Heta, whose first name was Maka, was both Nani's best friend and worst enemy.

'You ready to be taken down?' Mrs Heta would ask. 'Oh, the cards are really talking to me today.'

'Is that so, Maka?' Nani would answer. 'We'll have to see about that, won't we?'

The women would begin to play cards. No doubt about it: Nani Miro and Mrs Heta were the queens of the game. They also happened, whenever they didn't have the right cards, to be the biggest cheats I ever saw.

Mrs Heta would cough and reach for a hanky while slyly slipping a card she wanted from beneath her dress. You never saw anybody reneging as much as she did in five hundred — and expecting to get away with it! But her greatest asset was her eyes which were big and googly. One eye would look straight ahead while the other swivelled around, having a look at the cards in the hands of the women sitting next to her.

'Eeee! You cheat,' Nani would say. 'You just keep your eyes to yourself, Maka tiko bum.'

Mrs Heta would look at Nani, highly offended. Then she would sniff and say, 'You the cheat yourself, Miro Mananui. I saw you sneaking that ace from the bottom of the pack.'

'How come you know I got an ace, Maka?' Nani would say. 'I know you! You dealt this hand, and you stuck that ace down there for yourself, you cheat! Well, ana! I got it now! So take that!' She would slap down her hand. 'Sweet, eh?' she would laugh. 'Good? Kapai?' Sometimes she would do a little hula, making her victory sweeter.

'Eeee, Miro!' Mrs Heta would reply. 'Well, I got a good hand too!'

And she would slap her hand down too and bellow with laughter.

'Take that!'

And always they would squabble. I often wondered how they ever remained friends. The names they called each other!

Sometimes, I would go and see Nani Miro when she was by herself, playing patience. That was her game whenever there was nobody around to play with her. And still she cheated! I'd watch her hands fumbling across the cards. I'd hear her say, 'Oops,' as she turned up a jack or queen she needed, and I'd join her laugh of triumph: 'See, mokopuna? I'm too good for this game!'

Nani used to try to teach me some of the games, but I wasn't very interested.

'How are you going to do good things for your people if you can't concentrate?' she would ask. 'Here I am, counting on you to get a good education so that you can get the rest of our land back and you're just hopeless, he hoha koe —'

Not only that, but I didn't yell and shout at her like the women did. She liked the bickering.

'Aue,' she would sigh. Then she'd look at me, offer words of wisdom that didn't make sense like, 'Don't let me down,' or 'If you can't beat the Pakeha one way remember that all's fair in love — or cards,' and deal out the cards in the only game I ever knew how to play.

'Snap!' I would yell as she let me win.

Now, my kuia was sick.

I went to see Nani Miro that afternoon after I'd dropped my suitcase at home. The koroua, Nani Tama, her long-suffering husband, opened the door. We embraced and he began to weep on my shoulder.

'You talk to her, moko,' he said. 'She walked out of the hospital yesterday. She should go back there. It's no use me trying to persuade her; she's still as stubborn as, never listened to anything I say. But you —'

'I'll do my best,' I answered.

I walked down the hallway, past the sitting room to Nani Miro's bedroom. The room had a strange antiseptic smell. The window was open. Sunlight shone brightly on the big bed in the middle of the room. Underneath the bed was a big chamber pot, yellow with urine.

Nani Miro was lying in bed. Her pillow was flecked with small spots of blood where she had been coughing. She was so old looking. Her eyes were closed, her face was very grey, and her body was so thin, seeming to be all bones. Even when I was a child she must have been old, but I had never realised it. She must have been over seventy now. In that big bed, she looked like a tiny wrinkled doll.

Then I noticed the lipstick. Hmmn.

'You can wake up now, Nani,' I said sarcastically.

She moaned. A long, hoarse sigh grew on her lips. Her eyelids fluttered, and she looked at me with blank eyes . . . and then tears began to roll down her cheeks.

She took me by surprise. 'Don't cry, kui,' I said. 'I'm sorry. I'm here.'

But she wouldn't stop. I sat beside her on the bed and she lifted her hands to me. 'Haere mai, mokopuna. Haere mai. Mmm. Mmm.'

I bent within her arms and we pressed noses. Then she started to shake with mirth and slapped me hard.

'Snap!' she said.

She started to laugh and laugh and I was almost persuaded she was her own self. But I knew she wasn't. Why do people you love grow old so suddenly?

'What a haddit mokopuna you are,' she grumbled, sitting up in the bed. 'It's only when I'm just about in my grave that you come to see me.'

'I couldn't see you last time I was home,' I explained. 'I was too busy.'

'There's no such thing as being too busy to see your kuia,' Nani reproved. 'Next time, make time. If you don't I'll cut you out of my will. I'll give it all to Willie Jones, what do you think of that?'

'Go right ahead,' I answered. 'Willie will need every cent to pay his fines so he doesn't go to jail.'

Willie was my cousin. When I was growing up I always thought that I was the only one Nani Miro talked to about getting an education. Ha, it was Willie who told me she talked to everybody, but I was the only one to take her seriously. Nani liked to spread her bets. That way, one of her cards was bound to do the trick.

'Anyhow,' I continued, 'I heard Maka cleaned you out in your last game of poker!'

'Who told you that?' Nani scoffed. 'You know, now that she's old she's gone colour blind. Can't tell a heart from a spade.'

She gave a big, triumphant grin. She was my Nani again. The Nani I knew.

We talked for a long time. She wanted to know how I was getting on at university in Wellington. I told her I was doing really well with my studies, which was a lie, because I was seriously brainless and all the ambitions she held for me were rapidly going down the drain. She asked if I had a girlfriend so I made up more lies about who I was seeing and how pretty she was.

'You teka,' she said. 'Who'd want to have you!'

I brought up the subject of her returning to hospital.

'Tama's been talking to you,' she grumbled. 'Well, this is why I came home —'

She showed me all her injection needles and pills.

'I didn't like all those strange nurses looking at my bum when they gave me those injections. I was so sick, mokopuna, I couldn't even go to the lav. Better for Tama to give me my injections. Better for me to wet my own bed and not their hospital bed.'

I played the piano for Nani. She loved *Me he manu rere* so I played it for her and we had a sing-along. Afterwards, she held my hands tightly in hers as if she didn't want to let me go, and stared deep into my eyes.

'It's always the women who look after the land,' she said, 'but who will do it after I am gone?'

When I finally left her I told her I would come back in the morning.

But that night the koroua, Nani Tama, rang up. Dad answered the telephone and woke me.

'Your whaea, Nani Miro, she's dying.'

We all rushed to Nani Miro's house. It was already crowded with the other Waituhi families: the Tamateas, Tuparas, Waitaikis, everybody. All of Nani Miro's mates were crowded close around her bed. Among them was Nani's rival, Mrs Heta. Nani was lying very still. Then she looked up, saw Mrs Heta and whispered to her:

'Maka . . . Maka tiko bum . . . I want a game of cards.'

A pack of cards was found. Everyone sprang into action. The old ladies sat on the bed, began to gossip and, as usual, puff their clouds of smoke. Nani Tama suggested a game of poker in the living room, so all the men trooped in there to do some serious gambling. Wherever there was a table — in the kitchen, on the verandah, anywhere, games of cards started up. The kids played snap in the other bedrooms and, as the night progressed, so did the games, the laughter, the aroha. The house overflowed with card players, even onto the lawn outside Nani's window.

Suddenly, there was a commotion from Nani's bedroom. We all looked to see what was happening. The women had been betting on who would win the best of ten games and Nani and Mrs Heta were neck and neck — and Mrs Heta was squabbling with Nani because it was Nani's turn to deal.

'Eee, Miro,' Mrs Heta said, 'don't think that just because you can deal fast I'm not on to your tricks.'

'Quit moaning and start playing,' Nani answered. 'Well?'

'Dealing all the good cards to yourself,' Mrs Heta muttered. 'You cheat, Miro.' And she made her googly eye reach far over to see Nani's cards.

'You think you can see, Maka tiko bum?' Nani coughed. 'You think you're going to win this hand, eh? Well, eat your heart out and take that!'

She slammed down a full house.

The other women goggled at the cards. Mrs Heta looked at her own cards. She did a swift calculation and yelled:

'Eee! You cheat, Miro! I got two aces in my hand already! Only four in the pack. How come you got three aces in your hand?'

Everybody laughed. Nani and Mrs Heta started squabbling as they always did, pointing at each other and saying:

'You the cheat, not me!'

And Nani Miro said:

'I saw you, Maka tiko bum, I saw you sneaking that card from under the blanket.'

She began to laugh. Her eyes streamed with tears.

While she was laughing, she died.

Everybody was silent. Then Mrs Heta took the cards from Nani's hands and kissed her.

'You the cheat, Miro,' she whispered. 'You the cheat yourself —'

Ma wai ra e taurima
E te marae i waho nei?

We buried Nani Miro on the hill with the rest of her family. During her tangi, Mrs Heta played patience with Nani, spreading the cards across the casket.

Later in the year, Mrs Heta, she died too. She was buried right next to Nani so that they could keep on playing cards.

I bet you they're still squabbling up there.

'Eee! You cheat Miro!'

'You the cheat, Maka tiko bum. You, you the cheat.'

THE SEAHORSE AND THE REEF

THE HALCYON SUMMER

A TENT ON THE HOME GROUND

Here are three more stories about Maori, all from the same pastoral period of *Pounamu Pounamu*. All of them acknowledge the alternative histories of Maori, the histories that lie behind what you see, the unseen and unspoken rather than the seen and spoken.

'The Seahorse and the Reef' is another of those stories that bears my signature, one that people say of it, 'That's an Ihimaera.' People still stop me on the street to say 'I really liked the story about the seahorse.'

I've wrestled with 'The Halcyon Summer' through three versions. Although the central story deals nostalgically with rural Maori life and those universal values of aroha, whanaungatanga and manaakitanga, you have to look at the margins to see what was really happening to Maori during the 1970s, when we were endeavouring to hold on to our land, language and culture — our tino rangatiratanga. Other Maori writers also told what they saw — Rore Hapipi, Patricia Grace, Hone Tuwhare, Arapera Blank, J.C. Sturm, Katerina Mataira and Syd Mead are among them. They are a distinguished academy with stories to be treasured.

'Tent on the Home Ground' is from my second collection of short stories, *The New Net Goes Fishing* (1977), and deals with a time when Maori took their protests to the very heart of New Zealand's governance, Parliament.

Originally, I had planned a trilogy: *Pounamu Pounamu* begins the series by focusing on the exclusive presentation of Maori in a rural setting during the 1950s; Pakeha have no place in this setting. By contrast, *The New Net Goes Fishing* looked at the first generation of Maori living in an urban setting ten years later in the 1960s; the stories are explicitly political, dealing with the engagement of Maori with Pakeha, Pakeha life and Waitangi issues. The third collection, *Kingfisher Come Home*, was supposed to follow and to cover the 1970s, except that I placed an embargo on my work and stopped writing from 1976 to 1986, the year I came back with my novel, *The Matriarch*. I've often wondered what stories I would have written in those 'lost years', and only managed to pull some of the fragments and plot lines together into some semblance of what the third book was supposed to be some twenty years later; *Kingfisher Come Home* finally completed the trilogy when it was published in 1995.

Together, the three collections provide interrelated stories spanning thirty years of Maori experience, the rural to urban migration of Maori and the creation of postcolonial New Zealand.

Writing, too, is a Waitangi issue.

THE SEAHORSE AND THE REEF

S ometimes through the soft green water and drifting seaweed of my dreams I see the seahorse again. Delicate and fragile it comes to me, shimmering and luminous with light. And I remember the reef.

The reef was just outside the town where my family lived. That was a long time ago, when I was a boy, before I came to this southern city. It was where all our relatives and friends went every weekend in summer to dive for kai moana. The reef was the home of much kai moana — paua, pipi, kina, mussels, pupu and many other shellfish. It was the home too of other fish like flounder and octopus. It teemed with life and food. It gave its bounty to us. It was good to us.

And it was where the seahorse lived.

At that time, our family lived in a small wooden house on the fringe of the industrial area. On Sundays, my father would watch out the window and see our relatives passing by on their old trucks and cars or bikes with their sugarbags and nets, their flippers and goggles, shouting and waving on their way to the reef. They came from the pa — in those days it was not surrounded by expanding suburbia — and they would sing out to Dad:

'Hey, Rongo! Come on! Good day for kai moana today!'

Dad would sigh and start to moan and fidget. The lunch dishes had to be washed, the lawn had to be cut, and my mother probably would want him to do other things round the house.

But after a while, a gleam would come into his eyes.

'Hey, Huia!' he would shout to Mum. 'Those kina are calling out loud to me today!'

'So are these dishes,' she would answer.

'Well, Mum!' Dad would call again. 'Those paua are just waiting for me to come to them today!'

'That lawn's been waiting even longer,' Mum would answer.

Dad would pretend not to hear her. 'Pae kare, dear! How'd you like a feed of mussels today!'

'I'd like it better if you fixed the fence,' she would growl.

So Dad would just wiggle his toes and act sad for her. 'Okay, Huia. But those pipi are going to miss us today!'

Dad was cunning. He knew Mum loved her feed of pipi. And sure enough she would answer him:

'What we waiting for! Can't disappoint those pipi today!' Then she would shout to us to get into our bathing clothes, grab some sugarbags, don't forget some knives and take your time but *hurry up*! And off we would go to the reef on our truck.

If it was a sunny day the reef would already be crowded with other people searching for kai moana. There they'd be, dotting the water with their sacks and flax kits. They would wave and shout to us and we would hurry to join them, pulling on our shoes, grabbing our sugarbags and running down to the sea.

'Don't you kids come too far out!' Dad would yell. He would already be way ahead of us, sack clutched in one hand and a knife in the other. He used the knife to prise the paua from the reef because if you weren't quick enough they held onto the rocks really tight.

Sometimes, Dad would put on a diving mask. It made it easier for him to see underwater.

As for Mum, she liked nothing better than to wade out to where some of the women of the pa were gathered. Then she could korero with them while she was looking for seafood. All the long afternoon those women would bend to the task, their dresses ballooning above the water, and talk and talk and talk and *talk*!

For both Mum and Dad, much of the fun of going to the reef was because they could be with their friends and whanau. It was a good time for being family again and for enjoying our tribal ways.

My sisters and me, we made straight for a special place on the reef that we liked to call 'ours'. It was where the pupu — or winkles as some call them — crawled. We called the special place our pupu pool.

The pool was very long but not very deep. Just as well because Mere, my youngest sister then, would have been drowned, she was so short! As for me, the water came only waist high. The rock surrounding the pool was fringed with long waving seaweed. Small transparent fish swam among the waving leaves and little crabs scurried across the dark floor. The many pupu glided calmly along the sides of the pool. Once, a starfish inched its way into a dark crack.

It was in that pool we discovered the seahorse, magical and serene, shimmering among the red kelp and riding the swirls of the sea's current.

My sisters and I, we wanted to take it home.

'If you take it from the sea it will die,' Dad told us. 'Leave it here in its own home for the sea gives it life and beauty.'

Dad told us that we must always treat the sea with love, with aroha. 'Kids, you must take from the sea only the kai you need and only the amount you need to please your bellies. If you take more, then it is waste. There is no need to waste the food of the sea. Best to leave it there for when you need it next time. The sea is good to us, it gives us kai moana to eat. It is a food basket. As long as we respect it, it will continue to feed us. If, in your search for shellfish, you lift a stone from its lap, return the stone to where it was. Try not to break pieces of the reef for it is the home of many kai moana. And do not leave litter behind you when you leave the sea.' Dad taught us to respect the sea and to have reverence for the life contained in its waters. As we collected shellfish we would remember his words. Whenever we saw the seahorse shimmering behind a curtain of kelp, we felt glad we'd left it in the pool to continue to delight us.

As soon as we filled our sugarbags we would return to the beach. We played together with other kids while waiting for our parents to return from the outer reef. One by one they would arrive: the women still talking, the men carrying their sacks over their shoulders. On the beach we would laugh and talk and share the kai moana between different families. With sharing there was little waste. We would be happy with each other unless a stranger intervened with his camera or curious amusement. Then we would say goodbye to one another while the sea whispered and gently surged into the coming of darkness.

'See you next weekend,' we would say.

One weekend we went again to the reef. We were in a happy mood. The sun was shining and skipping its beams like bright stones across the water.

But when we arrived at the beach the sea was empty of the family. No people dotted the reef with their sacks. No calls of welcome drifted across the rippling waves.

Dad frowned. He looked ahead to where our friends and whanau were clustered in a large lost group on the sand. All of them were looking to the reef, their faces etched by the sun with impassiveness.

'Something's wrong,' Dad said. He stopped the truck. We walked with him towards the others of our people. They were silent. 'The water too cold?' Dad tried to joke.

Nobody answered him. 'Is there a shark out there?' Dad asked again.

Again there was silence. Then someone pointed to a sign.

'It must have been put up last night,' a man told Dad.

Dad elbowed his way through the crowd to read it.

'Dad, what does it say?' I asked.

His fists were clenched and his eyes were angry. He said one word, explosive and shattering the silence, disturbing the gulls to scream and clatter about us.

'Rongo,' Mum reproved him.

'First the land and now our food,' Dad said to her.

'What does it say?' I asked again.

His fists unclenched and his eyes became sad. 'It says that it is dangerous to take seafood from the reef, son.'

'Why, Dad?'

'The sea is polluted, son. If we eat the seafood, we may get sick.'

My sisters and I were silent for a while. 'No more pupu, Dad?'

'No more, kids.'

I clutched his arm frantically. 'And the seahorse, Dad? The seahorse, will it be all right?'

But he did not seem to hear me.

We walked back to the truck. Behind us, an old woman began to cry out a tangi to the reef. It was a very sad song for such a beautiful day. 'Aue . . . Aue . . .'

With the rest of the iwi, we bowed our heads. While she was singing, the sea boiled yellow with effluent issuing from a pipe on the seabed. The stain curled like fingers around the reef.

Then the song was finished. Dad looked out to the reef and called to it in a clear voice.

'Sea, we have been unkind to you. We have poisoned the land and now we feed our poison into your waters. We have lost our aroha for you and our respect for your life. Forgive us, friend.'

He started the truck. We turned homeward.

In my mind I caught a sudden vision of many pupu crawling among polluted rocks. I saw a starfish encrusted with ugliness.

And flashing through dead waving seaweed was a beautiful seahorse, fragile and dream-like, searching frantically for clean and crystal waters.

THE HALCYON SUMMER

Once there was a nest, floating on the sea at summer solstice, and happy voices to charm the wind. The nest is gone now, drifting away on the tides. But somewhere, somewhere must surely float scattered straws, even just a single straw, which I may light upon.

1

It was the year that Sir Apirana Ngata died. That summer the children's parents decided to go to the Empire games in Auckland. Tama was the eldest — an important eleven-year-old — and had two sisters, Kara and Mere. It was decided that the children would stay with their great-aunt, Nani Puti, while their parents were away.

'What about the land troubles?' their father asked their mother.

'The kids will be all right,' their mother answered.

The children had never been to Nani Puti's — all they knew was that it was way up the Coast somewhere, past Ruatoria.

'I'm coming with you,' Tama said to his father.

'No, you have to look after your sisters,' his mother responded.

'Then *you* go with them,' he answered.

He tried to pinch her but she only pushed him away. 'Just as well you're going up there,' she laughed. 'Nani Puti will sort you out.' But as a bribe — only if they were good children, mind — his mother said she would bring back some toys: a red clockwork train for Tama and a doll each for Kara and Mere. That decided the matter.

One morning, while the children were still asleep, their mother got up and packed a small brown suitcase with the clothes she thought they would need: a few shirts, shorts and a pair of sandals for Tama and some cotton frocks for his sisters.

'You kids won't need much,' she said. 'It's summer and it gets hot at Nani's place. Most of the kids up there run around with no clothes on anyway.'

At that remark the children started to kick up a big fuss because they were very shy and didn't relish the idea of showing their bottoms and you-know-whats to strangers.

'Oh, don't be silly,' their mother told them. 'You won't have to take your clothes off if you don't want to.'

Tama wasn't too sure about that either.

The children had to take a nap in the morning — they always took a nap if they were going anywhere, even to the two o'clock pictures at the Majestic. But they couldn't sleep. The thought of being deserted by their parents, and of being taken against their will to a strange relative's place in the strange country, frightened them.

When their mother found them awake she was very cross. 'It's about time you got to know your relatives,' she said. 'You kids are growing up proper little Pakehas. And your Nani is always asking me if she's ever going to see you before she dies. Don't you want to see her?'

Tama was not feeling very respectful and would have answered 'No,' if he'd been able to get away with it. This Nani sounded alarming — she was very old for one thing, being sixty, and had white hair and tattoos on her chin. How she ever managed to get married to Uncle Pani and have twelve children was beyond his comprehension. Not only that, but the whole family had names longer than Tama's mother, which was Turitumanareti something-or-other, and they spoke only Maori. How would he be able to talk to them? Thank goodness he had been to Scouts, and Kara had learned some sign language from Janet, the Pakeha girl next door, who was a Brownie. But Tama still didn't like the idea of going — it was all Maoris up the Coast, no Pakehas, and he and his sisters were used to Pakehas. Furthermore, Maoris wore only grass skirts and probably never even wore pyjamas to bed, and he knew that was rude.

'You kids are going and that's it,' their mother said. 'Nani Puti is expecting you.'

At that, the children knew their fate was sealed, because it was impolite not to go to someone's place when they were expecting you; just like the time when Allan had invited Tama to his birthday party and his mother got cross when he hadn't turned up.

So after their nap the children's father put their suitcases in the car and yelled out to them to hurry up as he didn't have all day — both he and their mother acted as if they couldn't wait to get rid of the children. Mere started to cry and was given a lolly. Tama and Kara told their mother not to forget the toys. Then the children all hopped in the front with their father and waved.

'Goodbye, Mummy.' They hoped that she would change her mind and take them up to Auckland too — but she didn't. Instead she fluttered her hand.

'Look after your sisters,' she cried out to Tama, and went into the house.

Tama wondered if he would ever see her again.

The children slept most of the way to Nani's place. The heat from the Ford always made them sleepy. But most of all they hoped that when they woke up they'd find that leaving home had just been a bad dream. It wasn't a dream though, because every now and then Tama would make a small crack in his eyes and look out and watch as Gisborne went past, then Wainui, and then Whangara. At Tolaga Bay their father stopped to refill the car with petrol. He bought some orange penny suckers for Tama and Kara because they had pointed out that Mere had been given one. At the shop Tama saw a newspaper billboard: *Trouble Deepens On The Coast: Arson Suspected*. For a while after that they sat quietly licking their suckers and watching the hills ahead. Then Tama realised that Mere had been given another sucker at Tolaga Bay and that wasn't fair either because it meant that she had had two and he and Kara had only had one. But their father wouldn't stop the car again. He said it was a long way to Nani's place and he was in a hurry.

Sometimes the children sang songs because their father liked them singing as he was driving. He said it helped keep him awake. The children stopped singing, but their father remained wide awake. It seemed as if years went past before they reached Tokomaru Bay. That was the furthest away from Gisborne they had ever been. They watched silently as the township slid past and they fell off the edge of the world.

The children must have been asleep for a long time — Tama having his usual dream about being chased by a giant green caterpillar — because when the car gave a big bump it was night.

'Where are we, Daddy?' Tama asked.

'Almost at Nani's place,' he answered. 'Hop out and open the gate.'

Tama peered out and saw the gate like a big white X. The gate didn't have a latch, just a piece of wire wound round and round a batten, but he managed to get it untangled and the gate swung open. When he returned to the car Kara and Mere were awake, and they all sat clutching each other and watching the headlights bobbing along the rough muddy track like a drunken man. Then all of a sudden Mere screamed. The track had disappeared and the car was at the edge of a cliff. Far below the sea thundered against the rocks, white-tipped and angry — hiss, roar, crash, *boom* — and on a small spit of sand shone the lights of Nani's place.

'Here we are,' their father said.

Mere started to cry again.

'Oooh, don't leave us here, Daddy,' Kara said.

'Bob, is that you?' a voice yelled, using their father's European name.

Their father yelled back.

'Hang on a minute,' the voice said.

The children looked down to the house and saw a man putting on his gumboots in the light of the doorway. He shouted in a strange language and a smaller shadow appeared from inside with a tilley lamp. The man took the lamp, and the children watched, mesmerised, as it glided along the beach and started to climb the cliff. They heard the man huffing and puffing and swearing when he slipped, and they clutched each other even tighter because he sounded just like the fee-fi-fo-fum man. Then he was there and although he didn't look like a giant, you could never tell. With him were some other children wearing pyjamas tucked into shoes — and one of the boys must have had two left feet.

'Tena koe, Bob,' the man said.

He shook their father's hand and, when Tama gravely extended his, shook that too.

'Here, give that suitcase to Albert,' he said.

But Tama shook his head. He didn't want to give over their clothes, just in case — the clothes might get thrown away and, with only one set of clothes left, what would they wear on washing day? The man laughed.

'Okay, boy,' he said. 'Well, let's all go down to the whare. Your Nani's been waiting for you all day.'

The children followed the man down the cliff, just like little billygoats trying to get over the bridge before the troll got them. The man looked at them and he and their father laughed. So did the other children — and Tama knew that they thought he and his sisters were sissies. Tama wanted to box them all.

They reached the whare. Tama bent down to take off his shoes.

'E tama!' the man said. 'Leave them on!'

25

THE HALCYON SUMMER

But Tama shook his head vigorously — he knew that Maoris were like people from Japan and taking your shoes off was a sacred custom.

Suddenly the light seemed to go out and a big mountain was standing there.

'Tena koutou, mokopuna,' Nani Puti said. She couldn't have seen Tama's outstretched hand because she grabbed him tight and squashed him against her and kissed him all funny because she hadn't put her teeth in. She held him away so as to get a good look, and mumbled something in Maori and English.

'You kids look just like June,' she said, referring to their mother's European name.

She pressed noses with their father — which Tama knew was the way Maoris kissed, just like the Eskimos — and then began to growl because they had arrived so late.

'Only ghosts arrive at night,' she said.

Ghosts? But she must have forgiven their father because she was soon speaking flat out in Maori and giving him playful smacks.

Tama observed Nani Puti carefully. She wasn't exactly the oldest woman he had ever seen but she must have come close. Her hair was certainly as white as he had expected. As for the moko, it was rather pretty really once you realised that it was supposed to be there and not to be rubbed off every night. Nani Puti must have known Tama was staring, because suddenly she stared right back, crossed her eyes and did a pukana. Kara got alarmed — even more so when Nani Puti mumbled, 'You kids are too skinny. Doesn't June feed these kids, Bob? We'll soon put the beef on them.'

Kara stared at the big black pot on the open fire. She had visions of herself sitting in it with an apple in her mouth just to sweeten her up. But then one of the girls went to the pot, opened the lid, and the pot was already full of stew.

Nani Puti gave a blessing on the food, and the children sat with their father eating the stew. They hadn't realised how hungry they were and ate everything — potatoes, mutton chops and some funny stuff which was seaweed.

'May I have a knife and fork please?' Tama asked.

The other children laughed out loud at his accent and, when he started to eat, copied his movements. They were mocking him, and Tama didn't like that. What embarrassed him most, though, was that his father forgot his manners and started eating with his fingers. Tama well knew that that could lead to the end of civilisation. Every now and then the other children would giggle and put their hands over their faces, look at Tama and his sisters, and giggle again. Tama decided to ignore them and to listen to what the adults were saying. The only trouble was that his father, Nani Puti and Uncle Pani were talking mainly Maori, and only a few sentences made any sense to Tama.

'It's good to know you've got support,' his father said.

'We may have lost the case in court,' Nani Puti answered, 'but no one's going to move us off.'

Uncle Pani laughed and Tama thought he saw him motion to a corner of the room where there was a rifle.

By that time Tama had been able to put names to his cousins' faces so that when, after tea, Nani Puti called to Grace, Lizzie and Sally to do the dishes he knew who they were. Grace was the eldest girl — she must have been eighteen — and when she moved she did so knowing how good she looked. Sally had short hair and was growing her chest. Lizzie was around Tama's own age and looked like a boy. Dutifully, Tama and his sisters asked if they could help — and the boy cousins fell about themselves at the thought of Tama doing the dishes. Tamihana was the big brother — he must have been about twenty and surely weighed ten tons. George came next, then Albert, Hone, Sid and Kopua. Phew! Two other brothers had already left home and were working on a local farm. Baby Emere was crawling on the floor. All these names to remember. But even more confusing was that the cousins with the European names also had Maori names and vice versa. Just as well, Tama felt, he had got good marks at school for memorising words in spelling.

'Well, I better start heading back,' their father said.

Mere had fallen asleep and had been taken to bed. Kara was crying and Tama felt like crying as well. He didn't like the idea of staying here at all. He and Kara walked with their father to the car. Their father kissed them.

'Be good,' he said.

'You will come back to get us, won't you?' Kara cried.

'Of course,' he answered.

'When?' Kara wailed.

'Soon,' he replied.

He stepped in the Ford, started the motor, swung the car around — and the children were left there, standing with Nani Puti. Insects buzzed and flitted in the lamplight.

That night Tama was very weepy. Nani Puti had said, 'Why don't you bunk in with the boys?' but he had said no. Tama had never slept with anybody else before. The trouble was that this got him off to a bad start with the boys, who then had to sleep in two beds while he slept in the third by himself — and that only made him feel lonelier than ever.

After all the lamps had been turned down, Tama heard the saddest sound in the world. His sister Mere had woken up and was calling:

'Mummy? Mummmmeeeeeee.'

Tama got up and went to her. 'We just have to be brave about it,' he said. 'We have to be brave little Indians.' He kissed her and went back to his own bed. Just as he lay down he saw Nani Puti — she had heard Mere too. Nani Puti had a candle in her hand and it floated into Mere's room and floated out again. This time Mere was in Nani's arms.

'Shhhh, shhh,' Nani said to Mere. She began to sing a Maori lullaby. The song was so comforting, sounding like something floating on the sea. Then it began to drift out beyond the point where Tama could follow it, and he fell asleep.

2

The next morning Tama was woken by angry voices outside the bedroom window. He looked out and saw that a policeman was standing there, leaning over Nani Puti. The policeman's face was swollen and red.

'You tell Pani,' he said, 'the next warning will be the last.'

The policeman strode back to his car.

Tama jumped out of bed and hurriedly got dressed. He called through the wall, 'Kara, are you there?' There was no answer so Tama crept slowly into the room to take a look. Kara was gone, but there was Mere, playing by the fire. Tama ran to give her a hug and that was when Nani Puti returned.

'Morena, sleepyhead!' Nani said. 'You must have had good dreams, eh?'

Tama nodded, 'Yes, thank you.'

'My moko, you're June's kid all right,' Nani laughed. 'You hungry for some breakfast? Grace! Come and get some kai for this kid.'

Tama felt a little ashamed about that, and when Grace appeared he said, 'I'm sorry, Grace.' He just didn't like the idea of her always being in the kitchen like Cinderella. Then Tama asked, 'What did the policeman want, Nani?'

A flicker crossed Nani Puti's face. 'What policeman!' she laughed.' No policeman has been here.'

While he was eating his breakfast Tama looked around the room. In the daytime everything looked smaller — how ever did Nani and Uncle manage to live with all their children in such a small house! It was even smaller than the one the Old Lady in the Shoe lived in. Gosh! There were just three bedrooms and this big room for eating and living in. The room was very plain with hardly any furniture except the table, two long forms, a settee in the corner, a few extra chairs, a cupboard for crockery, a wireless set and a small tin food safe. On one wall was a picture of the King. On a second was a colour magazine picture of Tyrone Power in *Blood and Sand* — Grace's boyfriend was supposed to look like that but handsomer. Just above the table was a photo of the whole family. Tama couldn't see Emere though, and when he pointed this out to Nani she laughed and said, 'Emere's there!' But Tama still couldn't see her so Nani pointed to her stomach, and Tama thought she was rude. Streamers from last Christmas were strung among the rafters. Hanging from the middle was a long sticky flypaper spattered with dead flies. On the mantelpiece above the fire was a piece of newspaper which had been cut into jaggedy patterns. Every now and then the wind would go *whoosh* in the chimney. Outside was the constant swish, swish, swish of the sea.

Nani Puti went out the back door, and Tama saw Kara playing with Sally and Lizzie. Tama felt she had forsaken him — and Mere too — and Kara made it worse by running in and laughing.

'So you're up at last.'

When she went to sit by him Tama pinched her hard. Her eyes brimmed with tears and she ran out again. Tama didn't know what to do. He had finished his breakfast but he couldn't really go out and skip over a rope with *girls*. Not only that, but Grace was wanting to clear up. 'You should go outside,' Grace said. 'The boys are somewhere out there.'

Tama stepped out into the light. He had to shade his eyes from the sun. He saw Hone, Sid and Kopua just beyond the back fence. He walked over to them. 'Hullo,' he said.

They pretended to ignore him and then Sid answered, 'Why, *hullo*,' in a put-on hoity-toity manner.

Kopua jabbed Sid with an elbow and, looking up at Tama, said, 'You must have had a good sleep, cousin.'

But before Tama could reply, Sid interrupted, 'Yeah, especially since he didn't have to sleep with any of his stink —' and he pinched his nostrils sarcastically '— cousins.'

Kopua again came to the rescue, saying:

'Easy, Sid. He's just a townie —.' He turned to Tama. 'Aren't you, Tama?'

But Sid didn't want to let it go. He stood up and shoved Tama so hard that Tama fell to the ground. 'Think you're better than us, eh? Just because you live in the town. Just because you speak all la-di-da . . .'

Tama felt the heat of humiliation on his face and he rushed at Sid, arms up and ready and fists bunched. He'd had a few boxing lessons at school and was rather proud of his prowess.

'Hey,' Sid said, pushing Tama away. But Tama's blood was up and he got a few lucky hits in. However, any betting man would have placed more money on Sid, who was not only taller and heavier but more experienced. With a great sense of shock and pain, Tama found himself floored with a bloody nose.

'You — you — rotter!' Tama cried. He launched himself at Sid again. This time there was no option for Sid but to knock his cousin down for the full count.

When Tama came around he found himself next to the outside pump by the horse trough. Kopua had a wet rag and was cleaning the blood from Tama's nose. He looked at Tama's left eye and whistled. 'That's going to come up a real beauty.'

Tama was still so humiliated that he pushed Kopua away.

'Hey,' Kopua yelled. 'What's up with *you* then! If you want to fight the lot of us, that's fine. But it will be better for *you* if we're friends. Okay?'

Tama shrugged his shoulders.

'Gee,' Kopua sighed, 'you're a hard fella all right. Come on.' He jerked his head to Tama. 'I said *come on*, willya! You don't want to stick around here so that your sisters can see you got beat, do you?'

Kopua started to walk away and then, like a jackrabbit, he charged up a tall hill. 'Yahoooo!'

By the time Tama caught up with him, Kopua was already sitting at the top, chewing on a piece of grass. Tama had cooled down a lot by then, the humiliation receding — and then he forgot all about that when he saw Nani Puti's house below.

'Your house!' Tama gasped. The sea appeared to be ready to snatch it with blue fingers. 'It's almost in the sea!'

'You *are* a townie!' Kopua laughed. 'Can't you tell a high tide when you see one? You want to come here in the winter time — we turn into a boat then!'

Tama felt awed. There seemed such grand *insolence* in the sight of that small tin shack — for it really was just rusting corrugated iron — sitting there for all the world like King Canute daring the waves to come any further.

'Don't you get afraid?' Tama asked.

'What of?'

'The sea of course!'

Kopua was surprised. 'Why should we?' he asked. 'It's only sometimes that our little toes get wet.' The twinkle in his eyes was a dead giveaway that he was teasing. Then Kopua stood up and pointed out to sea. 'Look over there, Tama!'

Tama shaded his eyes and saw a small rowboat bobbing like a broken straw on the glistening ocean. 'Is that Uncle and Tamihana?' he asked. Kopua nodded and said:

'They're getting us some crayfish for tonight.'

Tama looked again, puzzled. 'But they haven't got fishing rods,' he said. Kopua laughed again.

'Gee, don't you learn anything at that townie school of yours?'

Suddenly Tama saw a *flash* from the house. Nani Puti was there and she had a mirror in her hand.

'Huh?' Kopua said.

There was an answering *flash* from the rowboat.

'Mum must want Dad to come in early,' Kopua continued. 'Something must be up.'

The boys were silent for a while and then:

'How long have you lived here?' Tama asked.

'All our lives,' Kopua replied.

'Do you think you'll ever move?'

'What for? You don't understand, eh cuz. Didn't your mother ever tell you that she's from here? And that her mother was from here? In the old days there was a big Maori pa, right where our house is. It used to guard the whole Coast. It's famous.' Kopua puffed the words up with pride. 'And all the land —' Kopua described a large generous circle '— that you can see once belonged to us. Now, only this —' Kopua pointed down at the beach '— is left. The pa is gone, the land is gone, but our house and we are still here. And Mum's the big chief here. She'll never leave. Even if people are trying to get us out.'

Tama wanted to know more but Kopua appeared to want to go.

'Come on,' Kopua said.

'No, I don't want to go back to your house yet,' Tama answered.

'That shiner's still gonna shine even at night,' Kopua said. 'Okay, there's still lots to show you.'

Together the two boys walked along the cliff, with Kopua pointing out all the

31

landmarks — where the canoes used to be launched from, where the kumara pits once were, the palisades, the urupa — and Tama began to hear ancient voices calling from the land and to feel an absurd sense of exhilaration, of belonging, of *this* history being *his* legacy, of *this* place being *his* place. He felt cross that his mother had not told him all this herself.

'She probably did,' Kopua said. 'You probably didn't listen!'

Which might have been true, because Tama had always been more interested in the Celts and the Romans. But come to think of it, Nani Puti *could* have been a Maori Boadicea, yes, *and* Mummy too.

By that time it was mid afternoon.

'I have to milk the cows,' Kopua said.

The two boys returned to the house. Kopua went to bring in the cows and Tama helped him bail them up.

'What do you do at school?' Kopua asked from between the depths of Blackie's udder.

'I'm in form one,' Tama answered.

'So am I,' said Kopua.

Squirt, squirt, went the milk in the bucket.

'Oh,' Tama responded, because Kopua was at least thirteen to his eleven.

'And what are you going to do when you grow up?' Kopua asked.

Tama didn't want to answer, because if he opened his mouth the smell of the cow bail would get in and it was *atrocious*. 'A teacher,' he said quickly. How come Kopua didn't expire from the odour?

'You have to have a lot of brains to be that,' Kopua said. 'I think I'll be a racing-car driver. Brrmmm, brrrmmmm.' He began to fantasize on the cow's udder and Blackie glared at him as if to say, *Well if you drive your car like you pull my teats the only trophy you'll ever win is* — and she presented him with a cowpat.

For the rest of the afternoon Tama tried to hide his damaged nose and his black eye. But Mere screamed and Kara wanted to be his nurse — and she asked Nani Puti if she could have some bandages and chloroform.

'Your Uncle will have something to say about this when he gets home,' Nani said at dinner.

Sid shifted uneasily on the form.

But any displeasure of Uncle's was nothing compared to Tama's discomfort and, in the end, he just *had* to ask:

'Nani, may I use your toilet?'

Nani smiled and said:

'It's outside.'

This was exactly what he had been dreading.

'Hone will show you, otherwise you might fall in.'

This was even worse.

Tama put on his shoes and followed Hone to a tin shed at the end of a long track. Hone shone the torch inside. 'I'll wait here,' he said.

'Oh no,' Tama answered, 'I'll be quite all right.'

'Oh yeah?'

Hone shone the torch up to the top of the shed where a big black spider was.

'All right then,' Tama conceded. He dropped his trousers and just managed to sit down in time before Hone shone the torch accidentally on purpose in the direction of his you-know-what.

'Oops,' Hone said.

But he did it again. Tama wished the shed had a door on it. He felt so shy sitting there in full view of his cousin, the house and the whole *world*.

'Pass me a comic,' Hone said.

Tama reached down to the wooden boards and threw him a tattered western.

'Do you read comics?' Hone asked.

'Our mother doesn't let us,' Tama said.

'Gee,' Hone responded in a hushed voice, as if a world without comics was too awful to contemplate. 'What do you read then?' he asked.

'Oh classics,' Tama said, trying to brush it all off, 'like Rudyard Kipling and H. Rider Haggard. Have you read *She*?'

Hone rustled his comic. 'Phew,' he said. 'No *wonder*.'

For a while there was silence.

'I've finished now,' Tama said, dressing quickly.

'Just in time,' Hone answered. He shone the torch on the black spider. There it was, dangling right over Tama's head. Mere won't like *that*, Tama thought.

When Tama and Hone returned to the house they found that Uncle Pani had arrived back from town.

'Sid's for it now,' Kopua whispered as Tama walked in. And, sure enough, there was Sid, looking as if it was high noon and the hangman had come to Dodge City. But Uncle was mean and waited until the girls were in bed and there were just himself, Nani Puti and the boys in the big room. Then:

'Come here,' he said to Tama.

Uncle inspected the black eye. 'Who did it?' he asked.

Tama gulped. 'It was Blackie,' he said. *Please forgive me Blackie, you can kick me hard tomorrow morning.*

Uncle snorted and turned to Nani Puti, who was trying very hard not to laugh. 'Listen to the boy,' Uncle said to her. 'Did you know that Blackie could kick as high as Ginger Rogers?'

'Oh, it's true, Uncle,' Tama went on earnestly, 'honest Indian.'

Then Uncle frowned and said:

'Bring the Bible, Puti.'

Next minute, there it was, the Word of the Lord, right in front of Tama.

'Now, swear,' Uncle said.

And Tama thought, *Our Father which art in Heaven, I can't tell on my cousin, you won't send me to hell will you?* He closed his eyes, took a deep breath and — Uncle Pani took the Bible away. 'Nothing is worth telling a lie for, boy,' Uncle said. He looked keenly at Tama, but all that Tama could hear was the Hallelujah Chorus because he had been saved.

'Yes, Uncle,' Tama said meekly.

Then Uncle turned to the boys and said:

'All right, Kopua, go outside and get the biggest branch you can find. I know it was you.'

By this time Nani Puti was red with mirth — just as well she had taken out her teeth. It was then that Sid stepped forward.

'I'll go,' he said.

'Well, make it a big branch,' Uncle told him. 'You should know better than to pick on a boy younger than you.'

Later that night Sid told Tama that Tama was *okay* for not squealing on him.

'We'll be mates, eh?' Sid said, and they shook on it.

When they were getting ready for bed Tama asked if they could bunk together. But before getting into bed Tama walked into the girls' bedroom to check on Kara and Mere — they were both fast asleep. On his way back he saw the light still on in Nani's bedroom.

'So how long have we got?' he heard Nani ask.

'Maori Affairs is appealing the decision for us,' Uncle said.

'I was born here,' Nani replied, 'and I am not going to die anywhere but right *here.*'

Her voice was as eternal and as strong as the sea. Mere didn't cry that night.

Tama was horrified to find his cousin Kopua hauling him up from sleep at five o'clock.

'The cows,' Kopua said.

'Do you get up this early every morning?' Tama asked.

Kopua nodded, and Tama shuddered and was glad that in the town milk got delivered by the milkman. On their return from milking, Tama saw that Grace and Sally were also up, preparing breakfast. Grace was very beautiful — all dishevelled and untidy, but somehow attractive. Tamihana was awake too and dressed. Sounds of morning prayers came from Nani's and Uncle's bedroom. The rest of the household was still asleep. Then Nani came in and:

'Morena, moko,' she said. 'Kei te pehea to moe? Kei te pai?'

Tama looked at her curiously and he saw a shadow cross her face.

'You don't know, eh?' she asked.

'I beg your pardon, Nani?' Tama responded.

'You don't know your Nani's language,' Nani said.

'I know some French,' Tama said helpfully. 'Parlez-vous français?'

Nani smiled at him, a small smile which was only just there. Then Uncle Pani came in and started ordering everybody around. 'You want to come out with me?' he asked Tama.

'In the rowboat? Oh, yes please,' Tama responded.

Nani went to remonstrate, but Uncle just said to her:

'Oh, we'll just go to the point and back. Not far. Just for the morning.'

And Nani nodded that was all right then. 'I want to take the mokos to the reef later,' she said.

Tama went with Uncle Pani and Tamihana to the boat. The sea was like glass that had just been shined by the sun and polished by the wind. 'I've never been in a rowboat before,' he said.

'No?' Uncle asked, amazed. 'Gee, what do you do in the town!' He and Tama sat in the boat — and Tamihana pushed it out on the sea and jumped in with them. Uncle Pani took up the oars and rowed with a strong, easy rhythm. Sometimes Tamihana took over. Once Tama offered, but all he could do was make the rowboat go round and round in circles.

'Never mind, Tama,' Uncle laughed. 'Your Uncle's too heavy for you. Boy, you wouldn't have been any good in the old days.'

'I beg your pardon, Uncle?' Tama asked, not understanding.

'This was the Maori life, Tama,' Uncle replied. 'The men did the fishing and the women cooked the fish.' But Uncle Pani was wise enough to see that he had hurt Tama. 'Times change, moko,' he said. 'These days, the person who fishes with the brains is sometimes more successful than the one who fishes with the hands.'

The rowboat reached the first marker where the crayfish pots were waiting to be brought up. Tamihana began to pull up the line and, far down, Tama could see the wire cage coming up. The crayfish pot broke the surface, and Tamihana reached in and grabbed the crayfish. Tama thought he was very brave, because the crayfish were very fierce, waving their legs in the air and going click click *click*. Tamihana threw one at Tama's feet and he yelled, almost upsetting the boat.

'Just as well it wasn't a mouse,' Uncle laughed, 'otherwise you would have got on the seat and we would have been *over*.'

The seagulls thought it was funny too because they cackled and cawed and chuckled and squealed overhead.

For the rest of the morning Uncle and Tamihana rowed from one marker to the next, bringing up the crays, and while they were doing so, Uncle Pani reminisced about the old days. Up until that time Tama had thought that Uncle Pani was just, well, Uncle *Pani*. He hadn't realised that Uncle had been so handsome, so strong, so sought-after, such a fantastic rider of horses, the best athlete on the Coast, the greatest fullback that Ruatoria had ever seen and such an all-round sportsman.

'If it wasn't for me getting those two tries, drop-kicking that goal from halfway in the last five minutes and then going over again right on the whistle, the Coast would have lost,' he said. Tama's eyes were so wide with amazement that he didn't see Tamihana put his finger up to test the strength of the wind. 'That's why your Nani fell in love with me, Tama, right on the spot. She had to queue up for me though, I wasn't an easy catch, they were all after me, Maori and Pakeha girls alike. But I let her come first because she was the only one who was not after my *money*.'

At that, Tamihana let out a snort. 'Gee, Dad, dream on.'

But that enabled Tama to ask:

'Uncle, why do we call you Uncle, and Nani, Nani?'

Uncle Pani looked hurt. 'You mean you can't see how old your Nani is and how young and gorgeous-looking I am?' he asked.

Tama didn't want to offend his Uncle so he didn't answer.

'She was sure lucky getting me,' Uncle sighed. 'If I had know she was waiting in the bushes to lead me astray . . .' He tsk-tsked to himself. 'Tama, watch out for these Coast women,' he said. 'They're dynamite.' He grew reflective and looked back at the house, floating there on its spit of sand. 'But if you find a woman like her, Tama, you *grab* her, boy. You grab her and hold her so *tight* she can't get away. She's the one keeps us all together. Keeps the land together. Not just for our family but all our whanau. Your mother and you too. She's the one.' He took off his hat in a salute. Then he looked out to sea. 'E hoa, looks like you're out of luck today.'

'Why, Uncle?'

Uncle Pani smiled mysteriously. 'Usually a white shark appears. It's our kaitiaki. Our protector. I haven't seen it for a while. Perhaps next time.'

By the time the rowboat returned to shore it was filled with seething, clicking crayfish. Uncle and Tamihana took most of the catch on the truck to Ruatoria. Kara came running to Tama, dressed in her frilly swimsuit, crying:

'Come on, Tama, Nani's taking us down to the beach!'

Behind her, Tama could see Mere jumping up and down — she had a bucket and spade in her hand. Nani and the others were watching their antics as if they were creatures from another planet; they went to the sea just about every day and couldn't see what the fuss was about. There they were, all dressed in holey shirts and old black football shorts, and there were their city cousins all decked out like Christmas.

'All right, all right,' Nani said to Kara, trying to calm down Kara's boisterous glee. 'But work first and then swim.'

'Work?'

'You want to eat tonight, don't you?' Nani asked. 'Haven't you kids ever . . . You *do* know what pipis and pupus are? How about kinas? *What! What the blimmin'* heck does your mother feed you, you poor mokos!'

With that, Nani yelled instructions to Grace and Sid and then, like Boadicea, she led the way to the reef.

The reef was about a mile away and so isolated that the seagulls were outraged at this invasion of shouting children. *How dare you, how dare you!* they shrieked from the blue vault of sky. Unheeding, the town children ran on while the country cousins followed with the sugarbags and kits for the shellfish.

'Come on, Nani!' the town children cried.

The old woman only nodded her head, hoping that the gods of this place would understand that this was a new generation which knew nothing of the old ways and traditions, and she said to the gods:

'Be forgiving, e Tangaroa, of the ways of the innocent.'

As if to reassure her, a bright blue kingfisher scooped low across the inlet, flashing its reflection across the water.

'Oh look, Nani, look!' the children cried.

Then they were at the reef and the old woman issued instructions. The town children thought it was such fun and not like work at all. They had to pair up — Tama with Sid, Kara with Sally, Grace with Mere, Kopua with Hone, and Nani with Lizzie — and with Emere slung on her back, wasn't that just sweet? Then out they went to gather dinner.

Tama was wearing shoes to protect his feet from the sharp reef. Sid gave Tama a sack to hold. He reached into the water underneath a ledge and *tugged*.

'This is a paua,' he said. In his hand he had a big shell and inside was a long black piece of rubber. 'You have to be quick, because if the paua knows you're going to grab him he sticks tight to the rock. Then you have to use a knife to get him off. You try.'

Tama put his hand under the ledge and his face screwed up — what if there was an electric eel there or a giant clam? 'Oouchh,' Tama yelled. 'There's something prickly down there.'

Sid laughed. He grabbed underneath and pulled out a brown spiky ball; it looked like it would be good at puncturing tyres. 'This is a kina,' Sid said. 'We eat this too . . .'

Which was just the thing that Tama was afraid he would say.

Once the first sack was filled, the two boys hauled it back to Nani Puti.

'To Tangaroa goes the first of the catch,' she said, and she took some of the shellfish to a deep pool and returned them to the sea.

'Why did she do that?' Tama asked Sid later.

'It is always done,' Sid responded. 'Tangaroa is the Sea God. He gives us blessings. So this is our way of thanking him.'

It didn't take the boys long to fill their second sack. Sid did most of the work. Tama had to use the knife. But that didn't matter to Tama because he was feeling so happy and elated — and he just didn't know why. Perhaps it was the whole excitement of not having to go to a grocery store to get food but actually diving for it yourself. Or maybe it had to do with a growing sense of belonging — and of being accepted — by his cousins. Or perhaps it was because work brought with it a sense of achievement — as if he was doing something worthwhile. Perhaps, perhaps — and as he worked, he became more entranced by the reef and more akin with it. And his Nani, watching from afar knew what was happening and thanked Tangaroa for this *communion*.

'Kua mutu!' Nani Puti said. 'We have enough! Work is over! Now you kids can have a good swim and cool off.'

She sat on the beach watching for a while and she felt so glad that June had sent the mokos up to her. That was the only way the whanau would keep together. She heard Kara scream and saw that she had caught a baby octopus — or the other way around.

'Why don't you put it back?' Nani said.

Kara's eyes were large. 'Can Grace do it, Nani?' Kara asked. 'The . . . the mother octopus might be out there.'

Nani Puti glanced over to Mere, and there she was, building a sandcastle and looking for all the world as if she was on a beach at Brighton. *What future lies in store for you, my moko Pakeha?* Nani Puti asked herself. *What future lies ahead for us all?* And then Tama was there, shaking himself like a little puppy.

'You having a good time?' Nani Puti asked.

'Oh yes, thank you, Nani' Tama answered.

'Would you like to sit and korero with your Nani?' she asked.

Tama nodded his head vigorously. 'Uh huh.' He sat down with her and both of them were looking at the reef and the sea. The minutes went by but not a word was spoken between them, and yet Tama felt as if they had been talking for *ages*. What about? Why, sea and sky of course, earth and ocean, man and land, sea and land, man and man, kinsman and kinswoman, kin with kin.

'All your bones are here,' Nani Puti said, and Tama felt a great sense of *completeness* in her words, and he was falling through the blue well of the sky. 'No matter where you go in your life this is your home. No matter what you do with your life, these are your people. Whenever you need us, all you have to do is call. And whenever you are needed, you must come. Do you understand?'

'Yes, I understand, Nani,' Tama nodded.

In that mood of absolute enchantment the kingfisher came again, skimming its royal colour across the water.

The next days drifted past like a dream. Tama and his sisters grew strong and brown under Nani Puti's dictum — work first, then you can play later. It was therefore with a sense of surprise that the children received the postcard from their mother. They had been riding horses — or 'hortheth' as Mere would have lisped —

all afternoon and having bareback races with their cousins along the beach. Far off, Nani Puti had appeared waving her apron. As soon as they saw their mother, the cousins did a conjuring trick and disappeared into thin air — how were Tama, Kara and Mere to know that the horses belonged to the Pakeha neighbour, Mr Hewitt?

'Don't you worry,' Nani told Tama.' I know you kids got left holding the bag.'

She handed the postcard over to Tama and set off with a big branch to find their cousins. *Dear Tama, Kara and Mere*, Mum had written, *Daddy and I have just arrived in Auckland. We are missing our babies very much. Tama, I hope you are looking after your sisters. Kara, you do as Nani says. Mere, are you being a good girl? We will be back soon. Love, Mummy. XXXXXXX*

'Have Mummy and Daddy been away a week already?' Kara asked.

'Just about,' Tama said.

The children were a little disconsolate at dinner that evening — and matters were made worse when Uncle Pani told Mere she could cook her very own crayfish. Until that time Mere had quite happily eaten everything served up to her including crays. But when she popped a 'Mere-thized baby crayfith' into the boiling pot with her own pudgy hands and heard it *scream* she felt like a murderer. 'Put crayfith back!' she said, pointing at the sea. 'Put back, Uncle!' She drummed her fists against his chest. From then on she refused to eat crayfish, using her well-known complaint that 'my bottomth thtuck' — which was her way of saying she was full or had constipation. However, everybody brightened up when Nani said that she and Uncle had business with Maori Affairs (Nani didn't seem to be very happy about it though) and that all the family would be going to Ruatoria the next day.

'Can we go to the pictures?' Sid asked anxiously.

'The two o'clock and the eight o'clock?' Grace chimed in because she wanted to see her boyfriend, and night-time made him more daring.

'You kids are given an inch . . .' Nani sighed. 'Oh, all right. But I don't want dirty kids to shame me. So, bath-time!'

While the girls were doing the dishes Tama went with the boys to the wash-house, where they filled the copper and lit the fire beneath it. When the water was boiling they stood in a row and swung buckets down the line from the wash-house to the whare, where the bath was.

'Quick! Let's get in now,' Sid hissed.

But Nani saw him. 'Hey! You boys let Grace and the girls go first,' she yelled. 'You make the water too dirty with your patotoi feet.'

'Yes,' Grace continued. 'We don't want Kopua's kutus floating in our water.'

So the boys had to put on their clothes again and wait until the girls had finished.

There was something in the very idea of a 'bath' that always brought out the lady in Grace. She emerged from her usual place in the kitchen in a long pink robe and towel turban, positively t-rrr-ipping on her toes to the bath. Following behind her came Sally, Lizzie, Kara and Mere like adoring acolytes holding the scrubbing brush, shampoo and Sunlight soap which Grace would apply to her hair, face and person. This was no longer the Grace who tucked her dress into her pants when playing touch rugby with her brothers, nor the sister who yelled endearments like 'Hoi, kina head' or 'Gedoudahere, tutae face.' This was some other more divine creation. Anybody looking on and listening in as she slipped into the bath would have thought this was Cleopatra swimming in asses' milk rather than in a rusty tub with a candle on the rim. Surrounded by the smaller girls — all in awe of her voluptuous curves — Grace would sigh, 'Make more bubbles dahlings,' or 'Mmmm, more shampoo, sweetnesses,' or 'Oooo, just a little softer with the soap, babies.' And as they ministered to her Grace let them in on the secrets of How To Be Seductive or What To Do If He Wants To Go All The Way. And if she ever heard the irritated yells of her brother, 'Hurry up, Grace!' or the *thump* as a cowpat hit the roof, she simply sighed. There was a big difference between brothers and MEN.

Was it all worth it? Oh yes, for to see Grace transfigured by soap and water, gilded by the moon, queening it across the paddock and around the cowpats was to witness . . . a vision. Not only that, but one knew that one was only seeing part of the miracle. The full miracle would only be apparent after Grace had carefully plucked her eyebrows all off (and replaced them with black pencil ones), lipsticked her lips pink on the outside and deep red inside (to make them look narrower) and applied hair rollers (to substitute her straight hair with a style that approximated to the latest rage). For now, though, this glimpse of the Serpent of the Nile, Ruatoria-style, preparing to go by barge to meet a hick-town Mark Anthony the next day, was sufficient.

Once the girls had finished their toilette the boys emptied the bath and refilled it — Have a bath in girls' water? No fear! They were just about to hop in for the second time when Nani Puti and Uncle Pani came out. 'You boys last,' Nani Puti said.

Oh, the boys were so angry because had they known that Mum would pinch their water, they wouldn't have filled the bath to the brim. But finally it was their turn after all — and there was Tama, for the first time in his life, taking a bath with other people. Initially, he was embarrassed about being in the middle with Sid, Hone and Kopua, especially since they were always dropping the soap.

'Oops,' they would say as they hunted for it and ended up with a handful of you-know-what. They splashed each other too. But very soon Tama forgot about his inhibitions.

'Oops,' he said as he searched for the soap.

The next morning, after breakfast, Tama and the boys were the first to get dressed and to be waiting on the truck. There was a certain unspoken protocol to all this, as if it was expected that the boys should wait the longest. Five minutes later Uncle Pani arrived in tie, sports jacket and hat, followed another five minutes after by the smaller girls and Emere. Fifteen minutes passed until Nani Puti appeared.

'Ooh . . .' The little girls sighed on cue at the sight of Nani in coat and hat, stockings and white Minnie Mouse shoes, putting on her gloves and trying not to look too self-conscious in this unaccustomed elegance. Head down and still fussing about her seams, she was handed into the cab — an act reserved for occasions like this — by a gallant and proud Uncle Pani. Ten minutes after that one of the little girls was despatched to tell Cleopatra to shake a leg, returning to say, 'She's almost there' — wherever 'there' was.

Then, just before everybody's patience exploded, she appeared — Grace, the eldest girl and apple of everybody's eye, wobbling on red high heels and dressed to kill.

Not for our Grace a simple dress and a few accessories. Oh no, this kid knew she wasn't going to get to town for another couple of weeks, so she was making the most of it. Her hair was positively rolling in curls. The dress was lime green and the neckline was as low as Grace thought she could get away with. There must have been at least five petticoats to flounce that dress out as far as it went. Not only that, but the dress was surely five sizes too small — and knew it. And why wear only one bangle and necklace when you have a whole drawer full?

'Come on, Grace,' Nani Puti said.

Lost in a vision of her own beauty, jangling like a cowbell and walking as knock-kneed as a pukeko, Grace swayed and dipped and staggered toward the truck. Eyes never glittered as green-shadowed as hers, lips were never as luscious or greasy red, and if there was too much powder, don't forget that it had to last the whole day. Only one problem remained: all she had to do was to make sure that her beauty would not be destroyed by the dust on the way to Ruatoria.

Tama didn't have much time to appreciate Ruatoria because it was almost two o'clock — Nani Puti having stopped at a few relations' places on the way to take shopping lists to town — when they arrived. The movie was a double feature, hooray, with Audie Murphy in the first one and . . .

'Oh,' Grace screamed, 'Rory Calhoun!'

But while his cousins were jumping up and down, waiting for their picture money, Tama and Kara exchanged puzzled glances — was this *it*? This one main street with a few shops, picture theatre and hotel? Where was the *rest*?

'Here you are, mokos,' Nani said. She gave Tama, Kara and Mere five shillings each and Tama said:

'But Nani, we haven't got any change.'

'No, this is for being good mokos,' Nani answered. 'But don't forget it has to last the whole day.'

Tama had never seen so much money.

'Hurry up!' his cousins were saying, 'otherwise the picture will have started before we get there.'

Before they knew it, Tama, Kara and Mere found themselves being whisked off by their cousins, leaving Nani and Uncle standing in the dust.

'Come back to the truck after the pictures,' Nani called. She was biting her lips nervously and ruining her lipstick. By then Grace had got the tickets at the movie house and shooed them in, hissing:

'I don't want to see any of you till afterwards. And if you want to go to the lav, Lizzie, you find it yourself.'

With that, and in a flurry of hugging and screaming, Grace joined up with her friends and went into a huddle over The One And Only Subject: BOYS. Grace's boyfriend was already inside — it wasn't done for boyfriends to wait; apart from which, he would have to buy the girl her ticket, and he wasn't that dumb.

'Come on,' Kopua said, rolling his eyes.

Inside, mayhem was in power. The rules of the game were that the little children should go down the front where they could be pelted with peanuts and jellybeans — so off went Kara, Mere and other others. The big boys, who grudgingly allowed younger boys like Tama and Kopua to join them, all sat at the back. The middle territory was for the females of the attached and hoping-to-be attached variety — there they could be looked over or boasted about by the boys behind. Naturally Grace made a wonderful entrance, cracking gum and wobbling her way down the aisle with her friends. Without looking back, she hissed to one of them, *crack*:

'Where is he?' *crack.*

'On the left side,' *crack,* 'over there!' her friend responded.

The first feature was called *Adventure Island* and Tama fell in love with the red-headed lady in it — Rhonda Fleming. He was amazed how vocal everybody was, cheering, hissing, booing, offering advice like, 'He's just behind you,' or 'Hurry up and *kiss* her.' They cheered again and again, and threw peanuts everywhere.

During all this, Grace and her boyfriend sat staring at each other through the gloom (That was her, wasn't it, the one in green?) but not moving towards each other. That would look too forward. No, this was reserved for intermission. At that stage Grace was supposed somehow to be standing at the doors, her hand dangling somewhere in reach, so that — just before the lights went out — her boyfriend could grab it and haul her inside. Once that was accomplished, it was up to the boyfriend to show the goggle-eyed younger boys like Tama how to woo a girl, and up to Grace to make sure he left at least six cherries on her neck to prove he'd been there. As far as Tama could make out, the main object was to plant your lips on hers to stop her breathing, and when she was faint for lack of air, you started to move your hands downward. If you were lucky, despite her struggles, you got as far as the belt — but no further, buster. (The girls always relied on the brevity of the second feature to save them from a fate worse than you-know-what.) Watching all this, as well as the picture, it was no wonder that Tama was in a state of shock when the lights went back on. As for Grace, she had *triumphed* and there she sat in absolute adoration of her beloved. Nor did it matter that her hair, lipstick, eye-shadow, powder and eyebrows had been totally obliterated — she had *Prevailed*.

'Eeee, Grace!' Kopua said pointing at her neck, which looked like a vampire had attacked it.

Grace stared at Kopua as if he was a creature from another planet. 'Oh, go squeeze yourself,' *crack,* 'Pimple-face,' *crack,* she said.

Afterwards, Grace, Tamihana and George went off with boyfriend and girlfriends, and the rest of the children raced to the local shop, where they bought dinner — a pie, softdrink and doughnut each.

'Wasn't it neat when . . .' the young boys said to each other, reliving the two movies they had seen.

'Yeah, boy!'

As for Tama, he was still trying to recover. Then, remembering that they were to meet Nani and Uncle at the truck, they raced back. The truck was there, with the baby Emere sleeping in the cab, but Nani and Uncle were nowhere to be seen.

'They're in the pub,' Hone said, jerking his head at a large building, which shook with singing, boozing and laughing. 'But they'll be out by six.'

The children walked around a while with Kopua introducing Tama and his sisters to the locals. Tama decided that Ruatoria wasn't so bad. It was kind of like Dodge City or a sleepy Mexican town south of the Texas border, with the roughest, toughest, meanest, most colourful coyotes this side of Tombstone, *yup*. People still rode horses into town and swaggered in and out of the local cantina.

Then it was six o'clock and people began to burst out of the hotel, clutching crates of beer and each other.

'Here they come,' Kopua said.

Tama couldn't see Nani Puti or Uncle Pani, and while he was looking in the crowd somebody grabbed him. A bloated face peered into his and an overpowering smell of beer and stale sweat enveloped him.

'Keeoraa morgor, waz za pitcha kapai? Wherez za kidz —'

Before he could prevent it, the figure lurched towards Kara and Mere, who both screamed.

'Wazza madda, morgors? Iz only meee,' the face said.

Uncle Pani was there to rescue them. 'Hey, you haurangi moll,' he said as he grabbed her and pulled her away.

Were it not for the Minnie Mouse shoes, Tama would not have recognised Nani Puti at all. She looked like some huge macabre cray which had been scalded in hot boiling water and was still screaming. Her eyes were red and bulging and her face was hanging in ugly scarlet folds down her neck. Her hair was straggly and the hairline was thick with foam-like perspiration.

'Yezzzz,' Nani Puti said, 'iz only your Nanneee . . .' She went to lean on the truck and fell over. 'Fuggen hell,' she swore, 'Blimmen hell.' And she laughed and laughed in a horrible unfunny way, her lips blubbering and her eyes streaming with tears, just sitting there in the dust in her nice dress and coat. Uncle Pani went to pick her up and his voice was angry.

'Hey, *Mum*, snap out of it,' he swore under his breath. 'Lizzie!' he called. '*Lizzie!* Come and take your mother to the lav.'

Lizzie said, 'Oooo,' and wrinkled her nose as she and Uncle helped Nani over to the public toilet.

It had all happened so quickly that Tama was still bewildered. He felt that the real Nani Puti had been stolen away and a false Nani Puti had been put in her place. Kara came to him, shivering. 'I don't like Nani Puti like this, Tama,' she said.

Mere was still snivelling with fright. Uncle Pani returned and saw their fear. 'Don't worry kids. Your Nani will be right as rain.' He bent down to Mere's level and kissed her. Then, standing, he addressed Tama man to man. 'Your Nani was never able to hold her beer, and I couldn't stop her. She just wanted to drink her troubles away.'

Troubles?

'We've had some bad news, boy.'

Lizzie returned with Nani, who was looking much better. Even so, Uncle gathered everybody and told them he was taking Mum home but he had spoken to Auntie Trixie and she was going to the eight o'clock pictures, so she could bring them home afterward. The cousins were glad about that but Tama said:

'I think Kara, Mere and I will come back with you. Mere's just about asleep anyway and Mummy wouldn't like it if we didn't look after her.'

'Okay, Tama,' Uncle said. 'Well you kids get in the back then.'

Tama, Kara and Mere waved goodbye to their cousins and as the truck trundled out of Ruatoria they huddled beneath the blankets. Night fell quickly and very soon Uncle had to switch on the headlights. Tama wondered whether they were the only ones alive in the whole wide world. Nani Puti was sick three times, and at every *heave* Uncle would say:

'That's it, dear. Get it all out and you'll feel better.'

As heavy as Nani must have been, Uncle carried her from the truck into the whare when they got home.

Swish, *swish*, went the sea.

'Help me with your Nani,' Uncle asked Tama when he had lit a candle and put Nani on the bed.

Tama took off her hat and shoes, and while Uncle lifted Nani up he removed her coat and Kara took off her skirt. Nani flopped down in her petticoat. Mere got a flannel and cleaned her face. 'There,' Mere said.

That night Kara and Mere came to sleep with Tama. They were upset because adults were supposed to be strong. Yet Nani kept on crying and crying as if her heart was breaking. She must have known the children were still awake, because she called out to them.

'Yes, Nani?' they said as they stood at the doorway.

She was sitting up in bed having a cup of tea. When she saw them her face screwed up. 'I'm sorry, mokos,' she said.

'You don't have to be sorry, Nani,' Kara answered. 'You're big enough to do exactly what you like!'

46

'We can't be brave little Indianth all the time,' Mere added.

Nani smiled wanly. She kissed the three children on their foreheads. Just before they all left the room she shot Tama a piercing, smouldering glance.

'Never trust the Pakeha, Tama, never,' she said. 'When you get older, you learn all you can about the Pakeha law so that you can use it against him.'

The flame from the candle flickered, almost faltered, casting strange shadows on the walls.

Nani Puti recovered quickly and the next day no mention was made of her drunkenness. Tama's cousins had had a wonderful night.

'You would have loved the movie,' Kopua said.

As for Grace, she resumed her usual stance as Cinderella in the kitchen, dreaming of the next time her boyfriend would be able to attack her neck.

So the summer resumed, day after day, as if it was everlasting — a long glorious hot halcyon summer. Tama and his sisters continued to work in the mornings and play with their cousins in those joyous afternoons. Sometimes Tama would go out in the rowboat with his uncle and, recalling an earlier occasion, he asked:

'Uncle, do you think we'll see the shark today?'

Uncle looked toward the horizon, seeking a disturbance in the ocean. 'Something must be wrong It loves to come and scratch itself on our dinghy.'

Nothing but the sea ever glistening.

More and more, Tama found himself wanting to wander alone around the hills and bays. He would run to the top of the hill overlooking the whare and look across the beach which was so much a part of his cousins' lives. He envied them their living here, in this seeming timeless place, and would close his eyes hoping to imprint it all on his retina. To see Nani Puti sitting on her doorstep in the sun made him grin with happiness. To watch Uncle and Tamihana bobbing in the ocean made him want to be a fisherman like they were. The cup of his contentment would begin to bubble over, and he would run back down the hill to be with his sisters and cousins.

At the same time, despite the kingfisher days of forever sun, Tama began to notice that little things were going wrong — like, for instance, the long absence of the pet shark. Out of the corner of his eye, he would see a cliff face crumbling, or a stone falling into the sea, or a dead fish floating on the surface of the sea. The rowboat sprang a leak one day, and later Hone made a small gash in his leg with a fishhook. Nani Puti herself was cut by a broken bottle in the sand. Just little things — but both Nani and Uncle saw them also and seemed powerless to stop them

47

happening. Something was out there, something, somewhere, some *thing*. Then the policeman arrived a second time, bearing a government letter and was it Tama's imagination or had Uncle Pani picked up his rifle and ordered the policeman away? After that, Nani and Uncle seemed to grow older and darker before Tama's eyes, and he realised how vulnerable and how unprotected they were against the ills of the world.

In this mood of disquiet, with the edges of the world crumbling away, Tama found himself returning again and again to the sanctuary of the reef. He wanted to *know*, but know what? And just as he tried to memorise the landscape he did the same with the reef. In his own helpless schoolboyish way he would measure out the distances between one prominent feature and the next — six paces to the pool with the sea urchins, five strokes across to the next with the baby octopus — as if it were all going to disappear. He would watch the ocean and wish the pet shark to appear, as if such a supernatural event would stop what was happening and make it all right again. He read desperation in the normally routine prayers that Nani and Uncle intoned morning and evening. When they started to leave the children for long periods, travelling from marae to marae throughout the Coast, Tama wanted to know why. And then, when Maori kinsmen began to gather with greater frequency at the whare, debating and shouting through the stomach of the night, he wanted to join them. But his Uncle would say:

'Don't you worry, moko. This is for your Nani and me to sort out.'

Yes, it might all have been just his imagination — like the morning, just before dawn, when he felt the compulsion to visit the reef. He was running along the beach and there was so much earth and so much sky that he could have fallen into it all. Suddenly he heard a sound, a seagull calling. He looked out to sea. He had to shade his eyes because the sun was rising. There, framed in that golden aureole of light, bobbing on that blood-red sea, Tama thought he saw the rowboat. Nani Puti and Uncle Pani were in it. Nani was standing in the boat, dressed in black, and she was singing a Maori lament. It sounded like a farewell song to someone, as sad as Snow White's dying. The next day more kinsmen arrived. From then on, they began to stay.

The solstice came to an end. One morning when the sea was sparkling, a car appeared on the cliff. Waving to Tama, Kara and Mere from far away were their parents. The children were overjoyed to see their parents, who looked bronzed and happy and — like gods really. When Kara told her mother about all the adventures they had been on she laughed.

'I told you you'd like it at Nani's place,' she said.

Tama watched his parents with growing discomfort because they seemed unaware of what was happening, really *happening*. His parents had brought gifts for Nani and Uncle, who accepted them politely, and for the cousins — Grace gave a scream of delight at the new H-line dress that their mother had brought back from Auckland. The thought came to Tama that his parents were foolish people because they were so privileged that they could never see beyond themselves.

'We'd better go,' Tama's mother said. 'Nani and Uncle look like they're having a meeting.'

Only then did their father understand. He talked to their mother and she stared around her — and her eyes brimmed with tears. She went up to Nani Puti.

'How *dare* you,' their mother said. 'How *dare* you think that we would come and go just like that. We — I — my children — have as much rights as you over this place. And *you* were going to let me walk in and out without telling me? Don't you *dare* do this to me. Ever again.'

Nani Puti and their mother began to cry on each other's shoulders, and Nani Puti was firm.

'You would only get in the way, June,' she said.

'When do you expect the police to come?' their mother cried.

'In two days' time, but *sshhh*, we don't want to upset the mokos.'

Their father appeared to be arranging something with Uncle Pani about returning with their mother as soon as was possible, Uncle Pani showed their father how well oiled the rifle was. Their father looked grim and almost afraid.

'Okay, children,' their mother said. 'Time for us to go. Say goodbye to your Nani and your cousins.'

Suddenly Tama didn't want to go at all. He felt a sense of panic, as if the caterpillar train of his nightmares was catching up on him. Something was happening at the edge of childhood. It was just around the corner and, whatever it was, it would forever change all their lives.

'Nani? Uncle!' Tama cried.

But his Nani and Uncle and cousins were gently shepherding him, his sisters and parents along, away from the house and past the tent encampment of the kinsmen. Before Tama knew it, they were all standing beside the car.

'Goodbye, my cousins,' Tama cried. 'Goodbye, Uncle, Nani, goodbye . . .'

Nani gave a sudden hoarse cry, as if she were in deep pain. The ocean flowed from her as she grabbed Tama again and again.

49

'Never forget, my moko,' she said, 'never ever forget.'

Tama threw his arms around her. 'No, Nani, I'll never *never* forget. Honest Indian, Nani, honest.'

Tama, Kara and Mere crowded the back window waving and waving and waving. When there was enough spit in his mouth to make the words, Tama whispered:

'Oh, Mummy, oh, Daddy, it was the *best* summer I've ever had. Ever.'

For some reason his vision became all blurry as if, after the long summer, rain had finally come to the Coast.

Once there was a nest, floating on the sea, at the edge of childhood. Then it was gone, its straws scattered across the waves. And I have been a kingfisher searching, always searching.

TENT ON THE HOME GROUND

George had been drinking in the pub with his friends for about twenty minutes when, from out of the smoke, Api pounced on him like a panther.

'Aren't I good enough for your mates?' Api said.

George was taken aback. He hadn't seen Api since they'd quarrelled at Te Huinga. 'I don't know what you mean,' he answered. 'It's good to see you, Api. Been a long time.'

Api laughed. Mocking. Scornful. 'Well I've been sitting over there ever since you came in,' he said. 'Watching you. You and your mates.' He jerked his head at the others at the table.

'I didn't see you,' George answered.

'You didn't want to,' Api said.

'So why didn't you come over to me,' George flared. 'Bit of a snob aren't you?'

'I know when I'm not wanted,' Api answered.

George gave a gesture of helplessness. Api would never change. What was the use. All this suspicion. All this distrust. The wonder was that they were still friends.

He introduced Api to the others: Peter, Warren and David, all from the office where he worked. All members of the establishment that Api so despised. White collar. Middle class. The people climbing to the top. Elitist.

'I've seen you around,' David said. He put out his hand and Api gripped it in a test of strength. David gave a nervous smile.

Api filled his glass from a jug on the table. 'Up the lot of you,' he saluted.

'Quit it, Api,' George said.

'And up you too, mate,' Peter interrupted. He had met Api before and their antipathy for each other was obvious. Polarised from the beginning by their different backgrounds neither would give an inch to the other. Their meetings had always been characterised by the clash of flint against flint.

Hastily, George separated them. 'Look here you two,' he said. 'I came in here to have a nice quiet drink. Now simmer down.' He started to make small talk with Warren. The atmosphere began to cool, relax and spread itself out comfortably as if a belt had been let out a couple of notches. George smiled at Api. While Warren was talking with Peter and David, he turned to Api and said:

'You know, it really is good to see you, Api.'

Api shrugged his shoulders. 'What's the celebration? It's not like you to come to the pub, brother.'

'David's been promoted,' George answered. 'He's leaving us at the end of the week.'

'And you?' Api asked. 'You been promoted too?' There was a hint of derision in the words. Behind dark glasses Api's eyes pricked George with ill-concealed mockery.

'No,' George answered.

'So you haven't been sucked into the system,' Api said. 'Not all the way yet.'

'They don't want me,' George returned.

Apparently he still didn't fit in, still appeared to lack that special sense of administrative ability and those nebulous qualities which interviewers were instructed to seek out in those applying for promotion. What the hell. He was happy enough where he was anyway.

'George should have been promoted though,' David said to Api with a quick anxious smile.

At his words, Api exploded with anger. 'Don't you patronise us, man.'

'Api . . .', George began.

But once Api was started he was difficult to stop. His temper flashed out like a paw.

'Of course my brother should have been promoted,' he said. 'But he's a black man and this is a white system. And does the white man want us in positions of power? Like hell he does.'

'Hey, easy there,' Warren interrupted.

'Look,' David began. 'I didn't mean to . . .'

'No, you look,' Api growled. 'You take a good hard look at the system you've created. It's in your image, not ours. Everything about it is white. Religion. Education. Politics. You name it. And I'll bet you there's hardly any of us in it.

Why? Because you're scared of us. So you keep us down. At the bottom of the system. Eh. Eh.' The words cracked like breaking bones.

'Crap,' Peter muttered.

'What did you say?' Api asked dangerously.

'Forget it, Api,' George said. 'Peter, just shut up won't you? Both of you, drink up.'

But Peter took no notice. 'I said crap and I mean crap,' he said again. 'Just because you can't cope with the system, Api, you accuse it of being racist.'

'Hell, that's because it is,' Api answered.

'Prove it then,' Peter said.

Api began to laugh. His laughter rose above the hum of conversations in the pub, catching the attention of a few people in the crowded bar. Momentarily diverted, they watched Api curiously before returning to their drinking.

'What's the joke?' Peter said angrily.

'You,' Api answered. 'You ask for proof and there's so much of it I don't know where to begin.'

'Because there isn't any,' Peter said.

Api narrowed his eyes. Then he flashed the quick smile of a panther. 'Who discovered New Zealand?' he asked.

'Eh? Oh, Abel Tasman,' Peter answered startled.

Api grinned with triumph. 'Man,' he said. 'Your answer is your proof. Long before Abel Tasman got here, Kupe discovered this country. But you've probably never heard of him, have you. After all, he was only a Maori.'

Peter reddened with anger. 'Kupe? He's just a legend.'

'Your second proof,' Api answered. 'Anything that happened to us you call myth or legend. Anything that happened to you is called history. Cheers man. You better shut your mouth by drinking up.'

By now, Api was in tremendous humour. He drained his glass and winked at George. Then he turned to Peter and said:

'How about buying us another round, friend?'

Peter looked at him with eyes gleaming. 'Buy your own,' he said.

For a moment, George thought that Api would lash out with his fists. But no, Api was enjoying the extent of Peter's antipathy.

'Don't be like that,' Api mocked. 'Buy your *brother* another drink.'

Api. Circling Peter with his calculated comments. Teasing. Trying to draw Peter further out into the open. Waiting.

'Lay off him,' George warned Api.

But it was too late. Peter had had enough. 'You see racism in everything, don't you?' he said to Api. 'The system as you call it. Everything. And only because you haven't been able to make it.'

'The system won't let me,' Api taunted.

'Why not? Everybody goes through it. All of us must face it. But you? Oh no. You want to pull it down. Well you'll never do it.'

Api's eyelids flickered with growing anger.

'Yes,' Peter continued scornfully. 'I've seen you and your friends down at Parliament. You've set up an embassy down there haven't you. To protest for Maori rights, isn't it? Well, there's some of us who think you already have more rights than we have. And we all think your protest is a big laugh. A joke.'

'Come off it, Peter,' George said uneasily. 'Api, don't listen to him. It's the beer talking.'

But Api was moving in for the kill. 'You think you're so superior,' he said to Peter. 'Well, laugh while you can, man. The world won't be yours much longer. Maori rights? Man, we're protesting for *human* rights. And we want the white system to acknowledge our rights. We're no joke, man. And we're hitting you at the heart of your system. Parliament itself. Your home ground, man. And we'll win too. You've raped us long enough.'

'For God's sake, Api,' George said. 'Enough of that talk.'

Api turned on him. 'As for you, brother, whose side are you going to be on?'

'It's not a question of taking sides,' George answered. 'It's not a matter of winning or losing.'

'So,' Api mocked. 'Still sitting on that bloody fence. Come off it, brother. With me. Now.'

'You do things your way, Api,' George said. 'I'll do things my way.'

'How?' Api asked. 'You'll never get the chance. You'll never be promoted. We can't make it from the inside so we have to hit the system from the outside. Can't you see that?'

George closed his eyes. When he opened them he saw Api putting down his glass. Api's face was filled with contempt.

'Up the lot of you,' he said. Then he walked away. Silent. Padding out of the pub.

For a long time nobody spoke at the table. Then David and Warren began to relax. It was all over now.

'Well,' George sighed. He grinned at Peter.

'The black bastard,' Peter swore.

'Hey . . .' George began.

'The black bastard,' Peter swore again. 'He'll never win.'

The words punched into George's mind. It wasn't a question of winning or losing. It wasn't a matter of white against black. It wasn't a question of taking sides. Or was it? And if it was, which side was the winner and which was the loser?

'Shut up, Peter,' George growled. 'Shut up. And buy us another round, *brother*. Forget what's happened. For God's sake.'

Outside, the night grew dark. Down at Parliament, a tent had been pitched on the home ground. A banner flapped on a wooden fence: You Stole My Land Now Leave My Soul. From within the tent came the sound of a guitar, singing and laughter. The sounds did not seem aggressive at all. *We're protesting for human rights.*

George stood watching from the shadows. He had been there over twenty minutes. Then he walked to the tent, past a placard bearing an upraised hand, and opened the flap. The light from a tilley lamp blazed upon him. *He'll never win, the black bastard, Peter had sworn.* The guitar stopped. The people in the tent looked at him. Curious. Wary. In the corner was Api. George tried to smile.

'Api, aren't I good enough for your mates,' he said.

MASQUES AND ROSES

THE BOY WITH THE CAMERA

A NEW YEAR'S STORY

For a change of pace, I offer 'Masques and Roses' and two stories written in the noir tradition. I'm not much good at working with implication, understatement, subtlety and finesse. Of all my stories, 'Masques and Roses' comes the closest, in my opinion, to this kind of style, this kind of perfection. It's choreographed like a courtly dance, which is what a masque is. It came up and out without hitting the sides.

In 'The Boy with the Camera' and 'A New Year's Story', I also tried another kind of style — the psychological noir thriller. The term 'noir' relates to dark, brooding American movies, primarily of the 1940s and 1950s, a species of psychological crime film having certain story and stylistic qualities. Set usually against bleak cynical cityscapes, film noir explores the sexual pathology of male characters caught in a web of deceit and desire, centred on a femme fatale, criss-crossed with a sense of fatalism.

With both stories, I've tried to create characters who are seriously ambivalent and to surround them in the mood, lighting, tight cutting and exaggerated angles of film noir but transferred to New Zealand. I've also deliberately suppressed the dialogue and applied a certain style, elusive, low-key and polished with a deceptive sheen. Those of you who know the films of Alfred Hitchcock may see echoes of the great movies of his American period — *Rear Window*, *Psycho*, *Vertigo* and *Marnie* — in the stories where things are not always what they seem to be and people, as in the complex relationships of Hitchcock's supreme work of art, *Vertigo*, are often not who they appear to be.

There are, of course, other echoes. 'The Boy with the Camera' is the original version of the story of the same name which was published in *Dear Miss Mansfield*; it is an updated version of Katherine Mansfield's 'Woman at the Store', surely a noir story itself.

'A New Year's Story' is based on events which occurred when I was a university student on vacation in Tauranga.

MASQUES AND ROSES

'What time did you say Philip was picking you up, dear?' Mrs Grant called through the closed bathroom door. Behind it she could hear the steady thrum of water in the shower box.

'Half past eight,' Kate called back.

Mrs Grant looked at her watch. Quarter to eight. Goodness. 'You'd better hurry then,' she said. She listened for a moment and heard the shower being turned off.

'All right, Mum.'

Mrs Grant nodded to herself. She went back into the sitting room where her husband was reading the newspaper. The room was softly lit. 'You'll ruin your eyesight,' she reproved him as she snapped the standard lamp on. She picked up her knitting, sat down in her favourite armchair and began to rock back and forth. With irritation she noticed it was still squeaking. She looked across to her husband wondering if he could hear it. His eyebrows were arched and his face tight with concentration on the news of the day. The pages rustled as he turned them. 'Anything interesting?' she asked him as she continued to knit. But he didn't seem to hear her. With a sigh she shifted herself more comfortably in the chair.

The bathroom door clicked open and Mrs Grant heard the slippered steps of her daughter making her way to her bedroom. 'You'd better get a move on,' she called.

Kate appeared at the doorway. She had her dressing gown on and was pulling off her shower cap. She was clean-scrubbed and shiny with youth. She smiled at her mother and then peered with alarm at the mantel clock. 'Gosh, is that really the time?'

Her mother nodded, amused.

'Oh well,' Kate continued, 'Piri's bound to be late anyway.' For a moment she stood there, brushing her hair. She caught her mother's eyes and felt a wave of sudden affection for her. 'Are you going anywhere tonight, Mum?' she asked.

Her mother looked at her husband and then back at her daughter. Mother and daughter grinned privately at one another across the room.

'You taking Mum out, Dad?' Kate asked him.

Mr Grant looked at her across the top of his glasses and arched his eyebrows at his wife.

'It's a good night for television,' Mrs Grant said. '*Coronation Street*'s on. Now hurry, dear. Which dress are you wearing?'

'The dark blue I think.'

'But don't you think it's a bit, well *tight*?'

'Oh Mum. We're going to a club, not a church dance.'

'Well,' Mrs Grant said, 'you know best.'

Kate nodded and left the doorway. Mrs Grant put her knitting aside and reached for her cigarette case. She lit a cigarette and sucked it gently. A smile touched her lips. 'Girls these days,' she declared. 'They just seem to throw clothes on in a couple of minutes and hope for the best.'

Mr Grant harrumphed and folded his newspaper. For a moment he was silent, staring at his wife, and she began to feel a small panic rising within her. *Don't say it, Bill. Don't.* 'This Maori boy and Kate . . .' he began. 'Do you think it's serious?'

Mrs Grant felt something wither inside her and the façade to her feelings about her daughter and this boy, Philip, begin to crack. She tried to recompose the mask, one which she had applied with as much care as the powder and lipstick to her face. 'Kate's only nineteen,' she answered. 'This is just the third time she's been out with him.' She put her cigarette aside and stood up. She looked at the vase of roses standing on an occasional table. One of the roses was slightly out of place and the effect was irritating. She began to rearrange it, pushing at the bouquet with sharp angry movements.

'Whatever happened to that other fellow she was going out with?' Mr Grant grumbled behind her. 'He was a much nicer boy. More suitable too.'

Mrs Grant drew a breath. *I just don't want to think about it.* 'George Watson?' her voice quavered. 'I saw his mother in town today. She asked me the same thing. I don't know. I suppose they quarrelled.'

'Yes. Well. Perhaps this new friendship of Kate's will blow over too. Bound to. Yes. Hmmmn.'

The newspaper crackled again. When Mrs Grant turned, her husband was immersed in it. She went back to her cigarette and took it up. But the façade would not stay in place. She took several puffs. Short. Quick. Urgent.

It wasn't as if Kate was plain or unpopular. She could have her pick of boys. She'd always been as pretty as a picture. A lovely baby. People on the street would stop and admire her as she sat smiling in her pushchair. She'd never wanted for anything and, although maybe she'd been just a little spoilt, she was the only daughter after all. She'd been a bright little girl and, later, a very good student. And she'd had lots of good and suitable friends. Then *why*?

'Mum, can you zip me up?' Kate was at the door again, holding her hair away from the back of her dress. Her mother went to attend her and as she did, Kate looked at her father and giggled. 'Stop peeking, Dad!'

Mr Grant grinned. Oh she was a cheeky one, his little girl. Beautiful, too. Nobody could mistake that breeding. 'Why should I peek? When you were younger I saw all there was to see, my lady!' They laughed together and the mask was back in place and this was simply their little girl who was waiting for a friend to take her out.

'There,' Mrs Grant said. She stepped back to survey her daughter. Just lovely. Not too much makeup, the dress a little too informal for her taste but no, she was lovely all the same.

'Could I borrow your brooch, Mum?' Kate asked.

'Of course, dear,' Mrs Grant answered. She turned to go to the bedroom. The front doorbell chimed.

'Oh gosh, Piri's on time for once!' Kate wailed. She ran through the hallway.

Mrs Grant hurried to the bedroom. She opened the top drawer of the vanity unit and reached in to get the brooch. Her eyes glistened. She pricked her finger.

I would be worried about Kate no matter who she was going out with. She patted her hair and put a smile on her face. She walked out into the hall.

He was standing there.

'Hullo, Philip,' she said. 'Here we are, dear.' She fixed the brooch to her daughter's dress. Kate smelt like a rose. Then Mrs Grant looked into that dark face. That dark face with the hesitant smile that showed that he knew. He knew. And yet he could smile as she did and remain polite.

'Hullo, Mrs Grant,' he said.

'Will you come in for a while?' she asked.

'All right,' he answered. 'But I'm parked on a bus stop. Couldn't find any place else, eh.'

'You'd better hurry then, dear,' Mrs Grant said to Kate.

'I'll just get my coat,' Kate answered. 'Won't be long, Piri.' She ran down the hall, leaving her mother and Piri standing there by the door. With each other.

'Mr Grant is in the sitting room,' Mrs Grant said. She led the way through the carpeted hall. 'Dear? Philip's here.'

Mr Grant looked into her tremulous face, so pale and bright. His wife, waiting there, needing him. 'Hullo Philip,' he greeted. The heartiness of his greeting surprised him. He put aside his newspaper and rose to shake this boy's hand.

'Mr Grant,' Piri acknowledged. Then he stood there. In his dark jacket and open-collared shirt. Wondering whether his appearance was all right and whether or not the nick on his chin had stopped bleeding.

'Unfortunately,' Mrs Grant said, 'Philip can't stay long. He's parked on a bus stop.'

'Oh?' Mr Grant asked. 'Our off-street parking isn't what it used to be now that they've put up that block of flats further down the road.'

Piri nodded his head. He didn't know what to say. He looked round the room. 'Nice roses, Mrs Grant,' he offered.

'Why, thank you Philip.'

Her words glittered like pieces of broken glass.

Then, at last, Kate was there, smiling up at this boy. Putting her hand in his. Her hand in his hand. Her long fingers twining in his, interlocking, joining, pressing into his.

Mrs Grant turned again to her roses.

'Have Mum and Dad been looking after you?' she heard Kate ask.

'Yes.'

'What time will you be home, dear?' she heard her husband ask.

'About one I think, Dad.'

'Fine. I'll leave the hall light on for you.'

Then she felt her husband squeezing her arm and the small comforting press of his lips against her cheek.

'They're leaving now, dear.'

Mrs Grant turned. Her face was gay but her eyes were glistening.

'Are you all right, Mum?' Kate asked.

She hugged her daughter tightly.

'Of course, dear. It's just that you're so pretty,' she answered. She tried to laugh and to smile at this boy standing beside her daughter. But he knew. He knew.

'Well, we'll be off then,' Piri said. He followed Kate down the hall way to the front door. Mr and Mrs Grant went with them. The night was warm.

'Don't wait up,' Kate laughed. She blew a kiss to her parents. They waved back. 'Have a good time,' Mrs Grant called.

Mr Grant shut the door. He was silent for a moment. Then he put his arm round his wife. 'Well,' he said. 'That's that.'

Together they walked back to the sitting room. At the doorway, Mrs Grant gently moved from him and went to the bathroom. There she put a small sticking plaster over her pricked finger. The bathroom smelt like a little girl and she began to cry as she picked up the things her daughter had left on the floor. Surely Kate knew better than to leave the bathroom in a mess. Then she went into the kitchen to make a cup of tea.

'Aah,' Mr Grant smiled as she brought the tray into the sitting room.

Mrs Grant sat down on the sofa beside him. 'Was there anything interesting on the news?' she asked. She did not want to look into his face. She did not want him to see her face. She did not want to talk about anything except ordinary things. But her hand began to quiver and she had to put the silver teapot down.

'Dear?' her husband asked.

'Oh it's just my finger,' Mrs Grant said. 'I pricked it when I took the brooch out of the drawer.' She finished pouring the tea. She took her cup to where she'd been sitting in the armchair. She picked up her knitting and then put it down again. She began to sip at her tea. She lit a cigarette. She put it in the ash tray and took up her cup again.

Her husband smiled across at her. 'He's quite a nice boy really, I suppose,' he said to her.

Mrs Grant tried to smile back.

'And our Kate,' he continued, 'she's become a real beauty.'

Mrs Grant nodded.

'Yes, she's a good girl,' she said.

THE BOY WITH THE CAMERA

At her wits' end, the woman bought her son a camera. There, she said, go out and photograph the hills or trees or pond or birds, anything, but just *go*. The boy looked up at her with a hurt hangdog expression. He picked up the camera and, because he loved his mother, aimed and — *click* — took his first photograph of her tired, red and swollen face.

The woman had been living alone with her son for two years, her husband having deserted them both. She managed the motel that her husband had bought. In the middle of nowhere, on a cardboard plain two hundred miles out from the nearest town, the motel comprised an office and five double bedroom units — the woman and her son lived in one of the units. Apart from the motel, sitting there beside the black highway, there was nothing else to see but wave upon wave of yellow grass patched with stunted trees like babies' fingers reaching up out of the parched earth. Just the motel, that black line slicing the plain in half and the sea of *nothing*.

The motel had been built five years before by a brewery firm on the other side of the mountains. The firm had noted that the highway connected the city with a mountain resort one hundred miles away and had, perhaps justifiably, considered that a motel equidistant between city and mountains would do good business. What the firm had not counted on was that the package weekends offered by city travel agents — including air commuter service to and from the resort — would be a cheaper and quicker alternative for travellers. Indeed the only people who used the road were those who did it once out of curiosity (and never again), the large service trucks taking supplies to the resort and itinerant workers with nowhere to go. Very few people actually stopped at the motel and, if they did, they only stopped overnight — truck drivers needing a break or young men and women on their way to the resort, unable to wait to have each other. The television reception was poor, the units substandard, the refrigerators were not always working, there was no breakfast service — and then there was the woman herself and her son. There was something about both of them which was unpleasant, somehow depressing and *real*.

Once, the woman had worked in an upmarket bar in the city. In those days she had been as pretty as a wax doll and her figure and lascivious nature had made her an ideal hostess. She had been popular with men in the bar, did not mind being taken home if the guy was good-looking, and she herself boasted that she knew one hundred and fifty-five different ways of kissing. But she was only attractive as long as she was young and, in her early thirties, she began to look for some john to marry her. She found a fine big chap with a voice on him like a trombone but little upstairs. They married and produced a scrawny son and lived in a constant state of warfare. He would disappear for nights on end and she, in retaliation, would invite men to take his place. She was careless about her infidelities and that was when the beatings began. Nine years later she had been reduced to this: a woman who resembled a hungry bird, a thing of sticks and wires, chipped teeth and red pulpy hands. Certainly her eyes were still blue and what hair she had was still yellow. As for the boy, he looked a gangling and foolish youth, slack-jawed and dark-eyed. He followed his mother everywhere because he adored her so.

The motel was an oven in summer and a freezer in winter. Summer was worst because all day the heat was terrible. The wind blew close to the ground; it rooted among the tussock grass, slithered along the road and parched everything. Just behind the motel was a small copse of shaded trees and a little pond. Hundreds of larks shrilled there every morning, screaming a short time and shooting like poisonous darts in the slate sky before returning to perch in the trees again. When the woman's husband had accompanied the brewery's sales agent out to the motel to look it over, his decision to buy had been as much determined by that little copse as by the dreams of making big money — the sales agent was a slick talker and knew a sucker when he saw one. With the sales documents in his hands the husband couldn't wait to tell his wife what he had done and that they were on their way *up*. Did you look at the occupancy rate? she asked. No. How about the monthly takings? No, but the agent assured me that the motel was a goer under the right management and there were a lot of big trucks on the highway. Unconvinced, the woman allowed herself to be driven across the plain. As soon as she saw the motel she knew her husband had been conned. She asked him to stop on a small rise just above the motel. Well, she said, looking down at the huddle of buildings which was going to be her prison for the next three years, you've really done it this time. Then she started to laugh and her husband, mad with anger, began to slap her around. In the back seat, the boy closed his eyes and covered his ears so as not to hear his mother's cries.

A month later, after the sale had been confirmed, the man shifted his wife and son from their apartment in the city to the motel. There was nothing the woman could do except to hope for the best and she had even begun to fantasise that the motel would be successful — but the dream turned to dust when the car topped the rise and she saw the motel again. Nevertheless she got herself busy preparing the motel rooms — putting new curtains up, mending the linen, replastering the walls and replacing the carpets. It was invigorating work and she made two discoveries which she confided to her husband. The first was the darkroom, just off the office, which indicated that the former manager had been interested in photography. The second was the pile of photographs in the darkroom of couples having sex. The woman knew that the photographs were not professionally taken — they were too amateurish and the lighting was not good. When washing down the walls in the unit next to the office, she found a hole just large enough to poke a camera through. The woman and her husband laughed about that. Then the woman saw that her husband was becoming turned on by the photographs. They began to fondle and kiss each other.

In the first few months of ownership, the woman and her husband got lucky. They averaged at least four customers a week and five or six travellers a day wanting a coffee break and a bit of exercise. The truckers took a curious interest in the couple, particularly the woman, and got on their CBs to radio one another about the motel. The woman enjoyed the company of the customers and went out of her way to be attractive and fun. She encouraged her husband to put up signs three miles on either side of the motel so that people would know there was a nice rest stop just ahead with oh-so-cosy rooms and coffee cheap at $1.50 a cup. Indeed, in those initial months, the woman would make breakfast for her husband and son — Just like a regular family, she used to say — and then give the boy his morning school lessons, the motel being too far away from any school. Around lunchtime, there were bound to be people stopping for coffee, so the woman would pretty herself up, put on a little apron, a remnant from her days as a hostess in a bar, and make the customers feel right at home. Sometimes she flirted a little but, at that stage, it was all fun and nothing went further. In the afternoon the husband would

65

take a nap or read a magazine and the woman would take the boy through his lessons again. When sundown came, the man would put on the VACANCY sign, and together the woman and he would wait expectantly for the headlights of a car to come down the rise, go past, and then for the rear red lights to come on as the car backed to the motel. Why, hello, the man would say. Come right on in. The greatest thrill came when the air commuter service between the city and the resort broke down for five days. During that period the travel agents bused their customers to and from the resort. The PR man for the resort contracted the husband and the woman to cater two meals a day. The woman was in her element and the man, thinking that this was only the harbinger of greater things, beamed with pride.

Then the good luck ran out. The air commuter service resumed. Worse still, the off-season at the resort meant that traffic dwindled to a trickle along the highway. There was still the occasional trucker or hot and hungry couple stopping over, but time began to weigh heavily on the woman and her husband — particularly the husband. Nothing was worse for him than to sit in his office or out front, day by day, watching the cars go by and waiting for one of them to stop and back up. He would brace a smile on his lips whenever a car appeared at the top of the rise . . . and watch as it slid past and out of reach. He would think, The next car will stop The next car will stop The next car will stop — but it never did. The sight of the woman, all dressed up and waiting for customers who never came, only heightened his sense of failure and frustration. Nor was television or reading any help. The highway mesmerised him. It was like a long black straw and the motel was a small illuminated mouth waiting to drink.

In this mood the man grew mean and cunning. He started to slap his son around as if he was a fly. Whenever he had sex with his wife he tried to make it hurt. One night, the woman found him watching through the hole in the wall as two men and a woman groaned their way to climax. Very soon, any and all travellers were booked into the unit where he could watch. Then, quite by chance, one of the truckers, seeing the woman, vaguely remembered her from her days as a hostess. He came to verify — and the husband told the woman to put out to the guy. When she refused he held a knife to their son's neck. She went with the trucker, and the next. When her husband told her to use the room where he could watch she was already in too deep to object. After all, hers was the only income keeping them a going proposition. She went through a very rough time. The only person who loved the woman was her son, but he was too young and weak to help her. She tried to protect him when she could but, when she found that her husband was forcing her son to watch at the hole in the wall, she felt she had lost him. All the same, she was a woman with some respect for herself and she hoped that she would always remain, in her son's eyes, his *mother* and not some cheap whore. What she did not realise was that her son, seeing her with other men, loved her more not less. Then one night she told her husband, I'm not doing this again. He threatened the boy. She went for the knife. He beat up on her so bad that she ended up with two broken teeth. After that, her husband started to hitch rides away from the motel, anything to escape the monotony of the place and the ugliness of his wife, anything. He went away overnight. Then for weekends. Then for weeks at a time. At least his absences brought respite to the woman and her son. Then one evening the man took to the road carrying with him all the savings they had ever earned at the motel. He lit out. The boy felt a surge of triumph, because now he had his mother to himself.

The woman decided that she would stay because there was nowhere else to go. Battered as she was, and lacking in self-esteem, she knew that she would have to make the best of it for herself and her son. By that time, however, fortune was in a slowly descending spiral. The motel had already started to show its age and, despite her attempts with her son to keep it looking nice, no amount of repair or uplift improved it. The signs on the road faded in the hot sun so that travellers who may have stopped did not know the motel was there until they had passed it by. The rude paint jobs the woman tried to give the exterior peeled away one layer after another, giving the place the appearance of a diseased apple. The A in the neon sign slipped away, and then the N, so that nobody could understand the word VAC   CY. Even if they had, they would not have stopped. A motel whose sign was not kept up spelt trouble. In spite of all this, there were happy times for the woman. She took up with a Maori for three weeks and there were always men of a certain kind who liked women of her kind. Sometimes one of the truckers would bring some booze and they would make a night of it, drinking their cares away. The only thorn in her side was the boy — her son — who persisted in following her everywhere. No matter where she went, she felt she was never alone. He was always there. It was not his fault, of course, but she began to feel paranoiac about him. Why don't you do something? she would scream. Go somewhere! Get out from under my feet! Give me some space, let me breathe, do anything, but go *away*. She would push him from the motel and watch as he ran to the copse to shoot some birds or lay snares for rabbits. His rifle would shatter the copse, the larks shrilling and circling like a black shredded net in the sky. Make a garden, grow some flowers, plant a tree, go fishing, go anywhere. But the boy knew that his mother did not mean it and that she loved him. After all, who else was there for her to love?

Then a travelling salesman passed by and the woman bought her son the camera. From the very beginning it was a great success. The boy became camera mad. He took photographs of his mother, her lovers, the occasional overnight traveller, the copse, the passing cars, his mother, the truckers, the larks, the motel guests, the pond, his mother, the passing cars, his mother, the plain, his mother, his mother, his mother. Seeing his interest, his mother decided to renovate the old darkroom. One of the truckers, an amateur photographer himself, helped her out by bringing and installing photographic equipment he no longer had any use for. He gave the boy lessons and saw the wonder on the boy's face when he developed his first photograph. The photograph had been taken by the trucker. It showed the woman with a young man. The young man's left arm was possessively around the woman's waist. When the woman saw the photograph she felt a twinge of nostalgia and fear at the sight of this young man who, despite the fact that he was still gangling and foolish, had once been her little boy.

Two years is a long time in the life of a boy. The body strengthens and thickens, stubble grows in the armpits and crotch, the down on the chin becomes a beard, the voice deepens and nocturnal fantasies are accompanied by strong surges of desire. All these symptoms of manhood descended on the boy and the woman knew that he must leave. She wrote to a brother from whom she had been estranged many years asking if he would take her son in. A month later she received a reply saying, No, but send the kid for a vacation. When she told her son he thought he was leaving her forever. He began to whine and plead with her and, for the first time in her life, she struck him. She told him to pack and that he would be going the next day.

But that evening, the man who had deserted her two years before returned. I thought I'd see how my wife was getting on, the husband said. Get out, she answered. That's not a nice way to welcome your man, he said. Get out and stay out, she responded. Making a go of it are you? he asked. I'm still here, she taunted. Stashing it away huh? he continued. I'm doing okay, she laughed. At that point, the son arrived. So the brat has grown, the father laughed. You heard her, the son said, now get out. So he's a man is he? the father asked, then take me sonny, *take me*. The father and son fought and the woman tried to help her son. But the father's brutal experience gave him the upper hand. He struck his son to the ground and began kicking him. The mother managed to pull her husband away. She yelled to the boy, Go son go away go —

Bloodied and sobbing, the boy crashed out of the door and ran blindly through into the dark room. He shut the door and put his hands over his ears. He looked at all the negatives of his mother, hanging in strips around him, and pulled them all close to him, wishing that they were her. He felt that he had failed her.

How long he was in the dark room the boy never knew. But suddenly his mother was there, scratching at the door. He did not want to look at her because he was ashamed. When he did he saw that his mother's eyes had been blackened and her lip was still bleeding. The woman saw her son's alarm. Don't worry, she said, the bastard's gone. The boy asked, How? His mother answered, He only came for the money and I gave it to him. Then, without speaking, she tended to him and told him to go to sleep. Later that night he heard the back door opening. He saw his mother silhouetted in the light of a naked bulb.

The next morning the woman was up early to get her son some breakfast. She wanted him out of there and on his way to his uncle's in the east. She called to him, Your breakfast's getting cold. There was no answer. She shrugged her shoulders and thought that he must still be packing. She called again. There was no answer. Puzzled, the mother went in search of her son. She called through the house and realised that he must be in the dark room. Don't come in yet, he said. Not yet. But the woman was angry and wanted to know what he was doing. She opened the door.

The boy had just finished processing the negatives. He had blown two of them up. The woman saw that he had used an infrared film to take the photographs. Her face grew large with grief as she realised that he had followed her the night before. Why? she asked. One of the photographs showed her dragging the body of her husband toward the copse. Because I don't want to leave, her son said. Why? she asked again. The other photograph showed her removing the knife from her husband's chest. Because I love you, her son said.

At that moment, the woman heard the sound of a car horn. It seemed to be coming from far away. The boy ran past her to look. He pointed to the top of the rise. Three hawks were descending out of the sun.

A NEW YEAR'S STORY

And after that New Year's party, New Year could never pass without some memory of Max. No matter how hard Alec tried to forget, something always brought her back. Wine spilling from red lips. A streamer just the right shade of red curling through the jam-packed room. A girlish giggle, so brittle it was almost ready to break, just before the clock ticked to midnight, 'Happy New Year!' Just a glimpse of something, a *flick*, was all that was needed.

Alec was a student and had just completed his final year of law at the University of Auckland. He'd already been interviewed by a senior partner of one of Auckland's most prestigious law firms and had been offered a job. 'Apart from having the qualifications,' the interviewing partner had observed, 'there's a certain ruthlessness about you, young man, that will take you to the top. It doesn't hurt, either, that you've got a definite appeal that women will find attractive. You'll do very nicely.'

Any other student might have found that assessment objectionable but Alec was too self-aware to let it matter. It was only to be expected that he would start his career at the top, he intended to stay at the top and he would use whatever skill, charm and ruthlessness to do it. When he had gone as far as he could with the law firm he would go the next rung. Alec knew it and the interviewing partner knew it. Meantime they would use each other, draping their respective ambitions in the niceties of legal decorum and conduct.

'Thank you, sir,' Alec said as he shook hands. He looked firmly into the senior partner's eyes and, in that moment, thought of his father. After all, it had been Alec senior, a successful farmer in Gisborne, who had taught him that winner takes all. The fourth son in a family with dynastic connections in Poverty Bay, Alec senior had offered a loan to his oldest brother when he was having problems keeping the family farm going — and then bought the farm at the lowest possible price at a mortgagee sale. Family relationships and sentiment had no part in Alec senior's dealings; business was business.

From his father, Alec junior had not only inherited the same ruthlessness; he'd also inherited dark good looks and a frame whose power no clothes could hide. Women liked the look of him and he knew it and took advantage of it. When his womanising began, his father delighted in it. Alec's mother, however, disapproved. 'I never thought that a mother would say this of her son,' she said, 'but I must. I shall always love you, of course, but I don't think I have ever liked you, Alec.' Tenderly, she pushed at an unruly lock of his hair. 'I don't think I ever shall, really.'

Alec's mother died three months before that summer when he met Max. The prospect of spending Christmas and New Year alone with his father in Gisborne, was not attractive to Alec. He tried to persuade his live-in girlfriend, Helen, to come with him but, 'No,' Helen said, 'Mum and Dad are expecting me to be home.' Alec waited for her to invite him home with her. She never did. Three days before Christmas he packed a canvas bag, slung it into the back seat of his jeep, tied his surfboard on top and headed south.

For all his faults, Alec was a good and attentive son. Chiselled from the same stone, father and son understood each other well. Alec senior was busy with the shearing and his Maori workers respected him. Alec enjoyed the two days prior to Christmas working on the farm and, on Christmas Eve, to his surprise, he discovered that his father had booked a table for two at the best restaurant in town. The two men made a striking pair at dinner and the ease of their rapport made the evening a warm and affecting one. Many townspeople came over to wish Alec senior the best of the season. Near the end of the dinner Alec Senior gave his son the traditional gift: a cheque for a thousand dollars.

'Alec,' he said, 'you've done your duty. Now go, lad, there's nothing to keep you here.' Just as he was leaving, Alec saw his father's new Maori housekeeper join his father and slip a hand into his.

On Christmas Day, Alec telephoned his friend Josh in Tauranga, and told him he was coming up for New Year.

'Great, man,' Josh answered, 'but you've left it a little late. All the good-looking women have been taken.'

Alec hesitated. 'That's okay,' he said. 'But if you think of anybody, do me a favour, huh?' He didn't really need Josh to pimp for him but he didn't want to waste too much time hunting. He needed a woman. The sooner the better.

'I'll see if I can fix you up with Max,' Josh answered.

Alec made the trip back north nice and easy with a surfing stop just past Whakatane. The surf was up and the surfers were out. He hooked up with a couple of Aussies and, after some serious surfing, smoked some dope with them on the beach. They invited him to go with them on the never-ending quest for women but Alec declined — he wanted to hit Tauranga by midnight. By the time he reached the city it was just after one in the morning. The beach carnival atmosphere was evident in the crowded streets and throngs of holidaymakers. The whole place was jumping and gave Alec a frisson of anticipation. His nostrils flared and his eyes narrowed in heat. When he reached Josh's place there was a note pinned to the door:

GONE TO THE MOUNT. PARTY AT 163 BEACH TERRACE.

MAX WILL BE THERE.

Alec headed across town. There was no mistaking Beach Terrace or the party house. There it was, lights blazing and music booming. The windows were open and people were sitting on the sills. As Alec came loping up the path he saw someone vomiting from the window — a long golden arc dropping into darkness. Then he heard cheers from inside. The back door was open.

'Beer's in the kitchen,' a young guy said, 'and the action's in the sitting room.'

Alec nodded, squeezed through the crush and the gloom, grabbed a glass, filled it with beer, and made his way toward the insistent beat of the music. The nearer he got the more pulsating the music became: a foxy fuck-me Madonna number. But nobody was dancing. Instead, they were all watching, cheering and whistling as, above their heads, a young blonde girl rose and fell in a cone of fluorescent blue light.

'Ride him, cowboy,' everyone yelled. 'Ride him hard —'

Alec pushed through to the centre of the room. The girl was laughing, her head thrown back, eyes closed with joy, lips parted in ecstasy. She was astride the saddle of a mechanical bull. When it bucked high, her body arched, whipped and jerked, simulating sex. The blue light bathed her with eroticism.

Somebody crashed into Alec as he was watching. It was Josh, and he was already smashed. He slapped Alec on the back, gave a suggestive wink and, pointing to the girl, said, 'Alec, meet Max.'

At that moment, the ride came to an end. Triumphant, the girl stood on the saddle and jumped into the crowd. Hands came up to roll her across the room. She tumbled towards Alec and Josh, who caught her and swung her to the ground.

Laughing, she looked at Josh — and then at Alec. Josh whispered in her ear. He pushed some dollars down the front of her jeans. Max's eyes glittered.

'So you're Alec,' Max said, tossing her hair. 'I'm Maxine but people call me Max if they're lucky enough to get to know me better. Are you lucky, Alec?'

Alec smiled. Max's eyes narrowed like a cat's. 'I get so hot dancing, don't you? Doesn't it make you want to rip off your clothes, Alec?' She fingered his shirt and pulled. 'Do you mind getting ripped?' She led Alec away from the crowded room and down to her car — a sporty MG. In silence they drove to Josh's place. There, she stripped Alec, pushing him away whenever he tried to embrace her. He was surprised at the strength, the edge of viciousness, in her resistance. 'No,' she said, her teeth clenched, 'be a good boy now.' When Alec was fully undressed she took a few steps away to look at him. Pushed him on the bed. Went to the bathroom. Snorted a line of coke. Asked him if he wanted some. Came back and straddled him. Slapped him. He slapped back.

'Good,' Max smiled as the coke hit. 'I like to play rough.'

That had been Boxing Day, five days before that fateful New Year's party. When Alec woke in the morning Max had gone and he wondered whether he had dreamed it all. The girl on the bull. The girl riding him, spurring him onward. When he went into the bathroom he knew it had not been a dream. There were raw welts all over his body as if Max had flayed him with a bullwhip. Max had used her lipstick to write a message across the mirror.

Oh my Goodness!

Bemused, Alec showered, had breakfast and — when he saw that Josh had come back home from the party at some point to crash and had a girl beneath him — took his surfboard out to the beach. The sea was brilliant, aquamarine, and although there wasn't much surf Alec didn't care. He took his board way out and just sat there, watching the beach and the thin stretch of esplanade. Every now and then there was the flash of some car caught in the sunlight. It was almost as if someone was trying to semaphore to him, sending secret messages. The seawater, splashing on his skin, burned his welts. He'd had rough sex before but last night had bordered on sadism.

Around mid afternoon, Alec returned to Josh's place. The two friends grappled and slapped one another. Josh introduced Alec to his girl, Sylvia, a small redhead who scowled at Alec as if he had done something wrong. 'Did you get to the party?'

Josh asked. It was obvious that he had been too drunk to remember. In response, Alec struck a pose and let his shirt fall from his shoulders so that Josh could see the welts. 'So you met up with our Maxine then,' he grinned. 'Either that,' Alec answered, 'or somebody ran over me with a tank.' The two men laughed, but Sylvia didn't see the joke.

'Men are such arseholes,' Sylvia said. She kicked at her chair and left.

'Sorry, mate,' Josh said ruefully. 'I should have warned you. Our Max and Syl are twins. Syl hates people talking about Max as if she was a slut.'

Alec was stunned. He watched as Sylvia flounced down on a deck chair in the corner of the balcony and began sunning herself. Maxine and Sylvia were so unlike. One blonde, the other redhead. One slim, the other curvaceous. One beautiful, the other merely pretty. One dramatic, the other silent. 'I don't get it,' Alec said.

'Man, you don't know the half of it,' Josh answered. 'There was a third sister, more stunning than either Max or Syl put together. She was the *real* blonde. Her name was Barbara.'

Alec went to talk to Sylvia. 'You're in my sun,' she said.

'Listen,' Alec began, 'I'm sorry. I didn't know you and Max were sisters.'

Sylvia pushed back a red lock of her hair and stared at him. 'Look,' she said, 'I don't know you from Adam. You could be a nice guy for all I know but, personally, I wouldn't give you the skin off a grape. When Josh asked me to fix you up with Max I thought, what's the harm, because she's been through enough already. I don't know if you're going to see Max again or not. But if you do you better be good to her. If you're not, you'll answer to me.'

'Hey,' Josh called, 'go easy there, Syl.'

With a rush and a whirl, Sylvia stood up and spat her words at Alec. 'You think my sister's been an easy fuck, don't you.' Her voice was defensive, scornful. 'Well, I've got news for you, buddy boy. Max fucked *you*.'

Around five o'clock, Alec surprised Josh by asking if he had Max's address.

'You're not thinking of seeing her again?' Josh asked. 'Bad idea. My deal with her was that you were strictly a one-night stand. Now go out and find another woman.'

Josh was emphatic, and Alec wondered if Sylvia had been working on him. He persisted and, with some reluctance, Josh told him where Max worked. 'She wouldn't want to see you mate,' Josh yelled as Alec drove down the driveway. The trouble was that Sylvia's taunt kept coming at Alec. He hadn't liked that.

74

Half an hour later, Alec arrived at Max's office. Her red MG was parked outside. For a moment, Alec wondered why Max was working over the Christmas break. Then he saw the sign on a second-storey window — HASKIN BRYAN ASSOCIATES, REAL ESTATE — and realised why: for realtors, holidays mean brisk business. He parked opposite the office. At a window he could see young woman with short cropped red hair, talking into a telephone. Sometimes a man would appear, an executive type, balding, wearing a short sleeved white shirt, to give her some papers. There was no glimpse of Max.

As Alec was about to go up to the office to ask for Max, he saw an office boy come down the stairs and put the CLOSED sign on the door. Shortly after that the office boy left, followed by the bald man. The woman with the short red hair disappeared from the window. When she appeared at the downstairs doorway she winced at the sunlight and put on dark glasses. Alec was still watching the door and it was not until the last moment that he saw the redhead had stepped into the MG. It was only then that he realised she was Max.

Alec's mind was in a turmoil. This couldn't be the girl riding the Minotaur. This couldn't be the blonde with the figure which, last night, had practically whistled at itself. This couldn't be the Maxine who, high on coke, had slept with him last night.

Spinning the car, Alec went after Max's MG as it squealed through the homebound traffic — there was no doubt that the lady knew how to handle the wheel. Alec caught her at an intersection, drew up behind her, and flashed his lights to attract her attention. Max looked up, took off her sunglasses, stared, and put them on again. Alec was about to call to her but she roared off. Alec decided to follow her. This Maxine was nothing like the Max he had been with. This was more like her redhead sister, Sylvia. And Josh's words flashed through his mind that the real blonde had been Barbara.

Max drove fast, efficiently and oblivious of danger. She seemed to regard the highway as hers. She drove dangerously, taking chances, as if she didn't give a shit if she smashed herself up or not. Very soon she had her MG to full throttle and zooming down the Pacific highway. Alec lost her on the straight and, topping a rise, realised that she must have turned off somewhere. He backtracked and, on his left, saw a side road leading down to a small motel with a bar overlooking the sea. Max's MG was in the carpark.

When Alec walked in, Max had just bought a drink and was taking it out to the patio. Alec took a seat inside where he could watch her through the darkened window. Strong sunlight can be cruel to women and, in Max's case, it was very cruel. Her hair was coarse and its styling was butch. The chalk white skin that often comes with redheads was blotched and stained — and there were fine lines, like scars, patterning the left cheek, neck and shoulder. Her face, devoid of makeup, held nothing individual. Yet every action Max made — kissing the glass with her bottom lip, crossing her ankles, hitching up her short skirt — transformed her. She was not a beauty but she was certainly sexual. Alec made his move. He walked out to her and touched her shoulder. She looked up and at him as if he was walking out of a dream.

'Why, hello Alec,' Max smiled. 'Do you always go around leaving your fingerprints on a girl's shoulder? Not that I mind particularly. You've got such nice, strong hands.'

At that moment, a black sedan parked next to the MG. A dark, brooding man got out. Max stood up. 'Goodbye Alec,' she said. She put her drink down and walked across the patio to the man. They talked for a while and Max opened her bag and gave the man some cash. In return he held out to her a small package that Alec knew must be drugs. The man was playful, however, and kept teasing Max by holding the package just beyond her reach. She fell into his arms and he kissed her, long and strong. She began to struggle, and Alec saw the man put a hand into Max's dress. When Max finally broke away she spat at the man. He laughed and gave her the drugs. She turned, went to her car and drove out of the carpark. The man lit a cigarette, looked at Alec enquiringly, waited a moment, shrugged and then stepped into the black sedan.

The next day Alec telephoned Helen, his girlfriend in Auckland. It was almost as if he was attempting to establish some compass point in his life. Helen told him she was fine and happy. Would he see her after New Year? Alec asked. Perhaps, she said. Frustrated, Alec took his surfboard and, on the way, saw a young woman sunbathing on the beach. She liked what she saw. He liked what he saw. They smoked some dope together and then they made love in the dunes. When he got back to Josh's place, Josh wasn't there. But Sylvia was. Without really meaning to, Alec told Sylvia he had followed Maxine out to the motel. He mentioned the drug dealer.

Sylvia stared at Alec for quite a while. She had a glass of beer in her hand and she threw it at Alec. When she calmed down, she told Alec about Barbara, the third sister.

Every small beach town has a girl like Barbara. There are always girls just as beautiful but only one or two whose upward trajectory takes them like a comet through the sky, a comet everybody sees. Barbara is the local beauty, belonging to the genus Venus. She trades in beauty and the charisma that comes from beauty. She is the one who, second from the left in any competition, captures the attention of the judge and gets the crown. She already comes with a string of prizes from prettiest baby through Mount Maunganui Teen Queen to Miss Tauranga. Nor is she just an incredible freak of flawless skin and high cheekbones — her personality is gold-plated gorgeousness. Where other girls just walk into a room, Barbara lights it up. Other girls win hearts, Barbara torches them. She is incendiary, packing her own voltage, so that when she is not there you can taste the gap and see the empty space she has left behind. She has no peers because she is peerless. She has no equals because she is excellence unrivalled. She sets her own standard, and can only be measured against herself — Barbara on one day with Barbara on the next. Wherever she walks she walks in beauty. Whatever flaws she may have become distinctive characteristics of her total glamour. A girl like Barbara doesn't just happen to a family or community. She *impacts* on them and they are never the same again.

'When we were growing up,' Sylvia said, 'there was always me and Max, and then there was Barbara. Max and I were twins, three years older than Barbara, and Mum and Dad loved us both — but when Barbara came along they idolised her. We were pretty —' Sylvia's face assumed a self-mocking smile '— but we were made plain by comparison. I always had the feeling that Dad just couldn't handle the unbelievable beauty of Barbara. Anything was good enough for Max and me but nothing was good enough for Barbara. It was like having —' Sylvia shuddered '— a goddess in the house.'

'Weren't you jealous?' Alec asked.

Sylvia lit a cigarette and puffed nervously. 'Sure,' she continued. 'Max and I did horrible things to Barbara when she was growing up. You know, the usual acts of sibling rivalry. Once we cut all those cute golden curls off her head. Another time we shaved her eyebrows. The trouble was that we could never be jealous of Barbara too long. When she became a teenager I can remember saying to her, 'You are in danger, Barbara Louis, of becoming too gorgeous.' It would have been much easier on all of us if Barbara had grown up a downright bitch, done something which we could hate her for like steal our boyfriends, but she never did. What Max and I could never quite understand was that Barbara loved *us*. Although Mum and Dad favoured her she always made sure we were treated equally. If she got a blue dress, we all got blue dresses. If she got new shoes, we all did. But even in the same clothes, she was the one people looked at, that people loved.'

Four years ago, everyone's lives changed.

'Barbara had been winning beauty contests ever since she was a baby,' Sylvia said. 'But this time, the competition Barbara entered was for 'Miss New Zealand Cinema', and the winner's prize was a trip to Hollywood and a screen test. Barbara won the Tauranga regional semifinal and Mum and Dad planned to take her to the finals in Auckland. At the last moment Mum came down with the flu, Dad had to stay with her and, instead, Max and I went with Barbara. We were so excited. We stayed at the Sheraton and the ceremony was just wonderful —'

And Maxine was wearing a blue dress because Barbara had wanted her to wear it. Sylvia sat next to her in her white one. Their table was in front of the stage; right next to them were some *Shortland Street* actors, and Sylvia just about *died* when Temuera Morrison winked at her. The champagne flowed, the acts — Dave Dobbyn, Moana and the Moa Hunters and Crowded House — were great. All the Miss New Zealand Cinema contestants had to model a swimsuit and evening wear and, at the very end, they all lined up under the spotlights. Barbara was looking ravishing in a red dress.

A fanfare sounded and Paul Holmes, the Master of Ceremonies, appeared. The crowd went wild. 'Ladies and gentlemen,' he said, 'I have the judges' envelope.' There was a drum roll as he slit the envelope open. In that moment Barbara looked at Maxine and Sylvia and blew them a kiss. 'The judges are unanimous,' he continued. 'Miss New Zealand Cinema, the girl who will go to Hollywood is —' Oh, the suspense was *awful*. The drum roll seemed to go on and on. '— Miss Barbara Louis. Come on down, Barbara.'

'We couldn't help ourselves,' Sylvia said. 'Max and I jumped out of our chairs screaming and yelling our heads off. As for Barbara, she was so serene, smiling and turning this way and that for the cameras. Then, you know what she did? She came down to our table, and the flashbulbs were popping and dazzling our eyes, and Paul said, "Ladies and gentlemen, the beautiful Louis sisters." Barbara had to go back on stage and Max suddenly remembered, "We'd better ring Mum and Dad with the news." So she picked up her cellphone. "Hello Mum? Dad? Guess who's going to Hollywood! You already know? You're watching the ceremony live?" At that moment, Barbara came back. "Let me speak to Daddy," she said. "Hello? Daddy? I only wish you and Mummy were here to share this moment. Yes, Daddy, I was your little girl. I didn't think I would win though. The girl from Christchurch was so beautiful. Yes, we'll be starting for home as soon as we can." '

'Of course,' Sylvia said, 'there were television interviews, radio interviews and local press waiting to talk to Barbara. They wanted to know who her favourite film stars were and who she hoped to meet. So it wasn't until an hour later that we were able to get away from the reception. Maxine went to get the car while I checked us out of the hotel. It was just after midnight. We didn't bother to change. We went just as we were, in our evening dresses and Barbara trying to balance her crown on her head. I don't think we had ever been closer than we were that night. Max was driving, I was beside her and Barbara insisted on squeezing up front with us. We were laughing. Carrying on. Singing —'

It was Max who had thought of it. She gave a gasp, reached into the glovebox and pulled out the dictaphone she used at work. As they were driving along she pretended she was an interviewer. 'Miss Louis,' she said in a gruff voice, 'tell us what it is like to be a *star*.' And Barbara pouted, fluttered her eyelids, sucked in her cheeks and said in a squeaky voice, 'Well, I weely don't know, I'm shu-ah, but I'll ask my agent.' She passed the recorder to Sylvia who said, 'Waal, Miz Lou-izz feels just ger-rate and wants to thank all the liddle folks who ser-pported her, don't ya honey?' And, laughing, Barbara grabbed the recorder and said, 'Ah shure do, and ahm going to be up there with Mickey Mouse —' they all giggled '— and Lassie and Donald Duck and my all-time favorite Stuart Little —' By this time they were all having hysterics, the tears just pouring down their cheeks. '— and ahm going to make it to the top coz ahm not just tits and ass like those other starlets coz I've got intelli-genz.' And she turned to Sylvia and asked her, 'How du you spell that word, honey?'

Sylvia's voice dropped away to a whisper. 'That's when the truck *hit*,' she said, her eyes wide, unblinking. 'It came out of nowhere, like it had been waiting out there just for us. Just for her. Of course Max's reaction was to pull on the wheel hard and the truck smashed into the passenger side where Barbara was sitting. Max and I were thrown clear. Our only thought was to get Barbara out. But she was pinned there. Her back was broken. She must have been in terrible pain. There was blood everywhere. Hers. Ours. Max was screaming and screaming at the driver of the truck. "You bastard," she yelled, "didn't you see us?" Suddenly, Barbara's mouth filled with blood. Max gave a cry and wiped the blood away. "You can't die, Barb," she said, "I won't let you." Barbara tried to smile to reassure us. "I love you, Max," she said. "I love you Syl. I love you Mummy. I love you Daddy. I —" Then a great gout of blood poured from her lips and she was gone.'

The cigarette dropped from Sylvia's hand. She stubbed it out with her foot. 'Max took the blame,' Sylvia said. 'Doesn't the oldest always take the blame? She was in hospital quite a while and had to have some reconstructive surgery and skin grafting on her face. When she got out she had a breakdown and was institutionalised for quite a while. The Max who came back to us was not the same Max that I had known. But she's still my sister.'

Later that night, Alec went on the piss with Josh. He tried his luck with a Swedish backpacker but didn't get far. Around two in the morning, he went back to Josh's place to crash. Max was there, waiting for him, in his bed. Her blonde hair shone like gold.

'The twelve days of Christmas,' she mocked. 'One day of Christmas is horrible enough. You don't mind my coming, do you Alec? Tonight I'm alone and I don't like it. You're alone too. But look on the plus side. I'm a body and I'm warm.'

Max got out of bed and came towards Alec. As she kissed him he saw that her eyes were wide, unblinking. He tightened his grip on her so that she could not resist. He pulled at her hair.

'No,' Max cried.

Alec wiped the makeup from her left cheek, exposing her scars.

'No,' she cried again.

He said to her, 'I *know*, Max. I know about Barbara.'

Max began to scream and scream. 'Oh fuck me,' she said. Over and over again.

In retrospect, Alec came to realise that he and Max were lost souls. Sex, the raw need of one body to invade the other, had brought them together. That need expressed itself in rough, punitive and sadistic bouts. But after each bout, then what? There was no balance, none of the shared experiences and delight in finding something common in each other.

'You're a bad boy,' Max said once. 'I'm certainly a bad girl. We deserve each other. What I like about you is that you're rock bottom. I wouldn't expect you to understand this, but it's a great comfort for a girl to know she could not possibly sink any lower.'

Was that all they had in common? No, there *was* something — or, more to the point, someone — else: Barbara. Sometimes Maxine was Max and sometimes Max was Barbara. And as Alec got to know Max better, it seemed to him that the dead Barbara was more potent than she had ever been when alive. Her radiant bloom had been forever frozen, imprisoned at the moment of its greatest beauty, a rose encased in plastic, harvested before it could rust or wither. Dead, Barbara had become more exalted, transcendent. She cast her charisma like a giant shadow and wherever that shadow fell, all in its path was rendered a wasteland. Max was lost somewhere in it.

Somewhere in that valley of the shadow of Barbara, Max had picked up her drug habit. The drug dealer was Brian Cassidy and he was Max's supplier. If ever a girl was made for addiction, Max was, with her obsession with her dead sister. Alec thought he might be able to pull her out of it. Then, New Year's Eve was upon them.

On that morning of the thirty-first, Alec woke to find himself alone in bed. He went past Josh's bedroom and saw that he was still asleep. Max and Sylvia were talking on the terrace, Sylvia in her dressing gown and Max all dressed for work. Max was nervous. Sylvia was trying to calm her down.

'Don't worry, Max,' Sylvia said. 'I'll talk to Dad. It'll be okay.'

'No it won't,' Max answered. 'It never is. It'll be the same as it always is, every New Year. I just don't think I'll be able to do it this year.'

Alec stepped into the sunlight. 'Do what?'

'Syl will explain,' Max answered. She swept up her keys. 'I'll catch up with you later.'

In explanation, Sylvia told Alec that Max was anxious about New Year's Eve. 'We've always spent it at home with Mum and Dad,' she said. Tonight won't be any exception.'

'Does Max want me to come too?'

'Yes,' Sylvia answered. 'With you there, things might be different.'

The day was as high strung as an acrobat's wire. Alec telephoned his father in Gisborne to tell him that he would be thinking of him when the clock struck twelve. 'Thanks lad,' Alec senior answered. 'I'll not enjoy it much with your mother gone.' The answer surprised Alec because his father had never before referred to love or loneliness or need — and wasn't he having an affair with his Maori housekeeper? Wondering, Alec then telephoned Helen. Her father answered the telephone. Helen had gone north with friends. No, he didn't know where, sorry.

Pissed off, Alec turned to the beach. The sea was like glass and Alec felt he was floating on a huge mirror. No matter how hard he tried, all he could see was himself — no past and no future. It was as if life was moving in, swirling patterns of deception, and everything in his life led only back to self, self, self again. A rainstorm began, sending people on the beach scurrying for shelter. Out on the sea the rain dimpled the mirror, pitting it like bullets.

By the time Alec got back from the beach it was right on 4 pm. To his surprise

81

A NEW YEAR'S STORY

he met the two Aussie surfers he had come across on his way up from Gisborne. He grabbed at them because of the normality they represented. He squeezed time to take them for a few beers at a city bar. When they left, he decided to catch up with Max at her office. He thought he might tell her that he was taking a raincheck on going to her parents' place. The CLOSED sign was on the door. He returned to Josh's house. Nobody was home. By 7 pm Alec was like a tiger in a cage, prowling through the house, round and round and round. He'd have to go. He'd better get dressed. He went into the bathroom and turned on the shower. The room filled with steam.

Alec didn't know how long he was in the shower when the bathroom door clicked behind him. Through the glass of the shower door he saw a pale shape, Max, undressing, and his cock stiffened. She came to him through the steam, quickly, stepping into the shower with him before he changed his mind. When she kissed him he saw that she was Sylvia.

'You've had one sister,' Sylvia said. 'I'm making you a present of the other. You don't even have to waste time unwrapping it.'

And then the night pounced on Alec.

At nine, Josh arrived back at the flat. 'You ready to hit the New Year trail?' he said to Sylvia. 'The town's already jumping and we can get a couple of hours in before we head off to your folks.'

'Shouldn't we wait for Max?' Alec asked.

'Oh yeah,' Josh answered. 'She's phoned already to say we should go on without her. She'll meet up with us later.'

At that, Sylvia went ballistic. 'I knew it,' she said. 'I knew she'd do a runner on me. I'll bet she's with that Cassidy, snorting enough coke to shoot her to never-never land where she can just forget, let New Year roll on past, and wake up on the other side. Well, I'm not going to face Mum and Dad by myself. If Max doesn't turn up we'll have to troll every joint in town to find her. She's coming, even if I have to drag her home.'

Alec helped Josh put some crates of beer into Josh's wagon. The plan was to go to the house in Beach Terrace and drink as much as they could, and be at the Louis's house at 11.30. They would stay there until 11.55, then dash down to the clocktower to listen to the chimes ring out and sing 'Auld Lang Syne'.

You can live a lifetime in three hours, drink a lot of beer, shake hands with a hundred guys, kiss and fondle a thousand women and dream the undreamable. On

New Year's Eve you can do what you want with whom you want. That's what the Eve is all about — life, love, sex, fun and thumbing your nose at old age and that Eternal Bastard, Death. New Year's Eve is the prerogative of the young, the carefree and the careless. From Mexico to Reykjavik, Sugar Loaf to Mount Everest, New Plymouth to New York, New Year rules.

Beach Terrace was thumping. The house was so packed that partygoers had spilled out onto the surrounding streets. Alec, Josh and Sylvia pushed their way inside. It was so hot and smoky that Alec soon took off his shirt. Above everyone's heads the Christmas decorations — flags, streamers, silver foil — sliced and shredded the dark like glittering knives. Across the way, another bull rider swayed and screamed on the leviathan. Beer was flowing from the taps like a never-ending river. In the middle of the room, people were dancing, butting against one another. A fight started. Two guys slashed and flailed at each other, their movements choreographed semaphores of violence. Very soon there would be other fights in other places. Beer bottles shoved in people's faces. Some stabbed. Some drowned. Some shot. Regardless of the Eve, the same old dance of life and death went on. The rhythm was in their heartbeat. For most the rhythm pumped strong and on. For others it simply and quickly *stopped*.

Alec was well on the way by 11.20. His head was light and his eyes were bloodshot. A busty brunette, watching him down a beer, gave him a gentle pat on his bulge. 'Mmmn nice,' she said. 'You can drink at my spring any time.' Alec laughed in delight at the come on. At that moment, anybody looking at him would not have known how empty and out of it he felt. They would not have seen into his guts and divined, from the disarray of his entrails, that life had delivered him into some cul-de-sac. All they would have seen was a good-looking guy who looked like he could handle himself. A guy who had friends. A guy who had been rolling dice and rolling high numbers.

'Down the hatch, mate,' Josh said. 'Time to get to the Louis's.'

'But Max hasn't turned up yet,' Sylvia told Josh. 'I told you before, I'm not going to face Mum and Dad without her.'

'We've run out of time,' Josh answered. 'Perhaps Max is already there.'

Sylvia swore loudly. 'She'd better be,' she said as she led the way out of the house.

'What's the big deal?' Alec asked, puzzled. 'Why is Sylvia so agitated?'

'You'll see when we get to the Louis's house,' Josh answered. 'Home is where you go and where they have to let you in.'

83

Of course, when they got to the Louis's house, Max hadn't turned up yet. That meant Sylvia had to make the introduction, and it was clear that Ted and Dorothy Louis were not pleased. 'This is Alec,' Sylvia said. 'Josh's friend.'

'You know we don't like strangers here at this particular time,' Mr Louis said to Sylvia, ignoring Alec.

Alec hadn't known what to expect from Max and Sylvia's parents, but certainly not this. Not this large man with red hands and thickened features, who looked as if he'd been drinking all afternoon. Nor this small woman with nervous movements and odd lopsided smile who hung tightly onto her husband as if her life depended on it.

It was clear Ted Louis didn't give a damn what Alec thought of his behaviour. The silence lengthened. Sylvia tried to make small conversation.

'Max should be here any moment,' she said.

Ted Louis cast her a look. 'We wouldn't miss her if she didn't turn up,' he answered. 'Why don't you do something useful and get your friends some drinks before we go into the living room?'

Sylvia nodded and went into the kitchen. Mrs Louis followed her. Alec heard them talking. 'I don't know why you brought Josh and his friend. You know what Dad's going to do tonight.'

'But on the telephone this afternoon,' Sylvia answered, panicking, 'he told me he wouldn't. He promised me. He said that it was time to put the past behind us and try to be a family again. He *promised*.'

'You know your father,' Dorothy Louis said. 'Do you think he can let go that easily?'

Alec looked at Mr Louis and in those dark eyes was the look — the look — of madness. As soon as he and Josh walked into the living room he knew why.

The room was a shrine to Barbara. Everything in it was white: white walls, white drapes, thick white woollen carpet and white divan and armchairs. Small white wooden tables were scattered around the room. Their function was to provide stands for photographs of Barbara.

The focal point for the room was the huge full length oil painting of Barbara which hung in a gilt frame above the empty fireplace. The painting was highly romanticised, in full-blown colour. Barbara was in the evening gown she had worn on the night she was crowned Miss New Zealand Cinema. Beneath the painting was a vase of red plastic roses, never-wilting, ever-living plastic.

The room was silent. The atmosphere was claustrophobic. Alec wandered through it, looking at the photographs of Barbara. There was no doubt that she had been *it*, an authentic original. In group photographs, Maxine and Sylvia were merely facsimiles.

'She was so beautiful,' Ted said to Alec.

'Yes,' Alec answered, 'she was.' But beneath all this display of Barbara, Alec felt, was an obscenity. He wondered whether he should excuse himself, because whatever was happening was a family affair.

Josh must have known what Alec was thinking. 'Listen, mate, this won't take long,' he said. 'Just a couple of drinks and we'll be on our way.' Josh's eyes were pleading, so Alec nodded and took a seat. Silence descended again. Then Sylvia tried to make small talk with her mother. Dorothy Louis would answer 'Yes dear,' or 'No dear' or 'Oh really, dear?' like an automaton; her eyes were steadfastly on her husband, watching his every move. As for Ted Louis, he took an armchair opposite Barbara's painting and kept his eyes focused on it, looking neither right nor left, as if he didn't give a damn about anything else except that portrait.

Suddenly there was a squealing sound in the street outside and headlights blazed briefly as the red MG turned into the driveway. The car door slammed. High-heeled feet, on the run, clicked up the concrete pathway. The doorbell rang. Dorothy Louis answered it. Max's excited voice glittered through the hall.

'Sorry I'm late, Mum. The traffic! The city! It's a zoo out there!'

Then she was there, Max, standing in the doorway to the living room. To Alec, she'd never looked more beautiful. Her short cropped red hair was wet, as if she'd just come out of a shower. Her face was animated, alive, as if tonight was the beginning of forever. She saw Alec, Josh and Sylvia and gave a delicious gasp, 'Hello, you three!' She came across and hugged them all and then turned to her father. 'Hello, Dad —'

Ted Louis' face was demonic. 'It was all your fault,' he said.

Max took a step back, blanched, and shot a glance at Sylvia. 'But you said you'd spoken to Dad. You said, you said —'

She watched with horror as Ted Louis walked over to the video cassette recorder and television and switched both on.

'Shut your mouth, bitch,' Ted Louis said.

Max swayed like a reed and then she seemed to snap — a flower whose stem had been broken.

The silence of the room was suddenly broken by a loud orchestral fanfare. The picture rolling on the television set cleared, and Paul Holmes, Master of

Ceremonies, appeared. The crowd went wild. 'Ladies and gentlemen,' he said, 'I have the judges' envelope.'

Stunned, Alec looked at Josh.

'Sorry about this,' Josh said. 'You see, mate, it was on New Year's Eve when Barbara died —'

'Shut *up*,' Ted Louis yelled.

There was a drum roll as Paul Holmes slit the envelope open. In that moment Barbara looked at Maxine and Sylvia and blew them a kiss. 'The judges are unanimous,' Paul continued. 'Miss New Zealand Cinema, the girl who will go to Hollywood is —' The drum roll seemed to go on and on. '— Miss Barbara Louis. Come on down, Barbara.'

Ted Louis gave a deep groan. He put out his arms to the gorgeous blonde Barbara who appeared in close-up on the screen. The cameras followed her as she was crowned and took her bows before the crowd, dipping and swirling like a star. Then the cameras tracked with her as she left the stage, paused to be kissed by Temuera Morrison, and headed for two other girls almost as beautiful as she was. 'Ladies and gentlemen, the beautiful Louis sisters,' Paul Holmes said.

The videotape flickered to a close. The television screen went blank. Ted Louis gave a sob. Immediately, Dorothy Louis went to comfort him. He pushed her aside and went across to the tape deck.

'You made a promise, Dad,' Sylvia said to him. 'Dad, you promised you wouldn't do this.'

Max gave her a look. 'No, Syl, it's okay. Let Daddy do what he wants to do. You want any help, Daddy? Daddy?'

Max's voice was plaintive, yearning. She was like a little girl wanting to be loved, wanting to be picked up by her father.

'You're the one who should have died,' Ted Louis said. He started the tape. From out of the past came vampire voices, giggling, insinuating their ways into the present.

'Miss Louis, tell us what it's like to be a star?' a gruff voice asked. In the background were the noises of a car travelling fast towards Tauranga. Barbara's voice came on. 'Well, I weely don't know, I'm shu-ah, but I'll ask my agent.' And Alec felt his heart stir and become radiant at the sound of the voice. As Barbara kept speaking, in that high falsetto voice, he couldn't help feeling, yes, how much he loved her, even though he had never known her. The voices went on and on. Giggling. Breaking up. 'Ahm going to be up there with Mickey Mouse and Lassie and Donald Duck and my all-time favourite Stuart Little and ahm going to make it to the top coz ahm not just tits and ass like those other starlets coz I've got intelli-genz.' And Barbara had turned to Sylvia and asked her, 'How do you spell that word, honey?'

Suddenly the tape stopped, and there was a long scream. Whether it came from the tape or from Mr Louis, Alec couldn't tell. 'No, no, oh no —' Or maybe it came from Alec himself. He wanted to rewind the tape, make that glorious, funny voice come alive again, oh, please come back. It was too late. The tape crackled and hissed and then came the noise of the *thing* that had been waiting eighteen years for Barbara to come along that dark highway. It came with a roar and a hiss, thundering through the tape like a nightmare. *I have you now, my pretty, my princess.*

The crash came, as it inevitably had, with pain and blood and shattered bone. For a moment the tape hissed on in silence. Finally, that radiant voice came again, softly sighing away. 'I love you, Max, I love you Syl. I love you Mummy. I love you Daddy. I —'

The rest was silence. To his surprise, Alec found his face wet with tears. He saw Dorothy Louis get up and stop the tape. She went to her husband and he fell into her arms, mourning. Sylvia joined them. Then Max went across to make the circle complete, her arms outstretched to her father.

'You should have been the one,' Ted Louis said. 'You should have been the one to die on the road. It should be Barbara here today. Not you.'

At that moment, Alec saw how damaged the Louis family had all been by Barbara's death. And although he loved her, the dead Barbara, he wanted to say to her, 'Go now, depart, leave them alone.' Barbara herself would not have wanted to be kept here by Ted Louis in this unseemly manner. Above all else, she would have wanted her family to survive and go on living.

'You, Max,' Ted Louis said again. 'It should be Barbara here.'

Ted and Dorothy Louis were people out of whack. They were foolish, selfish people. They had already driven Max to go looking for her own deliverance, her own monster waiting for her as inevitably as it had been waiting for Barbara.

Max smiled a crooked smile. She spun on her heel, went out the door and there was a roar and a squeal down the driveway.

Every country, every city, town, family and person has a special way of celebrating New Year's Eve. In New York City, Times Square is the place to be with its glittering lights and huge mirrored orb flashing above the wellwishers. The Queen delivers a New Year's message in England, and Big Ben booms across the nation. Hong

Kong is all firecrackers and Chinese dragons. In Berlin the bars blossom with sexual nightshades of all descriptions and decadence. In most New Zealand towns, the climax is centred on the main street clocktower.

Alec stood alone among the merrymakers. When he, Josh and Sylvia had quickly exited the Louis house, all that Sylvia had wanted to do was to find her sister. 'You don't know Max,' Sylvia had screamed. 'You don't know what she's already been through. You don't understand what she's liable to do.' They had agreed that Sylvia and Josh would go back to the party house on Beach Terrace, and meet up later with Alec at the clock.

Two minutes to midnight. Alec elbowed his way through the crowd, the gay, beautiful, happy, lusty, funny, silly crowd. Looking over that mass of people it came to Alec that the year's end wasn't just being farewelled. It was also being slaughtered, dismembered month by month, and from out of the bowels of the old year would come the new. Was anything ever learnt? he wondered.

One minute to go. And Alec realised that having this short sexual relationship with Max, and coming to know her terrifying life, had taught him something. You either stayed trapped in the past or you went forward into the future. A huge sense of release came over him, a new kind of understanding, that he was a survivor. Unlike Max, he could, whenever he wanted to, get back into life.

The clock began to strike midnight. The crowd gave a cheer and, looking up at that luminous dial, started to chant away the year that had been. *One.* The whole street was like a sea filled with people drowning. Through the sea, being tossed above their heads, came a laughing blonde girl. *Two.* There was a man who was trying to catch up with the girl, a brooding dark man. He watched her as she lifted her arms in ecstasy to the clock. *Three.* The girl's eyes were glittering. Her face was in rictus with laughter and agony. On the perimeter, her sister and sister's boyfriend were calling to her. *Four.* The girl came tumbling toward Alec, tumbling, tumbling. A boy reached for her and pulled her down. He kissed her. *Five.* The girl's face sparkled and she placed one hand on her throat. The boy kissed her again. *Six.* All of a sudden there were other men and other hands circling the girl. The hands came from beneath the sea. One of them had a glass of wine, which was offered to the girl. *Seven.* The girl lifted the glass to her lips. Ruby red they glistened as the wine brimmed her mouth and moistened them. *Eight.* The dark man finally reached the girl. He was brutal, trying to spin her back with him. *Nine.* The girl pushed the dark man away, laughing. She began to spin like a top from one person to the next. *Ten.* Whirling, slipping, screaming, choking, kissing, being loved, across a sea of faces. *Eleven.* She was going to drown. She began to disappear beneath the waves.

Alec reached out to Max and pulled her to the surface.

Twelve.

The sky filled with fireworks. Max gave a gasp of surprise. The fireworks cascaded and spiralled through the night. The band at the base of the clock struck up. *Should auld acquaintance be forgot.* People were embracing, kissing, hugging. *And never brought to mind. Should auld acquaintance be forgot.* Alec pulled Max into a close embrace. He wanted to hug her forever, if only to protect her from all the ills and spites of a damned world. *In the days of auld lang syne.* He felt a tremendous compassion for Max, this lost soul who would never find peace. *For auld lang syne, my dear, for auld lang syne.* Max's face was wan. Her eyes were closed. She was very still. Alec wiped her face and the perspiration on her forehead. *We'll take a cup of kindness yet.* A lump caught in Alec's throat for Max, for Sylvia and the Louis's. For all those who were lost in the sea of the world. *For the days of auld lang syne.*

When Max's eyes opened, Alec smiled at her, achingly. He wasn't sure if Max knew it was him or not.

'Have you ever noticed,' Max smiled, 'if for some reason you want to feel completely out of step with the rest of the world, the best place to be is at a clocktower on New Year's Eve at midnight?'

Alec kissed Max long and sweet. She was already gone. Gone, gone, gone. The world expanded and blossomed with utter tenderness.

'Goodbye, Barbara,' he said.

BIG BROTHER, LITTLE SISTER

TRUTH OF THE MATTER

DUSTBINS

'**B** ig Brother, Little Sister' is another of those stories that bear what people have come to consider my imprimatur or moko. Together with 'Truth of the Matter', it comes from *The New Net Goes Fishing*, 1977. The structure of the story was inspired by Ryunosuke Akutagawa's *In A Grove*, made into the movie *Rashomon* by Akira Kurosawa; 'Truth of the Matter' itself was filmed for television as *Against the Lights* by Sam Pillsbury. 'Big Brother, Little Sister' was also filmed for television by Ian Mune.

I share with Albert Wendt and Haunani-Kay Trask the indigenous imperative. Haunani puts it this way: 'In my work, writing is both decolonisation and re-creation.' In all my Maori stories, the thematic formula I apply is Politics + Aesthetics = The Maori Story. In my opinion you can't write a story about Maori — which is a minority condition, equating with other indigenous peoples of the world — without both. Together they result in tino rangatiratanga, sovereignty.

From the 1970s to the 1990s I shared a national stage with many activists and writers committed to attaining that sovereignty. In Aotearoa, they were the times of the Springbok protest and the great work by Eva Rickard, Hana Te Hemara, Syd Jackson, Atareta Poananga, Tame Iti, Dun Mihaka, Ripeka Evans, Ngahuia Te Awekotuku, Donna Awatere and many others. I was also privileged to join protests in the United States, Canada, England, Australia and Hawaii. Once, in Australia with Aboriginal activist and writer Roberta Sykes, we were getting a stinging and hostile response from the audience over our criticisms of Australian racist politics. Roberta turned to me and said, 'Anyway, we should expect this. After all, we've broken the eleventh commandment.' I asked Roberta, 'What is that?' She answered, 'Thou shalt not survive.'

The three stories also offer reflections on the city in my stories. In *The New Net Goes Fishing* the city is a main character. In 'Yellow Brick Road' it is Emerald City, sparkling, as in *The Wizard of Oz*, at the end of the rainbow. In 'The Escalator', its metaphors are of seduction and desire. The city becomes a place of danger for Hema and Janey in 'Big Brother, Little Sister', at risk as they try to find their way out. It's a perilous, punitive city, full of trapped beings, in 'Truth of the Matter'. But in 'Dustbins' it reaches its apotheosis as a rubbish tip, a refuse pit for rampant consumerism.

All those who live in the city are in constant movement, on road or escalator, in a taxi, riding a rubbish truck. Their lives shuttle between highway and railway station, airport and bus stop. This was, and for many still is, what life really *is* like at the end of the rainbow.

BIG BROTHER, LITTLE SISTER

He burst out of the house and was halfway down the street when he heard Janey yelling after him, her cry shrill with panic. He turned and saw her on the opposite pavement, appearing out of the night. As she passed under a street light her shadow reached out like a bird's wing to ripple along the fence palings toward him.

'Go back, Janey,' he called.

She cried out his name again, and pursued her shadow across the street. A car screamed at her heels and slashed her with light as she fluttered into her brother's arms. 'I'm coming with you,' she said. She wore a jersey and jeans over her pyjamas. In her hands she was carrying her sandals. She bent down and began strapping them on.

'You'll be a nuisance,' Hema grunted. 'Go home.' He pushed her away.

'No.' She wrapped her arms and legs tightly around him. He wrestled her off and she fell on the pavement. He began running, down that long dark street of shadowed houses, away from Berhampore towards Newtown.

'Don't leave me,' Janey cried.

He turned. His face was desperate. 'You're too small to come with me,' he yelled. 'Go home, Janey.' But she was pursuing him again. He picked up a stone and threw it at her. She ducked. He picked up another stone. 'Go back,' he raged.

'No.' She gritted her teeth, opened her eyes wide with determination and launched herself at him. Hema felt her trembling in his arms.

'You'll just be a nuisance,' Hema growled.

A year ago. Hema had been asleep when Janey began to peck at his dreams. 'Hema,' she whispered. 'Wake up.' The two children slept in the same bed in one of the two bedrooms in the flat. Hema turned on his side away from her. She began to shake him.

There was the sound of a crash. Hema sat up. He saw a crack of light under the closed door. Mum and Dad were back from the party. They were quarrelling again. Mum must have found out about Auntie Lena.

'Don't be scared,' Hema said to his sister. He went to the door and pushed it open. How long Mum and Dad had been fighting he didn't know. He'd never heard them as violent as this. He went back to the bed and sat on it. Janey crawled into his arms. They watched and listened as their parents fought.

'Don't you talk to me like that, Wiki,' Dad was threatening Mum.

'I'll talk to you any way I like, you rotten bastard.'

'And don't you answer me back, Wiki.'

'You don't own me,' Mum yelled. 'You and your black bitch, you were made for each other. Next time I see her I'll smash her face in.'

There was the sound of a tussle. Janey began to whimper.

'Keep your hands off me,' Mum said. She was panting and struggling with Dad. There was a ripping sound. A helpless woman-cry. A sudden crack of Dad's open hand against Mum's face. 'You bastard.'

'Shut your face, woman,' Dad said, 'or I'll crack you one again.'

'That's all you can do, eh? Big man aren't you. Why don't you go and pick on somebody your own size. Get out. Get out.' Mum spat into Dad's face. He slapped her again and threw her against the wall. Janey gripped Hema with fright.

'Damn bitch,' Dad said. 'You want me to go? All right, suit your fucken self.' Dad's shadow cut through the lighted crack of the door. Mum's voice suddenly was filled with fear.

'No, Jack. Don't leave me.'

Dad laughed at her, scornful. Again, Mum's voice changed. 'All right then, you bastard, go to her.' She pulled open the wardrobe and began to throw Dad's clothes at him. 'Here then. And here. See if I care.' Dad turned the handle, ready to leave. Seeing that he really meant it, Mum's anger became ugly. 'You bastard, well, two can play that game.' She ran to the telephone and dialled a number. 'Hello? Is that you, Pera?'

Dad's laughter stopped. 'You been playing around, eh Wiki?'

'You're hurting me.'

'You and Pera? Eh? Eh, you bitch?'

Hema ran to the door and opened it. Dad was holding Mum against the wall. He had one knee against her crotch. Both hands were around her neck.

93

'Dad. Mum. Don't.'

'Get back to bed, you damn kid,' Dad yelled. He pushed Hema back into the bedroom. The door cracked shut against Mum and Dad's faces. Blood was streaming from Mum's mouth.

'Leave them alone you bastard,' Mum screamed. She fell heavily to the floor. When Hema opened it, Dad was standing there, fists clenched, kicking at Mum. Hema tried to protect her by lying on top of her. For a while Dad kept on kicking and kicking. Then, 'Oh, Jesus,' he said to himself.

Mum stood up. Her face was bruised and bloodied. She hugged Janey and Hema close to her.

'Get out,' she said to Dad. 'Don't think we'll miss you. Get out, Get out.'

Uncle Pera came to stay.

'I knew you'd be a nuisance,' Hema said.

Janey tugged at his hand and, when he looked down at her, she was squirming and fidgeting and holding her other hand across the front of her jeans. Hema ignored her and pulled her along with him.

They reached Newtown Hospital, pushing fast through the tangle of busy streets. A taxi swerved into the curb in front of them. Inside was a man with a smashed face. As the taxi driver helped the man out of his cab the man started to scream through the red hole where his mouth used to be.

Janey tugged again at Hema's hand. 'I can't help it,' she said. 'I never had time to go.'

'There was a public lav a few streets back. Why didn't you tell me then?'

'You were in a hurry,' Janey said. 'Anyway, I didn't want a mimi until *now*.'

'You'll just have to wait until we get somewhere less crowded.'

Newtown was busy. Cars were double-parked all along the shopping centre, impeding the stream of traffic. People spoke in a babble of strange, frightening languages. They spoke past each other, their conversations not connecting, hostility brimming over: Go back to the country you came from. Shops spilled their crates of fruit, bolts of cloth and other wares into the street. A Salvation Army band exhorted passers-by to embrace God. A man in a fish shop swung his cleaver and cut off the gaping head of a large grey fish. Crayfish seethed in a tank. A small dark boy sold evening newspapers.

A woman haggled over the price of an old cabinet stacked with other junk outside a secondhand mart. In this alien land, her face was wan and desperate as if her very existence depended on getting the cabinet. Secondhand wares for secondhand people.

Janey began to fidget again.

'Hema,' Janey wailed.

'Hold on, willya?' Hema answered. He pulled her after him through the littered pavement towards the pedestrian lights at the corner of John Street.

While waiting to cross, he took a look back at the Hospital clock. Eight o'clock. He had left the flat immediately after Mum and Uncle Pera had caught a taxi to go to the pub. The pub didn't close until ten and, if Hema was lucky, Uncle Pera would take Mum to a party. So there was plenty of time to get away, even if Janey slowed him up.

Not that Mum would miss them. She'd probably be glad they'd gone.

The lights turned red, the 'Cross Now' signal buzzed, and the traffic punched to a stop.

'Come on,' Hema said to his sister. Car motors revved and roared at them, ready to leap on them and crush them if they didn't get to the other side in time. They made it. The lights turned green and the traffic leapt and sped through the intersection.

For a moment, Hema stood undecided. Which way should they go? They better take a detour. If they kept to the main street it would take them past the Tramways Hotel. Mum and Uncle Pera might be there. Be safer to go up John Street. But first, attend to Janey.

'There's some trees over there,' Hema said, pointing to the nearby park.

'It's dark. Will you come with me?'

'No. You'll be all right. Just hurry.'

Janey rushed into the shadows and was swallowed up by them. Hema kept a lookout. Emerald lights were strung across the façade of the Winter Show Building. Suddenly, he heard Janey scream. She was struggling in the arms of an old man. The predator was pulling at her dress.

Frightened, Hema looked for a weapon. Saw a loose paling and pulled it away from the fence. Ran to the rescue and faced off against the man. 'Fuck off,' Hema said. 'Fuck off or I'll smash your head in.' He threw the paling at the man. A lucky hit. The man yelled in pain and staggered back. Janey ran to Hema. Heart pounding, he pulled her after him. Only when they had turned the corner did he stop and hug his sister, brushing her down and checking to see if she was okay. 'Let's get out of here,' he said.

Cars slewed past in a steady stream. A few streets ahead, people were arguing on the pavement. Two snake-sheathed girls began to fight. A beer bottle smashed on the asphalt. Hema and Janey skirted the arguing people, their sandals crunching on broken glass.

'So where are we going, Hema?' Janey asked.

'I'm thinking,' Hema answered. His mind was working fast. He'd planned just to run away, find some shelter under a bridge and live on the streets. Maybe he could find a gang house and become a gang member, yeah, that would be cool. Now that Janey was with him, he couldn't do that. So what should he do? He checked in his pocket and felt the dollar notes he'd stolen from Uncle Pera's wallet. 'We're going to the railway station,' Hema decided. Yes, that's what he'd do. He'd take Janey down there and put her on a train to Gisborne to Nani George. After all, she couldn't live on the streets with him.

Onward they walked, past the lighted windows, the singing windows of the city.

Six months ago. When Uncle Pera came to stay, for a while life got better. He was younger than Mum and flattered by an older woman's attentions. He even liked the idea of being called uncle by Wiki's two kids, and staying in with his woman on the weekends, playing the guitar while she cooked the kai. After a while, however, his eyes flickered with boredom and so he began telling his mates to come over to Wiki's for a party. Hema would watch Mum drinking, dancing — her hair swinging free, sweat dripping down the neck of her dress, thighs grinding — and wish that everyone would go away and leave her alone. In the mornings, while Mum and Uncle Pera were still sleeping, he and Janey would clear up the debris, sweep the floor, wash the glasses and open the windows to get rid of the stink of beer and marijuana. Once, they found Mum, pissed and doped out of her brain, flaked out on the floor; Uncle Pera had made it to bed and had left her there. Hema wiped her face and mouth with a flannel.

'You bastard,' Hema said to the sleeping Pera as he put his mother beside him. He wanted to smash Uncle Pera's face in.

But partying at home was not enough for Uncle Pera. He began pulling Mum out on the usual pub and party circuit. Before Hema realised it, he was back to the familiar routine of being home alone with his sister.

'Hema, look after your sister, eh? Uncle Pera and I are going out for a while. Can you get tea for yourselves? Here's some money. Get some burger and chips, eh?'

As for Janey, she hadn't minded Uncle Pera at first. She liked the way he made Mum laugh. But when the boredom came, and when Uncle Pera began to demand Mum's time, Janey became frightened. What frightened her most was that *Mum* was frightened, watching Uncle Pera with scared eyes as if he was going to walk out the door at any moment. His lips had always been moist for pleasure, his eyes always reckless for fun.

'What was that, Pera? You want some biscuits with your tea, honey? Hema, go down and get some biscuits for Uncle Pera. Don't be too slow. He wants them now.'

Mum's anxieties to please Uncle Pera began to affect Hema and Janey. They were careful when he was around, treating him with as much caution as Mum did, because if he left Mum he also left them — and Mum didn't have a job. Trying to please him, trying to make sure he would stay. None of them realised they were turning into his slaves.

But Uncle Pera knew it, and he began to play on it. Whenever he was irritated with Hema and Janey, all he had to say was, 'Do your kids always have to eat with us?' and Mum would push them away from the table and tell them to have their kai in the sitting room. Or, whenever he wanted to watch television, Mum would say, 'Go to bed now. Uncle Pera and I want some time to ourselves.' To make things easier, the kids began to have dinner before Uncle Pera came home. They watched television but, when Uncle Pera came into the sitting room, they went to bed without being asked.

One night, Uncle Pera played his trump card. Mum was cuddling him in the sitting room. Uncle Pera had one hand up her dress, stroking her thighs, but his eyes were on Hema, taunting him.

'I'm the man, aren't I, Wiki,' Uncle Pera said to Mum. 'Not many men would take on an older woman and her two kids, eh.' All the time, those eyes on Hema. You get the picture, boy? You get the score?

'You're my man,' Mum answered. 'My sweet, loving man.'

Uncle Pera smiled at Hema, stretched his legs and began to unbutton his trousers. 'Show me how much you love me, Wiki,' he said, winking at Hema. 'Show me. You know you love it.' He twisted Mum round his finger whenever he wanted to.

Later that night, Hema watched his mother making herself up, readying herself to go out to another party. Uncle Pera had twisted and twisted until, *snap*, Mum came to him at his every command. She had become his.

Wiki was smiling at herself in the mirror, trying to look pretty. When she saw

97

Hema, her smile dropped away. She might be strong at times, but she was not strong when it came to men. She needed a man to affirm herself. She couldn't survive without one. All she had to trade was her looks, the kind that appealed to male vanity, and her sex. She looked at her reflection again. Saw the desperation written in it and how dependent she had become.

'I'm sorry, son,' she said to Hema. 'Your mother was always lousy at picking her men.'

Hema and Janey watched from their bedroom window as Mum got into the car with Uncle Pera and zoomed off into the night. Janey went to sleep. Hema watched the lighted windows across the road and the people sitting or laughing behind them. He glanced at Janey where she fluttered in her dreams. For them there were no lighted, singing, windows.

The night cracked open. Through the gap came helmeted bikies on silver-chromed wings. Their bodies were carapaced with leather and studded silver. As they roared through the dark they trailed scarves from their necks like clotted blood.

'My feet are sore, Hema,' Janey said. She sat on a ledge beneath some huge billboards on Taranaki Street. Taggers had been at work. Across the smiling paternal face of the local Member of Parliament, someone had sprayed the words: THE TREATY IS A FRAUD. On another, a picture postcard scene of New Zealand: AOTEAROA, LAND OF THE LONG WHITE SHROUD.

Hema and Janey ran across the road to Pigeon Park. The bikies rumbled on down the steel canyons of the city. Janey unstrapped her sandals.

'Let me have a look,' Hema said. He found a small sharp stone in one of the sandals. It had bruised his sister's left heel. He rubbed it. 'No wonder your feet are sore,' he said. 'All better now. Why didn't you tell me before?'

'I've already been a nuisance.'

The two children sat watching laughing people walk past and the traffic glittering in the streets. Further along, on another bench, some Maori kids were laughing at a mate who was vomiting his guts out. The ground was splashed with his vomit. Hustlers stood on the corner, touting the crowds heading for Courtenay Place, fifty bucks a blow job, a hundred bucks a fuck.

Suddenly a police car screeched to a halt. Two cops got out and waded into the Maori kids. 'We'd better get out of here,' Hema said. He wasn't frightened by the attack. What he was more concerned about was that the cops would turn on him and Janey and ask questions. Quickly he pulled Janey towards Cuba Street. Neon signs announced layby, discount, bargain, sale price, special for one day only. Further along, a window display showed an underwater grotto. Plastic mermaids gambolled within it, trailing price tags from their swimsuits. An octopus languidly waved its arms. On each arm were draped watches, bracelets, fake diamonds. Hema and Janey's reflection swam into the octopus's arms. On the outside looking in.

'Shall we take a bus to the railway station?' Janey asked.

'I haven't got enough money.'

'I have,' Janey answered. She reached into the pocket of her dress and showed her brother some coins. Hema smiled at her. 'Better keep it for later,' he said. 'Just in case we need it for something else.' Nine dollars and fifty-two cents, yeah, that would get them a long way.

'Okay,' Janey said. She grinned proudly and put the coins back in her pocket.

At the intersection, Hema saw a man thumbing through green notes and stuffing them carelessly into his wallet. He hated the man for being on top of his world and not needing to worry about the next day. If Hema had been older, he would have done the arsehole.

The intersection was crowded. 'I don't want you to get lost,' Hema said to Janey. 'If we get separated stop right where you are and don't move. I'll find you.' Thrusting through the crowd was like struggling through a land of giants. 'Are you following me?' Hema shouted. Janey nodded back. She was getting cross. Couldn't people see her down here? Over her head she saw a movie poster of a grim-faced man pointed a gun at her. In a television shop a woman was being stabbed to death. A gaunt youth staggered out of a pub, knife in hand, shoving past her. Suddenly she couldn't see Hema at all.

Hema looked back. Adrenalin pumped. Where the hell was Janey? He pushed against the crowd and saw her fluttering far back among them. She was in the middle of the intersection — and the lights were changing. The intersection cleared. Only Janey was there, turning round and around, looking for him. As if she was a bird trapped in a cage with nowhere to go.

'Janey —'

Hema rushed out from the pavement. The traffic roared on both sides, drivers yelling at the two kids. This time, the traffic would really get them, but Hema didn't give a shit. A car braked in front of them. The traffic came to a stop.

'Get your sister off the road, boy,' a voice called.

Hema picked Janey up. Someone muttered something about mothers who let their children roam the streets at night. Eyes pierced him like sharp needles.

'You told me to stop right where I was and don't move,' Janey said.

Hema tousled her hair. 'You did right,' he answered. 'Not far to go now.' He pulled her down Lambton Quay. Behind the glass-paned window of a coffee bar a woman jabbed at her blood-red steak with a fork.

Last night. Mum had jabbed at her food in the same way. Over the table, Hema and Janey watched her, silent. Over the last few weeks they'd stopped talking when they got home, too afraid that anything they might say might lead to a reprimand. It wasn't just Uncle Pera they were cautious about; it was Mum as well.

Mum's face was tight. Her hands kept smoothing down her dress, moving down her thighs and up again, brushing the room with tension.

'Is there any pudding, Mum?' Hema asked.

But Mum didn't hear him. She never heard them anymore. She was looking at the clock on the wall. The week before, Uncle Pera had moved out. He was tired of her, he had said. He was sick of having the kids around. He was pissing off. But Mum had been telephoning him every day, asking him to come back. Please come back to me, please, please, please. Tonight, he had said he would. He'd just wanted to teach Mum a lesson. Just to let her know who was boss. Did she really want to see him? Oh yes, she'd crooned. Yes. Yes.

'When Uncle Pera comes,' Mum said to Hema, 'I want you both to go to bed and I don't want to hear you or see you until tomorrow. You got that, son?'

The door opened downstairs. Mum gave a cry and ran down the steps to her man. He was drunk. She didn't care. She kissed him and started to bring him upstairs. Her eyes were shining with happiness and tears.

'Go to bed now,' she said to Hema. 'Take Janey with you.'

Uncle Pera was already mauling her. A hand up Mum's dress, feeling her. His lips whispering to her, 'You wet for me, honey?' He looked at Hema and winked.

'We don't want you,' Hema yelled. 'Janey, Mum and me, we can look after ourselves.'

Mum hadn't understood what Hema was doing. Her eyes were filled only with terror that Pera might leave, go back out the door, just when she had managed to get him back in. 'Go to bed Hema,' she screamed.

'No.'

'Do as your mother says,' Uncle Pera said.

'You're not my father,' Hema answered. 'I don't take orders from you.'

Who knows what triggered Pera's rage? Maybe, at the pub, he'd tried a line on some younger woman and had been rejected. Or maybe he'd got into an argument with a mate and lost. Whatever, he came roaring up the stairs and chopped at Hema's windpipe with the back of his hand. Stunned, gasping for breath, Hema fell to the floor. Pera grabbed him by the throat and threw him into the bedroom.

'Pera, no,' Wiki called. 'Hema didn't mean it.' Janey ran to her and hid her face in her mother's dress.

'The little bastard needs a lesson,' Pera answered. 'He needs to know that even though I'm not his fucken Dad I'm the one who puts the meat on the table. You got that, kid?' He took off his belt and began to thrash Hema with it. He kicked the door closed.

'Mum —'

The *pain*. Hema held his body tight against the blows. The belt whistled and whistled.

Half an hour later, Hema limped to the bathroom. He stood shivering in the shower. He was towelling himself when Mum came in.

'Me and Uncle Pera are going out,' Mum said. She reached out to caress him.

'Don't touch me.'

'Try to understand, Hema.'

'Don't touch me.'

'Never interfere, son. You only get hurt if you interfere.'

Finally, the railway station. Fists thudded in a sudden fight outside the main entrance. Two men argued over ownership of a taxi at the rank. Within the pillared shadows thin faces gleamed.

Mum had never even come to stop Uncle Pera. She had let Uncle Pera give him a hiding. She let him.

Above the clamour, the loudspeaker announced departure times, platform numbers, welcomes and farewells to passengers. Everyone seemed to have a place to go, a destination. Everyone, except Hema and Janey. Of course he hadn't realised that at that time of the night no trains went to Gisborne. Trains only went as far as Napier anyway and from there you had to take a bus. Gisborne where Nani George lived was a faraway land, remote, at the other side of the rainbow.

Meanwhile, train after train pulled out of the station, carriage after carriage of lighted windows flowing past, dream after dream.

'I'm hungry, Hema,' Janey said.

Nodding, Hema took Janey into the station cafeteria. He bought a pie to take

101

away and a Coke. They went outside and sat on the entrance steps.

'I wouldn't have gone without you,' Janey said. 'You could have thrown all the stones you like, but I wouldn't have left you.'

'Yeah,' Hema answered. 'You've always been a nuisance.'

The railway station began to grow silent. It became a derelict place strewn with cigarette butts, spilled food, ripped porno magazines — all the rubbish discarded by people, piling up at the huge door of the night. The luggage depot, florist, bar and cafeteria began to close down. Only a few people remained. An old tramp who had nowhere else to go. A young couple who had missed the last unit to the Hutt. Three skinheads looking for fun.

A late-night porter whistled his way across the concourse. He cast a curious look at Hema and Janey.

'Do you think Mum will be home yet?' Janey asked.

'Too early,' Hema answered. *And when she got home and saw they weren't there she would cry out their names and run from room to room and down the street looking for them and . . .*

'Where shall we go?' Janey asked. 'We can't stay here, eh Hema.'

Looking around, Hema felt so lost, so utterly lost. There was nowhere to go. All around were street signs: ONE WAY. TRAFFIC LIGHTS AHEAD. NO STOPPING. NO PASSING. NO EXIT. He began to think of his mother. Understanding of her overwhelmed him. Their mother was a weak woman. She needed men. One day when they had all left her, she might need Hema and Janey again. But until then, there was no safety at home either.

Hema made up his mind. He and Janey would just have to make the best of it. He took his sister's hand.

'You'll never leave me, eh Hema?'

'No,' he answered. Not now. Not ever.

They hurried through the night. A patrol car screamed along the street. A star burst across the sky. The lights of the city tightened around them.

TRUTH OF THE MATTER

The taxi driver to a friend after the trial

Two years they got for what they did to me. Less for good behaviour. Justice they call it. I tell you, there should be harsher penalties. People think they can get away with anything these days. Assault. Murder. And why? Because they don't fear the law any more.

Yes, they'll both be out on the streets, happy as Larry, in a couple of years. Me, I'll carry these scars for the rest of my life. Not a pretty sight, are they. That's where they hit me. Almost split my skull open. Almost killed me. I hope they both rot in hell.

As I said, there were two of them. Black as the ace of spades. The wife was always getting at me for driving in the early mornings. Thought it was too dangerous. I wish I'd taken more notice of her now. But the bills were piling up, see. And another kid was on the way. We needed the money.

I'd just finished taking a fare to Kilbirnie, a nice couple I'd picked up from the Opera brasserie. Friendly types they were. Put me in a good mood. Actually, I was going to call it a night after dropping them off. Then the call came through from the office about these two guys in Newtown wanting to go to the railway station. So I said I'd do the job. Bloody fate dealt me a lousy hand. But I was in a good mood and thought I'd do these guys a good turn.

I should have guessed there was something fishy about that call. I mean it was after two in the morning. The trains had stopped running for the night. Why would two guys want to go to the railway station at that hour? They never wanted to go there in the first place. What they did to me was planned right from the start. Premeditated, the word is. They meant to do me over, my oath.

Actually, I knew the place where I had to pick those two up. You soon get to know some addresses because of the number of calls you get. This place was like that — a regular party house. Parties from Thursday to Saturday. Always the same kind of people. You know the kind. They all look the same to me. The money that must have been wasted on booze.

I parked outside and waited. You know, people ring up for a taxi, have a couple more drinks and forget about us. The music was really loud. You wouldn't catch me living in that street, my oath. There was a red bulb in one of the windows. Black shadows were moving behind it.

Well I'm as patient as the next guy, but I got a bit tired of waiting. So I sounded the horn. After a couple of minutes I gave the horn another blast.

Then they came. The door of the house burst open. These two guys, staggering out. One was helping the other to walk. Swearing at each other. Apes, they looked like.

I put on the inside light. One of the guys, big, built like one of those Japanese wrestlers, yanked the back door open and heaved his mate in. He slammed the door before I could ask him not to. But when he got in, I said, friendly like, Hey, mate, don't do that again. I mean, you have to put these people in the picture about treating property with respect. He looked at me with that ape face of his and know what he did? He pulled his door shut with another slam. He wanted trouble. Wanted me to say something about it. Give him an excuse to do me right then.

I don't look for trouble, so I shrugged my shoulders and started the car. I said, Railway station is it? The big guy answered, Don't you know? And his mate said, What took you so long, man?

Those voices! Black like the guys themselves. The anger in them. But why be angry with me? I hadn't done anything to them. Didn't even know them.

As I say, my other fare had put me in a friendly mood. And driving a taxi in the early mornings can be pretty lonely. So I thought I'd strike up a bit of conversation. You've got to give people another chance, I always say. I said to this big guy, Good party was it? I wasn't prepared for his answer though. What's it to you, man? he said. What's it to you? So I answered, Just asking, mate.

Well, he'd had his chance. So I shut up. If a fare doesn't want to make conversation that's his privilege. After all, he's the one who pays the bill.

By that time we were just coming up to Courtenay Place. I had to stop at the lights.

There was a young girl standing at the corner waiting to cross. A pretty little thing she was. Don't know what she was doing out at that time of night. She was wearing a blue raincoat. And as she walked in front of the taxi the flap of her coat opened to show her legs.

I often wonder now whether I would have been done if that hadn't happened. That is, if you take the view as the judge did that what those two guys did to me wasn't premeditated. You see, the girl didn't seem to be wearing anything under her coat. It's the truth I tell you. And God, those legs were beautiful.

When those two guys saw her they were away. They whistled and laughed and gestured at her and punched each other as if they'd never seen a girl before. The smaller guy yelled to her, You want a ride, honey? And the big guy said, Hop in, baby. And all the time they were laughing and whistling and grinding away.

The girl didn't even bother to look at them. She kept on walking without looking back. That's what riled them, I think. Because when the lights changed and I drove the car off the big guy yelled at her, On your back and grunt, bitch.

By that time I'd just about had enough of the pair of them. They were just animals. Filthy. They were talking about girls. White girls. Girls they'd had, girls they'd shared, girls they'd had in a pack with their other friends. It churned me up to listen to them.

So I stopped the taxi and told them to get out. Don't bother about the fare, I said. Just get out, I said

That's when they turned on me. Both of them. Called me all the names under the sun and added some I'd never heard of. And believe you me, I've been around. White shit, they called me. I mean, what sort of talk is that?

Then the big guy asked me if I had a daughter.

Get out, you filthy sod, I said to him.

He laughed at me. Okay, boss, he said.

They made as if they were opening the doors of the taxi. Suddenly, I heard one of them whispering. I turned to look.

I felt an arm snap around my neck. My oath, that big guy was strong. And the pain. Give it to him, he was saying to his mate. Give it to him.

That's when I saw the beer bottle.

I tried to fight back. I managed to jerk free. I reached for the mike to call for help.

That's when they hit me. Hit me. Hit me.

The blood. The pain.

I heard the front door open. One of the guys was feeling in my pockets. The other grabbed the cash on the seat. Just before they ran off, the big guy whispered to me, You deserve this, you bastard.

He smashed his hand in my groin.

Then they were gone.

Some time later, I don't know how long it was, I heard the taxi door open again. I thought they'd come back to finish me off. I heard someone say, Oh Jesus.

The doctors didn't think I would pull through. Well, I did. But what for, I ask you? Two years they got. Only two years.

The big guy to his cellmate in prison

I thought I'd seen the last of this bloody place. Two years in this rotten hole. All because the jury believed the crap that cab driver threw them. Bastards the lot of them. Justice? There's no such thing for the likes of us. Justice is a joke in this country when a white bastard can get away with his side of the story. Two years.

Me and my mate, we were in the pub. The Oxford. You ever drink there? This brother of ours comes over and says, Feel like a party? Well, my mate and I didn't have anywhere else to go, so we latched onto our brother and that's how we ended up at Wilson Street. Some Ngatis live there and you know what those Ngatis are like. Drink piss like water. And the women, *man*!

About one o'clock in the morning the piss began to cut out. Those Ngatis started up a collect to get more. My mate and I, we're not free riders, but my mate thought it was about time to move out. He'd been trying this woman all night but she wasn't coming across. I was doing okay, though. With this woman, Arlene was her name. Brother, those tits. She really wanted it. But my mate, he called us a cab. Two years before I even touch another woman. By the time I get out I'll have forgotten how to do it.

The cab sure took its time coming. I thought we'd have to come across with some dollars before we left, and Arlene was coming hot and strong for me. But then we heard the horn outside. I didn't want to go but my mate pulled me out. She's got the pox, he told me. Bloody liar, Arlene said. Well, something smells rotten, my mate answered.

And it was true, eh. So I started to laugh. Thought it was a great joke. Arlene couldn't see it though. Piss off, she said.

We buggered out of there, laughing, to the cab.

The white guy was sitting there. Built like a bull. Smoking a cigarette. Had these massive hands. Looked like he could handle himself in a punch-up. Couldn't handle us, though. We fixed him, me and my mate.

As soon as I saw him I knew he was a cunt.

He saw us coming and he flicked his cigarette at us. Have you ever seen those eyes that look at you but don't see you? Those are the kind of eyes he had.

And as I opened the door he said, Don't slam it, hori.

Then he said, What took you so long? I haven't got all night.

Before we could even get into the cab he'd started moving it off.

Hey man, I said. Take it easy.

He laughed, the bastard. He was enjoying playing the boss man. He reckoned he'd been waiting for over twenty minutes for us to show. Lies, all of it. Just a trick so he could wind on the clock so we'd have to pay him more than we should have. They're all like that. Think you're dumb. Easy.

I should have smashed him right then. But my mate didn't want any trouble, eh. Cool it, he kept on saying to me. Cool it. Never been inside before. Shit, he has to learn. Soon be thinking of this place as home.

Yeah, well my mate said something like sorry to cunt-face in the front. You'd think that would be the end of it. But he kept going us. Started to throw his weight around. Acting the big man. What the hell for, I'd like to know. We'd done nothing to him.

You horis and your parties, he said. You're all the same, aren't you. You hit the big city and all you can think of is your parties.

I was getting wild with the bastard. So was my mate. I said to the bastard, What's it to you, man? What's it to you? And my mate said, Why don't you just drive the cab and cut the talk? That's what we're paying you for.

That shut him up for a while. It's the colour of the money, not the person, that counts. The bastard knew it too. Thought he was the boss man. But we were the ones with the dollars, yeah.

We were coming up to the hospital by then. The bastard should have turned up past the Winter Show building into John Street. I've taken cabs before and that's the way they usually go when you want to get to the railway station. It's quicker, eh. But what happens? He keeps on going towards the Basin Reserve, the long way.

So I says to him, You missed your turning didn't you, man?

Just to let him know that I was up to his game, eh. The dirt in his look. And he starts going us again. Said that he'd just finished taking an old couple to Seatoun and if he'd known we were wanting to go to the railway station he wouldn't have taken the job. You're lucky I came, he said. You wouldn't have got another cab at this time of night. He expected us to believe him.

My mate said, Forget about it. He didn't want any trouble. If it was the long way, what the hell. What was a coupla dollars to us.

So I settled down. Things got pretty quiet. I almost forgot about the bastard.

Until we got to Courtenay Place. The bastard could have made it through the lights but he slowed down. On purpose. To add more time to the clock.

That's when he saw her. This girl. In a black raincoat. Crossing the road. As she ran in front of us the wind caught at her coat and opened it up. Her skirt was so short you could see her arse.

Old Whitey, he began to act like a crazy man. I've never seen anything like it. Maybe his wife wasn't giving him any at home. He blasted this chick with his horn. Then he wound down the window and began yelling at her. You're walking the wrong way, honey, he said. Honey baby, I'll give you something you'll never forget.

He was laughing to himself and moving around as if he was wanking himself off.

But the girl sure didn't want any of him. She stood there for a moment. The headlights were shining full upon her. And she smiled this crazy smile and opened her legs wider.

Then she laughed right in his face and shoved two fingers at him. As if to say, A look is all you'll ever get.

My mate and I, we couldn't help it. We really cracked up.

You sure missed out there, man, my mate said.

By a mile, I said.

The bastard was so wild that he gunned the motor. The car leapt forward, almost knocking the girl down. I tell you, the bastard was crazy. He sure didn't like us laughing at him.

I wouldn't have touched her with a twenty-foot pole, he said. And then he began to talk about hori chicks. How they were all easy.

He was looking at us and enjoying making us wild. Looking at us. Laughing at us.

My hands started to clench themselves into fists.

But my mate said, Don't listen to him. He wants us to go him.

My mate didn't want any trouble, eh. He told the bastard to pull over. This was as far as we were going.

Old cunt-face drove into the kerb. We got out.

What do we owe you? my mate asked.

The bastard named the price. He was laughing as he said it. He knew and we knew that he was doing us. But my mate, he's a calm fella. He grinned back and said, Okay, *boss*. He pulled out some dollars, wiped them on his arse, and threw them at the bastard.

We began to walk away.

But I heard the bastard call to me.

Hey, hori, he yelled. You got a sister?

That was it. My mate couldn't stop me. I bunched my fists and walked back. Cunt-face saw me coming. He kept on smiling as he picked up his mike. He wanted me to do him, to give him an excuse to call the cops. But he still thought he was the boss man. Didn't think I would smash him up.

I had a beer bottle in my hand. As he was talking into the mike, I threw it at him.

Jesus, my mate yelled.

He ran at me. But I shoved him away and opened the cab door. The bastard was moaning. The blood was pouring down his head. Blood everywhere.

I said to him, You deserve this, you cunt.

I did him over. Good. Then I took his cash. I knew the cops would find me and my mate sooner or later. But we had a good time before they caught up with us, spending the bastard's money.

But the jury believed his side of the story. What the hell. Two years. At least I showed him he wasn't the boss man he thought he was. I wish I'd killed the bastard.

The other guy to his father during prison visiting

Two years, Dad. I don't know how I'll stand it. You do believe I'm innocent, don't you Dad? You've got to believe in me. Someone has to.

Yes, I know that other fella calls me his mate, but it's not true. He told me that I should go along with his story for the sake of both of us. I was a fool. I didn't know any better. He said nobody would believe what really happened that night. Two years! I should have told the judge the truth.

I'd seen that other fella a couple of times around the street. Then, that night, I bumped into him again. I was just waiting for the other guys from karate club to come. I was at the Franklin pub, where we usually go. But they never showed. You know I don't drink much, Dad. Just a few beers now and then. Because of my friends, see.

I was drinking by myself when this fella comes in. He started to talk to me. I got to like him. No matter what he did that night, he was a friendly fella. Even you used to say that everybody's got some good points, Dad. So there we were, drinking together at the bar. Around closing time he turned to me and said, You want to come to a party? I didn't see any harm in it. So I said, Okay.

We caught a bus to Newtown. That's where the party was. At a place in Wilson Street. I didn't know it was a rough joint. Didn't look too bad from the outside. Some fellas from up the Coast flatted there.

I was a bit shy at first. But this fella kept on saying to me, What's wrong with you? Enjoy yourself, man. So I had a few drinks and got to know some of the people. Friendly people. Lots of them too. I didn't see this fella for a while. Then, through the smoke. I saw him. He was doing a line with a girl who wasn't interested. As for me, I met this really nice girl, Arlene was her name, and we got to talking. That's all we did. Just talked.

Round about one o'clock, these other guys came in. Me and this other fella, we didn't know it at the time, but the two girls we were talking to belonged to two of these guys. And while I was talking to this Arlene, I saw something being thrown at me. It was a beer bottle, Dad. Just misses me. Smashed against the wall.

I looked at this fella and he looked at me. He said, We'd better split. I mean, we didn't want any trouble, Dad. So he called us a taxi.

We waited and waited. The party got a bit wild. There was a fight. My mate threw a punch. Those Coasties began to crowd in on us. I gave one a karate chop.

Then we heard the taxi outside. We rushed out, this fella and me. We were sure glad to get away, I can tell you.

The taxi driver was waiting there and he smiled.

Sorry I took so long, he said.

And this fella said, That's okay, man. Hope you haven't been waiting for us. We had a bit of an argument in there.

The taxi driver laughed. He told us that everybody knew the place at Wilson Street. They have fights all the time, he said. And then he said, You're lucky I came along to pick you up. Not many drivers accept calls from this address.

Thanks, I said.

We hopped into the taxi and closed the doors behind us. The taxi driver said, Railway station is it? I nodded.

He was a real friendly man, that taxi driver. Told us that this was his last trip for the night. His wife was pregnant and he wanted to get back to her. Just before picking us up, he'd taken this couple to Lyall Bay. He didn't mind taking us to the station because it was on his way home. He was a big man with friendly eyes. He'd lost a lot of his hair though. What little he had left was combed over his bald spot at the back.

Then he asked, Good party was it?

He winked because he knew it wasn't true. After all, he'd seen us running out of that place. Then he asked, How did you two guys manage to get mixed up with that lot?

He began to tell us how he'd seen many young guys like us who come to the big city and fall in with the wrong crowd. He said that after a while you could pick the ones who would get into trouble. They mightn't even intend to, but it happened. He hoped it wouldn't happen to us. Didn't think it would.

Round about that time, we were coming into Courtenay Place. Hardly anyone was around. Hardly any wind either, because I looked out the window and saw that some flags flying above a used car lot were still and not moving.

The lights were against us so we had to stop.

That was when we saw this girl. She seemed to come out of nowhere. She was wearing a dark raincoat and was hurrying to cross before the lights change. She looked quite a nice girl, long legs, and as she hurried in front of us her raincoat flapped open.

And she smiled, Dad. A soft smile it was, like mist. I felt that it was just for me.

She looks nice, I said.

The taxi driver gave me a disbelieving look and this other fella laughed out loud. The taxi driver said she'd been wearing nothing at all and this fella said, Just about. And they began to talk about the girl. That she was probably a stripper on her way home. Or that she was a prostitute.

No decent girl would be walking round alone at this time of night, the taxi driver said.

And this other fella said to me, You want to watch it. Not a good judge are you!

They began to laugh at me.

Well, I didn't like it when they did that. Especially when the taxi driver sounded his horn at the girl and this other fella began to call to her. When the lights changed and we started to move, I decided to get out of the cab and walk the rest of the way home.

They kept on laughing at me, see, Dad. I don't like being laughed at.

So I asked the taxi driver to slow down and let me off.

What's wrong? this other fella asked.

I didn't answer him. As soon as the taxi stopped I opened the door and made to get out. He put his hand on me, this fella.

Hey, how about giving me some money to pay for the cab? he said.

Well I didn't have any money on me. I'd told this fella I hadn't any when we first met in the pub.

I haven't got any money either, he said.

But he was lying. I'd seen him pull out some notes when he bought some beer. And another thing. He'd made sure not to share his beer at the party either. He still had the bottles with him.

The taxi driver began to get a bit scared.

Come on fellas, he said. He thought I was having him on.

I'm broke, I told him.

I made to get out of the taxi again. The taxi driver reached over and stopped me.

Look fellas, he said. Somebody has to pay me. Now who was it who rang for the taxi?

Him, I said, pointing to this fella.

Wasn't me, he said.

I could see that the driver was getting angry. But I didn't want any trouble. So I said to him, If you drive me to my uncle's place I'll wake him up and get some money to pay you. Okay?

But he wasn't having it on. He was getting pretty mad and I don't blame him. He started going me and this other fella. Saying how he had thought we were different from the rest but instead we were just the same.

This other fella was getting angry too about what the taxi driver was saying. They started to shout at each other.

Suddenly, this other fella laughed.

He turned to me. He winked. Then he said, Looks like we'll have to hit this taxi driver over the head.

It was just a joke, Dad. But the taxi driver thought we meant it. He reached over to grab his mike.

Hey, this other fella said.

He leaned over to reassure the taxi driver. The taxi driver pushed him away.

This fella, he got scared. He'd already been in prison before. He grabbed the driver round the head and pulled him away from the mike.

For Christ's sake help me, he said. Give it to me. Give it to me.

He was pointing at one of the beer bottles. Without knowing what I was doing, I gave it to him.

I heard the bottle smash as this fella hit the taxi driver over the head. Oh God. The blood. The blood.

And this fella kept on hitting the taxi driver. Hitting him. Hitting him. I tried to stop him.

I couldn't stand it any longer. I opened the door and started to run.

Hey, wait, I heard this fella call.

I turned. He had gotten in front with the taxi driver. Then he was running after me.

We ran together. I was crying, Dad. And this fella, all of a sudden, he pushed me against a wall.

We're in this together, he said. You and me, we did this together.

But it should never have happened. We didn't mean to do it at all. You've got to believe me, Dad. It's the truth. I swear it's the truth.

The girl in the raincoat to her boyfriend

I can't keep it to myself any longer. I've got to tell you. After all, it was your place that I was coming from that night.

It was about five months ago it happened. You probably don't remember it, but it was after that party at your flat. We'd had some drinks, smoked some marijuana. I wanted you to take me home. But you were really out. So I decided to walk.

God, I felt fantastic. I was floating along the streets. Nobody was around. It was really late. The street lights looked like emeralds and I felt they all belonged to me. I felt as if I was walking in a dream. The whole city loved me. Those dummies behind glass windows all loved me. If they had the chance they would have broken out of their crystal sheaths to make love to me.

The feeling was so strong that I didn't notice the three men. They were in a car, stopped at the lights at Courtenay Place. I thought they were dummies too, with eyes like fires burning behind glass windows. One of them sounded the horn and it was like a fanfare. They all began to shout at me.

I couldn't help smiling at them. I laughed and danced in front of them, opening and closing my coat.

It wasn't until later that I discovered I was almost naked.

Well, I heard the car roaring past me. I watched as it turned the corner. I went on walking home.

I turned into a side street, the usual way home, and that is when I saw them. The three men. The fires in their eyes were flaring high, brightly burning. They were arguing.

I didn't want to be seen. I hid in the shadows. All of a sudden I could hear conversation cracking through the glass. One voice saying, No girl would want you, man. Another voice saying, She didn't even look at you, hori. A third voice saying, She'd wrap her legs around me anytime.

They were quarrelling. With each other. The three of them at each other. As they quarrelled they were hissing at each other. Come on, man. Come on hori. Come on fella. Show me. Show me. Show me.

They began to fight. They ripped at each other. They slammed into each other, two against one, one against one while the other rested before joining the battle again. The sounds as they banged against each other jarred against the walls of my mind. I pressed myself further into the dark.

Then I heard one of them shout, You rotten bastard.

The one he was shouting at had grabbed a bottle and smashed it against the pavement. The fragments showered. The other two began to back away from him. He jabbed at them, spinning light through the air as he slashed.

Okay fellas, he was saying. Which one first? Or both of you at once? Come on. Show me. Show me.

I felt angry and frightened. I screamed at them. Stop. *Stop.*

The man with the bottle looked up. The bottle was up-raised in his hand. One of the others leapt at him and kicked him back toward the car.

The man with the bottle fell back. He gave a loud cry. One of the others ran past me, his arms arcing slowly through the dark. The other ran towards the car. He grabbed something. Then he ran off too. I heard their footsteps clattering out of my mind.

I was trembling. I heard the man who had fallen, moaning in the car. The sound was so terribly frightening. I went to him. Are you all right? I asked. Wait here. I'll go and get help.

I ran home, planning to call the police. However, when I got home I changed my mind. I wasn't sure whether what I'd seen was real or not. And I was scared about the drugs in the house.

But if it wasn't a dream then what I have told you is what really happened that night. Believe me, I saw it.

DUSTBINS

You can always tell what people are like by what they throw out in their rubbish. Take it from me, I should know, I'm an expert. Me and my bros work the dustcarts day in day out Monday to Friday. I've been doing the job for, how long now? Seems like years but it's probably less. Actually, I was pretty lucky to get the job in the first place. I came down here from the Coast. No brains, no money, no job. Dumb as. Me and the old man weren't getting along all that good and whenever he got drunk he beat up on me. Well there's only so much a man can take. So one night when he was getting stuck into me I took a poke back at him. He told me to get out. So I did.

newspapers/plastic cups/the Evening Post/*rotten apples/Watties cans/old magazines/old chicken drumsticks and bones/* North&South

I landed down here at my cuz Crazy-Joe's place. He took one look at me and said, Not another Ngati and I suppose you're skint too. But he opened the door and said, Any space you find on the floor is yours.

You know Wilson Street? That's Crazy-Joe's place. It's the biggest party house in town. All the bros drink there, straight after payday Thursday to Monday morning, one long party. The women, man, they's easy. And the fights are the best. Last Friday the cops came twice. Hardcase, man, you should have seen it. Some girl screaming she'd been assaulted.

Anyway, I'd been here two weeks when Crazy-Joe kicked me awake one morning. Hey kid, he says, you been bludging off us for too long, freeloading, and it's time you started paying your way. I asked him, What you mean? And he says, The boss, Harry, sacked one of the bros and there's a vacancy so I told Harry I got a meathead cuz, strong as. And Harry says, Can he hack the job? And I says, Sure, you should see the legs on him. Big as. So you got the job kid.

That's the way with us cuzzies. Man, Crazy-Joe really looked after me. They don't come more staunch than him.

Used condoms/rusting razor blades/Knight riders/catshit/Gillette/decaying vegetables/ Kentucky Fried/shampoo bottles/hair recently cut/Cold Power/mouldy bread/New Zealand The Way You Want It

Do I remember the first day? Do I what. I used to think I was pretty fit but not for these hills. I was on the truck with Crazy-Joe, Bill and two other guys, so I thought I was sweet. I mean Bill was as skinny as, and Crazy-Joe had a gut so big he couldn't see his thing unless it was hard. I was the fifth man, the spare they called me.

We must have got to the yard about six. Harry, the Pakeha boss, signed me on and read me the rules and then said I could be on Crazy-Joe's round. Crazy-Joe said, Just my luck to have a rookie but I know he didn't mean it. Bill took first shift as the driver and me, Crazy-Joe and the other two guys were on the back, standing on the ramp of the truck. Hey, it was great standing there with the bros and hanging on. Crazy-Joe said, If you want to smoke have one now because as sure as eggs you're not going to get the chance until we get back to the yard. So I took one from his pack and it was really choice to be one of the bros. But I was careful to watch Crazy-Joe and Bill and, when they threw their butts onto the road, I knew we were pretty close to getting into it.

Our round started in Kilbirnie on the flat ground. We did the domestic rubbish. Another cart did the commercial stuff, you know, picking up the rubbish from the shops, factories and industrial areas. I wanted to impress so I watched Crazy-Joe a few times until I got the idea and then told him I wasn't a kid. Him and Bill winked and Bill laughed and said, Then we better let you off the leash.

So Crazy-Joe and I did the left side of the street and the other two guys did the right. I'd do four houses, Crazy-Joe would be ahead doing the next four, and we'd bunnyhop each other up the street. There I was, running in and out of people's gates, round the backs of their houses to where they kept their rubbish tins, upending their tins into my sack or fadge, crashing through to the next backyard and then taking the filled fadge back to the truck. Then I'd bang on the side of the truck and yell 'Squeeze' so our driver would know to start the hydraulic ram. I loved hearing the sound of the compressor, the whine of the motor and the crunch as it came down to claw the rubbish into the body of the truck so that there was room for more. Once you've heard that sound you never forget it. For me, the sound was sort of like paying back. Paying back who or what, search me, but there was something really cool about it.

That first hour I got into the swing of the job. Bill asked, No sweat? I nodded, No sweat. Easy as.

Then we struck the hills. It wasn't long before I realised that you can be as fit as, but that running up hills hits the muscles at the backs of your legs and thighs and sucks the breath out of you. Before you know it you're gasping for air. I mean. Really. Gasping. Until the air is so dry it's like razorblades in your throat.

That's when I really admired my bros. They taught me how to pace myself. To figure out the places where you can go easy and conserve your strength for the places where you need it. You know those guys who go to gyms? They wouldn't last five minutes on the dust. Their muscles are in the wrong places. And they can't let go of their image of what they might look like to people. To be a dustie you have to kiss goodbye to thinking about how you look and just keep your head down and get the job done.

And I'll tell you what. Being on the dust sure makes you appreciate water. When we got back to the yard there was nothing better than to strip off and take a shower. Really mighty.

combs/tossed out clothes/Keep New Zealand Clean/stinking fish and fishheads/old shoes/ New Zealand Woman's Weekly/building materials/Persil Washes Whiter/broken crockery/ orange peels/rusted irons/blood-soaked sheets/old books/chipped glasses/hypodermic needles

I can tell you that by Thursday payday I felt I had really earned every cent. I had learnt a few more things too. Take dogs for instance. There are some mean hounds around and sometimes you don't know until you're around the back and they leap up at you wanting to take an arm and a leg. People with dogs like that don't get their rubbish lifted unless it's outside the front gate.

People, they're another hazard. You can be picking up the rubbish when some guy comes out thinking you're breaking in or he turns up with some sawn-off shotgun mistaking you for someone who's having it off with his wife. Or you're on the truck and some up himself bastard comes up behind the truck in his car and wants to get past. They can be pretty abusive, some of them.

But, hey, did you know that in the old days people didn't have rubbish collectors? The boss, Harry, was telling me. In London and other cities people used to throw their rubbish out the window and if you were walking beneath you copped the lot. Harry said that you could tell you were approaching a city by the smell. Makes you think twice about the importance of your job. Us rubbish collectors are at the arse end of society. We're like the night cart men who came every Tuesday to pick up the crap cans. Undertakers are like us too. I mean, just think about it. If you didn't have undertakers to pick up the dead they'd pile up at the doors of the living. Just imagine how that would have been way back when there were plagues and the Black Death. You'd have nobody going around crying, 'Bring out your dead! Bring out your dead!' Same with us. If we weren't here to pick up the rubbish it would pile up and pile up until it towered over the living. The stench, God, it would be real stink.

A mate of mine, Selwyn, puts it this way. One day he asked a group of us, What is the most important part of the body? Some said the eyes, others said the heart or the brain or your thing. But he said, No, it's the arsehole, and for a moment we thought he was a homo. But then he told us this story of how the rest of the body laughed at this idea, so the arsehole decided to prove its point by going on strike. Very soon the whole of the body started to feel the symptoms. The head started to get headaches, the heart started to have palpitations, the stomach started to get bloated by all the gases and poisons of waste matter piling up inside it. The kidneys and liver started to malfunction and the blood started to turn green. The body discovered that without the arsehole it was poisoning itself. So all the other organs of the body finally accepted that the arsehole was the most important of them all.

Whenever I saw people looking at me as if I was shit I used to think of that story. I felt like stuffing a cork up their bum. Going on strike. Believe me, it wouldn't take long before they give me some respect.

But hey this story is about the girl in the white dress, not about my life as a dustie. I mean, nobody's going to make a movie about me but that girl, well she was as pretty as. About sixteen I guess. I used to call her Mary although that wasn't her name at all. It just struck me that she was a Mary sort of girl. The kind you see in a church. Who makes you think about love and not sex. Sweet. Smile as bright as. Nice teeth. Long hair that shone. Clean smelling. Not like some women who used to party at Wilson Street whose breaths could kill you and who still smelt of the guy who's been there in front of you.

It must have been on my fourth day on the job that I saw her. We'd just done the street that everyone called Nappy Valley because of all the disposable napkins that used to get chucked out in the rubbish. Talk about stink. Anyway, we were doing the better part of the suburb, where the houses are white and two-storeyed. Mary was up early putting out the rubbish as I was coming around the back. She was in a clinging white dress. It sort of flowed all over her concealing everything but also showing everything, you know? Bare feet. Bare arms prickling with gooseflesh. When she saw me she was so modest. She pulled her dress around her with one hand. With the other she pushed a wing of her hair back. Then she gave me the sort of smile that curls around your heart.

stale bread/Do Not Take Without Doctor's Advice/broken toys/glass/car parts/Playboy/ ripped blankets/broken bottles/throwaway biros/posters/maggots in meat/You Have To Be In To Win/carpet squares/DB Is Better/branches and leaves/sanitary napkins/Vogue/ polystyrene mugs/stale fish and chips/thrown-out correspondence/Be A Tidy Kiwi

As I been telling you, you see all kinds of people when you're on the dust. Pensioners, they're the best, I guess because they want to please. Some even have little gates so you can go through their backyards easier. But other people, well they seem to take a lot of care about the front of their houses, I guess because that's what you see from the road, nice paintjob, nice fence, roses in the garden, lawn nice and tidy, venetian blinds and curtains. But nobody gives a stuff about the back. It's sort of like a person who's wearing something in the front but when they turn around they've got a bare bum. Backyards? I've seen them all. Full of dogs and doggie doo doo, kids' prams and toys, trash, smashed-up motorbikes, garden waste and other unmentionable compost muck, mattresses that have been thrown out because somebody has been smoking and the mattress has caught fire. Some of those backyards smelling because the owners haven't been bothered to go to the toilet and just let fly out the window. Lines full of clothes, some of the underpants brown from who knows what. Beer bottles all over the place. Windows wide open.

You know, it's funny about people. They'll close their front curtains if they're doing it in the sitting room but they leave the curtains wide open when they're doing it at the back. And when do the guys like to do it? In the morning, of course, when his bladder is full and helping to give him a boner. I tell you, the boys and I seen some sights. Funny as. I used to think there were only a coupla ways of getting your load off. But sometimes, watching, I had to wonder to myself, How do you get in that position? Sometimes the people would see me and the woman would scream blue murder. But other times they'd just keep humping and pumping, loving us looking on. I saw Mary's older brother once, with some girl. He had her against the wall, pulling at her hair and slapping her around. I never saw her face.

Yeah, Mary had a brother and a father but her mother had died a few years ago. The father was a rich man, some bigwig banker, very respectable, making megabucks. Had a Jaguar in the drive and a yacht down at the marina. He was one of those who hated it when, if he was running late, our truck was blocking his way. Complained about it once to the boss. Never left any booze out for us at Christmas. And the son was just as bad. Worked with his Dad in the same bank. Had a mouth on him. An attitude. I heard he was pretty good with his fists. Could believe it too. But you'd never tell when you saw him in that suit of his, smiling at his clients. All charm and clean up front but when he turned around, pure arsehole. Mary had left school the year before. She didn't work. Maybe she was between jobs. I don't know.

The next time I saw her, a few weeks later, she was combing her hair in the mirror. She saw me go past and poked out her tongue and grinned. When I got back to the truck Crazy-Joe saw the stars in my eyes. He says, So you've met the madonna? I says, The who? The madonna, he replies. Haven't you ever been inside a church?

That's when I realised Mary was special. Not just to me but to all the boys. But you know, the funny thing was that none of us ever talked to her? It was as if, in talking to her, she'd have to come down from her pedestal. I mean she used to try to get me to talk but I'd get all tongue tied. There she'd be, putting the rubbish in the rubbish tin and she'd say something like, 'Hello again.' Or, 'I'm sorry I couldn't fit the bottles into the tin last week, thank you for taking them.' Or, 'Isn't it a nice day?' Or, if it was a really hot day, she'd offer a beer or an orange juice.

Squeeze, I'd yell. I loved the sound of the hydraulic ram.

Did I tell you that she always wrapped her rubbish? Believe me, you never know about people's habits until you've seen both their backyards and inside their rubbish tins. We had some Indians on our run, they were as clean as and their rubbish smelt of curry, and yet Indians have a reputation for being dirty. The same with Samoans, they'd fill their tins with leftover taro and vegetables and maybe they weren't wrapped, but at least they didn't spill maggots all over the place like at some of the better houses. You'd think that Maoris would be clean but I tell you some of my bros are as dirty as. I've had my hands cut up from some of the beer bottles they've thrown into the rubbish. I mean, you'd think they would appreciate the fact that one of their own was doing their rubbish. No way, man.

One of the houses I liked doing was actually full of trannies. I met one of them and I knew straight off that she wasn't a woman. But they're good for laughs, those trannies, and their rubbish. Man, some crazy things there. Like falsies and torn lingerie. They didn't stay too long because the cops came and cleared them out. The next tenants were even funnier. They were prostitutes and one of them was a dominatrix. Their rubbish was even funnier. Leather harnesses. Broken chains. Crazy-Joe used to love doing their rubbish.

The worst rubbish was Nappy Valley and the street where Mary lived. In Nappy Valley, sometimes I'd see fond grandparents coming to see their grandchildren and walking up the clean paths to the clean houses and I'd think, If only you could see what your nice clean grandchildren did today. All those disposable nappies.

And as for the rich houses. Broken bottles after swanky parties. Condoms. Cigarette butts. Leftover meat swarming with maggots.

One morning, as I was taking a tin down I heard a mewling sound. I looked in, and there were these kittens wrapped in a sack. Crazy-Joe cursed and spat and said, It happens all the time, why can't people do the job properly. He took the sack and swung it against the side of the truck until it was stained red with blood. I was a bit sick just watching but he said, Better to get it over with than have them suffocating to death. He saw that I was shaken so he said again, Listen, it happens all the time so get over yourself.

Back at the yard I took an extra long shower. I thought, How sick people are, what bastards. I could have given up on the whole of mankind if it wasn't for my bros. If it wasn't for people like Mary.

Squeeze, I'd yell, and I'd bang on the side of the truck.

bring out your dead/old flowers/Tip Top Icecream Is Best/cereal/broken wine glasses/ mewling cats/stale cake/What Every Housewife Wants/sanitary napkins/inorganic waste/ plastic roofing/Your Baby Will Love His Treasures/Jif/Choysa Tea Tastes Better/Poisonous substances/dead budgies/fish bones/days-old food/kerosene tins/broken records/used electrical appliances/Look For The Silver Lining/dead pups/clothes/soiled blankets/Keep Away From Children

It was Bill who noticed it first. The dark rings under Mary's eyes. The way in which she would look away whenever I was doing her rubbish. He said to me and Crazy-Joe, Something's happened to Mary.

Whatever was happening, it didn't happen quickly. Not so quickly as you would catch on. But when Bill pointed it out, he put into words what I had been thinking for some weeks. I'd noticed that she wasn't smiling so much. Her hair seemed more dull. Whenever I came across her, she sometimes didn't bother to hold her hands across her white dress. It was as if a light was going out inside her.

The trouble is, you see, that dusties only pick up people's rubbish once a week and it's a long time from one week to the next and, I know it now, Mary was such a good actress. She could still muster a smile and, sometimes, you only see what you want to see. I used to say to her, 'How goes it?' And she'd say, 'Fine.' And then I'd say, 'See you next week.' And she'd say, 'Okay.' I mean, a few minutes each week is not much to go on, is it. But I knew something was really wrong when I upended her rubbish tin one week and saw that none of it was wrapped. Everything was raw. Bleeding. Exposed.

Even then I really didn't cotton on until that morning when I heard, as I went round the back, Mary vomiting her guts out in the toilet. And the sound of her weeping. Then, after that I didn't see much of her at all. Only sometimes a shadow at the door as her father swept out or the flutter of a curtain as she sat in the sitting room with her brother.

I suppose I was, as my boss Harry would have said, too occupied with the comedies of life. I reckon your mind prefers to see only the funny things. Like Mary's brother with his girlfriend in the mornings and, one morning, even her old man with some woman. Or like the dominatrix down the road locking some stupid fella into a closet so that he could enjoy the dark, good grief. And then there were people who had moved in next door to Mary's, and the woman was always screaming and yelling to her husband that she didn't want to have the baby. Sometimes you try not to see the things that are bad because it's easier to laugh than to cry. Easier to look at what's happening that you can fix rather than at the things you can't fix. And I'd also met this new girl and was having a good time with her.

Then came the day, just like any other day, as beautiful as. We'd done Nappy Valley and were doing the street where Mary lived. Her dad passed us on the street, his horn blaring away. His son was in the front with him, laughing. Mary wasn't around when I took her dustbin. It would have been good to see her but I moved on to the neighbour's place. And then on to the next. I was feeling really good as. Feeling good to be alive.

Then it happened. Crazy-Joe looked at the rubbish in the truck and yelled out to Bill, Squeeze. I've always loved the sound of the hydraulic ram. The whine of the

123

motor. The way the claws come down. The crunch as the rubbish is crushed into a tight mass and pushed to the insides of the truck.

Then, out of the corner of my eye, I saw the rubbish move.

I heard this mewling sound.

I thought, Another kitten. But it was too late to get it and kill it.

Then as the hydraulic ram began to churn rubbish I saw something erupting from the rubbish. A wet pillowcase, with blood stains and shit and — oh God, maggots from God knows where. I thought . . . the kitten. Ah well, the thing would suffocate soon enough.

But then I saw the eye.

It was looking out of a rip in the pillow case at me. Just staring. A little bloodshot eye, swimming in blood and rubbish and maggots, and I knew, even before I saw its bloodied little hand reaching out for me, that the thing wasn't a cat.

The squeezer was still doing its job squashing all the rubbish and pushing it back into the hopper. Crazy-Joe hadn't seen what I had seen. He said I screamed at him to tell Bill to switch the hydraulic ram off. He thought I was crazy because I leapt in, as it was doing its job, into all that churning mass, coming down on top of the sack, and rolling with it into the rest of the rubbish.

Crazy-Joe ran round the driver's side, reached into the cab and pressed the stop button. He and Bill came back and tore the rubbish apart until they got to me. What the hell, Crazy-Joe yelled, What the hell . . .

I was crying so much, bawling my eyes out, because I thought maybe it was too late. Bill saw the pillowcase and the little hand. He said, We got to get to the hospital. I'll radio ahead. Stay put. Crazy-Joe leapt in with me and Bill went back to the cab of the truck and took off. The back was still open and rubbish was spilling out everywhere and rubbish bins were bouncing all over the road. Bill drove like a maniac, screaming at other cars, Get the hell out of the road. Past Nappy Valley. Down the hills onto the flat. We totalled a Honda on our way through red lights and the Council has a huge payout to make on it. Winged a few other cars too. I can laugh at it now but at the time I just couldn't stop shivering and holding that little bundle in my arms. Even when we got to the entrance of the hospital I didn't want to let go.

When they took the baby I cried like hell. Then I spewed my guts out.

Of course, I knew whose baby it was. I didn't want to tell the cops my suspicions but they found out, in the end, that the baby was Mary's. She'd not told her father or brother, but they must have known she was up the duff. When the baby had come, two days earlier, she'd gone to the toilet and had it there, sitting over the bowl. She hadn't looked to see if it was alive or dead. She just wrapped it up in a pillow case and put it out in the rubbish.

There was more. It all came out later. I hope her father and brother rot in prison.

The baby lived. I went to see it in the hospital. It was a little girl. She was all bandaged up except for her eyes, mouth and one tiny hand. The doctors told me she was going to be okay. She kept staring and staring at me. I put my little finger down and that tiny hand closed around it and wouldn't let go.

After that I chucked the job in. Why? Because every time I picked up a dustbin I kept thinking, There may be a baby in here. I would think back on all the other dustbins I'd emptied. I had nightmares for weeks, dreaming of lifting the bins and that in every bin were babies and the hydraulic ram coming down and down and down, whining like a monster clawing their heads off and churning them away into darkness. The whole world turned into a dustbin and there I was, burrowing further and further down into it, into that churning world, grabbing dead and decapitated babies under my arms, holding my breath, trying to grab one more before getting back to the surface. Just one more.

I don't know what happened to Mary's baby. Or to Mary.

One day I'd like to find out.

And one of these days I'd like to say to Mary: It wasn't your fault, Mary.

Not. Your. Fault.

*Bring out your dead/newspapers/plastic cups/*Evening Post*/rotten apples/Watties cans/ old magazines/old chicken drumsticks and bones/bring out your dead/*North&South*/ stale bread/Do Not Take Without Doctor's Advice/broken toys/glass/car parts/*Playboy*/ ripped blankets/broken bottles/throwaway biros/posters/maggots in meat/bring out your dead/DB is Better/sanitary napkins/*Vogue*/condoms/bring out your dead/Be A Tidy Kiwi/bring out your dead/*
bring out your dead/your dead/dead dead/
deaddeaddeaddeaddead/
dead

THIS LIFE IS WEARY

THE AFFECTIONATE KIDNAPPERS

THE WASHERWOMAN'S CHILDREN

The next three stories come from *Dear Miss Mansfield*, my third short story collection, published in 1988, the centennial of Katherine Mansfield's birth. I wrote it in Narragansett, Rhode Island, while spending Christmas and New Year with Henry and Leni Spencer.

Six of my books have actually been written overseas. *Pounamu Pounamu, Tangi* and *Whanau* (which was originally a short story called 'Village Sunday') were all written at 67 Harcourt Terrace, South Kensington, London when Jane and I were on our honeymoon. *The Whale Rider* was written in New York for my daughters, Jessica and Olivia, who were coming for vacation. *Bulibasha, King of the Gypsies* was written while I was the Mansfield Fellow in Menton, France; I got sidetracked from doing *The Dream Swimmer*, an absolutely psychotic novel, by the sight of gypsy caravans just outside Nice. The words of the aphorism by which I try to live my life are written on the door of the villa where Mansfield once worked: 'Risk! Risk everything! Care no more for the thoughts of others. Do the hardest thing on earth for you to do. Tell the truth.'

As far as *Dear Miss Mansfield* was concerned, I wanted to offer my own personal centennial tribute. I have always felt that every writer in New Zealand must confront the mana and brilliance of Katherine Mansfield; for young Maori writers of the future, that writer will be Patricia Grace. When the book was published, I had scathing reviews. One critic berated me at a conference and said the book was one of the most subversive acts perpetrated on New Zealand literature. Another said it was a very unfair thing to do to a dead white woman who couldn't defend herself.

'This Life Is Weary' revisits 'The Garden Party' from the perspective of two children who live in the working-class lanes below the Sheridan house; the title comes from a song sung by Jose in the Mansfield original.

'The Affectionate Kidnappers' looks at 'How Pearl Button Was Kidnapped' from the perspective of the kidnappers themselves. The great African writer Chinua Achebe, after reading British novelist Joyce Cary's *Mister Johnson* with its bumbling Nigerian character, wrote that 'it dawned on me that although fiction was undoubtedly fictitious, it could also be true or false'. 'How Pearl Button Was Kidnapped' was the only story of Mansfield's with recognisable Maori characters. When it was published in England, readers thought the kidnappers were gypsies.

'The Washerwoman's Children' is the original title considered by Mansfield for her great story, 'The Doll's House'.

THIS LIFE IS WEARY

1

The little cottages were in a lane to themselves at the very bottom of a steep rise. At the top was the house that the children called *The Big House* — everybody called it that because it was oh so lovely with its lovely house and gardens lived in by its lovely owners — like another world really, one much nicer than down here below the broad road which ran between. But Dadda would always laugh whenever the children were too filled to the brim about the goings on up there, and he would remind them that 'We are all equal in the sight of God' or 'Remember — the lilies of the field — ' This was Dadda's way of saying that no envy should be attached to *The Big House*, nor malice against its gilded inhabitants.

The children loved their Dadda so much, especially Celia the eldest, who thought he was the most wonderful, most handsome, most perfect man in the whole world. Truth to tell, Celia was not far wrong about him — Jack Scott was a fine man. His face was strong and open and was topped with blond curly hair. His shoulders were broad and, altogether, he was a fine figure of a man. But Dadda was more than physically attractive — he possessed a sense of goodness and wholeness, as if his physical beauty merely reflected an inner purity untouched by coarseness. 'When I grow up, Dadda,' Celia would say, 'I shall marry someone just like you.' To this Jack Scott would laugh again — her dear, laughing Dadda — and caution Celia that beauty or handsomeness faded with years and, 'Oh, my sweet Celia, follow your heart and, wherever it leads, to ugly plump thin or brown, there lie you down.'

This kind of simple honesty was what made Dadda so greatly loved in this land of chocolate-brown houses. Although the very smoke coming out of the chimneys might be poverty-stricken — not at all like the great silvery plumes that uncurled from *The Big House* — one could hear the larks sing whenever the carter, Jack Scott, was around. ' 'ere you, Old Faithful,' the washerwomen would call as Dadda whistled past. ' 'ow come you're always so 'appy of a mornin'?' Dadda would answer, 'God has given us another beautiful day, ladies, and there are so many beautiful things in it.' And the washerwomen would blush, for they took his remarks as declarations of romance and they loved him all the more — not lasciviously, mind, because they were decent women and beyond the age of temptation. 'Oh my, Jack Scott,' they would call, 'you 'ave a way with the words, but be off with you!' Ah yes, and the men loved Dadda too because of his uprightness and fairness. 'You're a good lad, Jack,' the old pensioners would tell him whenever he was able to spare them some victuals. 'Yes, you're a good mate,' the young men agreed. There was not a finer friend to the young men than Dadda

He was not old, was Dadda, being only twenty-nine, and his responsibilities as a good husband and father had not brought weariness to him. In the case of Mam, though, Celia could see that life's travails had changed her greatly from the little slip of a thing whom Dadda had met on the ship bringing settlers from England. Romance had blossomed below decks between Jack and Em — and Em's parents had not put a stop to it, for they could tell that Jack would make honest passage through the world and, given his good head for business, a profitable one. Nobody could want better for a daughter of fifteen years. So, on arrival in Wellington, Jack and Em had become man and wife, and they had fulfilled God's commandment to be fruitful by producing Celia, Margaret and Thomas within the first three years of marriage. The doctor had cautioned Jack, saying, 'Give Em some peace now, lad, and let her body recover from the child-bearing.' Dadda had laughed and said, 'It's not for my want of trying, Doctor, but the babies just seem to come and, if it is God's will — ' And God willed that there should be two more, the babes Matthew and Mark.

The Big House was regarded with simple awe by many who lived in the little cottages below. Others were not so awestruck, looking upon *The Big House* with a sense of grievance, for it represented everything that they had hoped to escape from when they had left England. Even Dadda was not untouched by the angry murmurs of the working men at meetings of an evening. But above all else, he truly believed that Work and Self-Improvement would win the changes that all strived for.

Dadda went to work every morning before dawn. He would slip out of bed and creep with candle up into the loft to see his little ones. 'Blessed be the new day,' he would whisper, 'and God keep you all safe and well.' Then he would be gone, often not returning until long after dark. Mam had the babes to tend to and, whenever she could, she took small mending work from *The Big House* — she had artistic fingers for embroidery. As for the children, they went off to school during the week. Mam was very firm about this and did not want them swarming in the little crowded lanes like many of the other children who were kept at home.

However, Saturday afternoons were free for the children to do as they pleased and, without fail, this meant going up to *The Big House*, crossing quickly over the broad road between, to watch the house and the comings and goings of the lovely people who lived or visited there. Celia had found a special place — you had to slip between the rose bushes and under the karaka trees to get to it — right by the tennis court. Under the trees was an old wrought-iron loveseat, just ideal for the children. The seat had obviously been thrown out many years ago but it was comfortable enough — once you wiped away the birds' droppings — and perfect to observe from. There was the house, side on to the sun, gleaming like a two-storeyed dolls' house. The driveway was at the front with a circle of green in the middle. Oh, what excitement was occasioned whenever the front gateway opened and a carriage came in! There was a back gateway also and, there, the delivery vans and storemen would enter, bringing the groceries, meat and other supplies to Cook. Once, the children had seen the familiar figure of Dadda himself, and that night they couldn't wait to tell him, 'Dadda, oh Dadda! We saw you at *The Big House* today!' — as if grace and divinity had been suddenly bestowed on him. The house was surrounded with broad swathes of bright green lawn bordered by daisy plants. Just beyond the borders were the roses — hundreds and hundreds of glorious dark red roses of the kind that the children had seen on chocolate boxes.

It was Celia, of course, who thought of keeping notebooks on *The Big House*. Celia had always been an imaginative child and it only seemed natural that simple observation should lead to something more formal — like setting it all down in writing. Dadda and Mam were amused at first but grew to be thoroughly approving. 'Better that the children should be constructive,' Mam would say, 'than down here wasting their lives away.' And Dadda had said, 'Who knows? Some of what they see might rub off on them!' So it soon became part of the Saturday routine for Mam to sharpen pencils and, when the children became more serious about keeping notebooks, to let them take a simple lunch — a crust of bread each and a bottle with water in it — with them. 'Be back before dark!' Mam would cry as the children scampered off. 'We will, Mam, we will!' Celia would reply — because telling Mam and Dadda, right after supper, about what they had seen at *The Big House* became part of the Saturday excursions also. The children knew that Mam and Dadda welcomed their reports, taking them as signs that their children would do better than they had to make good lives for themselves.

Although Celia had never been to any theatre, watching *The Big House* was just as she imagined a play would be. Like all theatrical settings, the weather was always ideal up there and the days perfect and made to order. The backdrop was windless and warm, with a light blue sky flecked with gold. It was all so unlike the dark and dirty eyesore which cluttered the area the children came from. Indeed, sometimes it was difficult for the children to accept that this world was as real as their own — it really was as if they had paid a penny to go to His Majesty's Royal Theatre for a few hours of a drab Saturday afternoon. But what fun! Naturally, the house itself was the main stage prop, particularly the verandahs, top and bottom, and the french doors on to the verandahs. From out of these door would come the lovely people of *The Big House*, the main actors of every Saturday afternoon performance. Head of the Household was Mr Sheridan, who worked in the city and never seemed to be around very much. He generally slept late on Saturdays, sometimes not appearing until 2 p.m., all hairy and drumming his chest after a wash. Mistress of the House was Mrs Sheridan, prone to sitting on a chair off the main bedroom and fanning herself like a lady in a magazine. Once, so Margaret swore, Mrs Sheridan actually waved to the children where they sat. 'Impossible,' Celia replied. Her version appeared that night, after supper, when she produced a sketch of Mrs Sheridan trying to swat at something going bbbzzzz — Mam and Dadda thought that was very funny, but Margaret was cross.

Mr and Mrs Sheridan had three daughters, Meg, Jose and Laura, and a son, Laurie — and it was on these four fascinating golden creatures that the children focused all their attention. Celia would scribble like mad in her notebook as Margaret and Thomas described every appearance: 'Meg has just washed her hair,' Margaret would say, in awe, because washing one's hair in the afternoon was the prerogative of the wealthy. 'Oh, look, there's Jose! She has put on her lovely silk petticoat and the kimono jacket.' And Thomas would reflect, 'Do you think she got the jacket from the Chinamen who play pakapoo?' To which Celia, the expert on fashion, would say, 'Kimonos come from Japan, Thomas, not China.' But Margaret might interrupt, 'Oh, quick, here comes Meg again! Doesn't she look pretty? I'll bet

131

a beau is coming to call.' Sure enough, half an hour later, the gateway would open and a fine hansom would deposit a grave but hopeful young man. 'Oh, he's not right for Meg,' Celia would say. 'Pooh, no!' Thomas and Margaret would agree, for they knew that without doubt Meg was going to be a famous pianist. Her life was not to be squandered away on silly young men! Wasn't it true that every afternoon Meg practised the piano and showed signs of improving? — why, only four mistakes in the 'Für Elise' last Saturday! As for Jose, oh dear, she would just have to give up any thought of an operatic career. While her voice was strong enough, alas, her sense of timing was woeful. Worse still, she could never hold the tune. Apart from which, nobody could sing 'This Life is Weary' better than Dadda —

This Life is *Wee*-ary,
A Tear — a Sigh.
A Love that *Chan*-ges,
This Life is *Wee*-ary,
A Tear — a Sigh.
A Love that *Chan*-ges,
And then . . . Good-bye!

No, Jose would be better off receiving silly young men herself. In this manner, the children would observe, ponder, dream and hope that the characters whom they had come to love would grow, prosper and make the right decisions.

The children's main interest was in the heroine of the Sheridan family, the one who they thought was most like themselves — Laura. Her every entrance was greeted in the same way as a diva by a star-struck audience — with a hushed indrawn breath, moment of recognition, long sigh of release and joyous acclamation. Laura was Celia's age — at least, that's what Celia insisted — and could do no wrong. She was the one whom the children most wanted to have as a friend, if class would ever allow it. Their notebooks were filled, positively to the very margins, with anecdotes, drawings and notes about Laura in all her moods. To even get a good likeness was difficult enough, for Laura was always flying in and out, here and there, to and fro. Often the children would have to compare their drawings for accuracy and, 'No, she didn't look like that,' Celia would say, 'she looked like this.' Then Margaret would interject, 'But she wasn't wearing the blue pinafore, she was wearing the yellow one with the tiny wee apron.' To which Thomas would respond, 'Well, she was just perfect as she was, a perfect little princess.' This was, in fact, patently inaccurate, because perfect little princesses were not tomboys — and there was a streak of this in Laura. Perfect little princesses did not do cartwheels on the front lawn or thumb their noses at beaux they didn't like. Oh, she was such a character sometimes! 'I wonder what her bedroom is like?' Margaret would wonder. 'Does it have a huge bed and are all her dolls propped up on the pillows?' Interrupting, Thomas would venture, 'And would there be a rockinghorse?' To which Celia would purse her lips and say, 'Perhaps. Rockinghorses are really for boys but — yes, Laura is bound to have one.'

On most occasions, the appearances by the Sheridans were seen from afar. There was one magical moment, however — the children had to pinch themselves to make sure they weren't dreaming — when Hans, one of the servants, brought a small table and four chairs on to the tennis court right in front of the children. Laura appeared with three of her dolls, placed them on chairs and proceeded to have afternoon tea with cakes and biscuits. 'Lady Elizabeth,' Laura said, 'would you care for some milk? Sugar? One lump or two?' Then, with a laugh, 'Oh, quite, Countess Mitzi, quite.' And Celia almost fainted away with pleasure when, turning to the third doll, Laura said, 'Princess Celia, how was your last visit to Paris?' For the rest of the afternoon the children were just transported, bursting with ecstasy — and they could hardly wait to tell Mam and Dadda. 'Oh, slow down, lovey,' Mam said to Celia. 'Do slow down!' And that put the seal on the entire afternoon, for it was exactly the sort of comment that the children were constantly passing about Laura herself.

2

One day, the children came running back from an afternoon watching *The Big House* with the news 'Oh, Mam! Dadda! There's going to be a garden-party! At *The Big House*! We heard Mrs Sheridan reminding Cook! Next Saturday! Oh, can we go for the whole day? With our notebooks? In the morning? So many people have been invited! Please, Mam! Please, Dadda!' As it happened, Em had hoped the girls would mind the babes while she visited her parents but, 'Let the little ones go,' Dadda said, adding with a wink, 'and I shall try to come home early in the afternoon, eh, Em love?' Trying not to blush, Em said, 'All right, children, you may go,' and the children clapped their hands together with glee. Then a thoughtful, twinkling look came into Mam's eyes and she suddenly left the kitchen to rummage in the glory box in the bedroom. When she came back she had some velvet and other material in her arms.

'Come here, Celia lovey,' Em said. 'My, you've grown — ' and her eyes sparkled with sadness, mingled with pride, at the thought of her eldest daughter growing into womanhood. 'What are you doing, Mam?' Celia asked. 'Why, measuring you, your sister and brother, of course,' Mam said. 'You can't go to a garden-party in your everyday clothes.' And Margaret said, 'But Mam, we're not invited — ' To which Em said, 'Hush, child. We can dream, can't we?' And Jack came to hold Em close and kiss her. 'That we can, Em love,' he said, 'that we can.'

The children could hardly contain themselves. All that week they conjectured about the garden-party — who would come, what food would be served, what Laura would wear, would there be a band, how many waiters — and they were so fidgety that Mam had to say, 'Do keep still, Margaret, or else your dress will not be ready in time!' Then Margaret would stay very still indeed, hardly drawing breath, because green velvet was her favourite colour and she wanted to look her very best — and Mam even made a green bow for her hair! Thomas, reluctant at first, also got into the swing of things. He knew that he was going to look a proper guy — and how was he going to get up to *The Big House* and back without the other swarming children seeing him — but, oh, there was such a delicious silky feeling to the new shirt! As for Celia, she had determined, 'Mam, I can make my own dress and hat.' So while Mam stitched costumes for Margaret and Thomas, Celia worked on a cloth that had once been a curtain. When Celia completed her dress Mam trimmed it with a lace ribbon she had been saving for herself.

When all the stitching and sewing was completed, didn't the children look just lovely, parading in front of Dadda and Mam that Friday night before the garden-party? Hardly a wink was slept, so that when Dadda came to wake them, why, the children were already dressed and waiting! And wasn't Dadda the most perfect man? He had transformed the cart into a carriage and placed cushions on the seats. Bowing, he handed the children up, saying, 'Lady Margaret, if you would be so kind — Princess Celia, charmed — Sir Thomas, delighted — 'And Mam, trying not to laugh too much, came from the doorway with a hamper of cordial, sandwiches and a dear wee cake. 'Oh, Mam. Oh, Dadda,' was all that Celia could say because the words got caught in her throat. 'Have a lovely time, children,' Mam said. 'And Thomas, don't worry — your Dadda will pick you all up before dark from the gateway of *The Big House*. Byeeee — ' She blew a kiss as they left.

And after all the weather was ideal. When the dawn came creeping across the sky, the children knew it was going to be a perfect day for the Sheridans' garden-party. From their position under the trees they saw it from beginning to end. They saw the

Maori gardener already at work mowing the lawns and sweeping them. 'Oh, he's missed a piece!' Margaret wailed but, joy, he returned to sweep the swathe so that the lawn looked all combed the same way — not a lick out of place. 'Nothing must go wrong,' Celia nodded. Then the children saw movement in *The Big House* and knew that Mr and Mrs Sheridan, Meg, Jose, Laura and Laurie were at breakfast. Mr Sheridan came out the front door with a BANG to go through the gateway. At the same time the men came to put up the marquee. And who else but Laura, the little princess herself, should appear to give the men their instructions! 'Oh, she's so pretty!' Thomas said, 'and look, she's eating bread and butter — just like we do.' The next few moments, though, were anxious ones for the children because at one point, Laura pointed to the tennis court. Yes, it was certainly the most appropriate place for the marquee but, 'It will spoil our view,' Celia whispered. Why, Laura must have heard, because the workmen set the marquee near the karaka trees instead!

'Message, Laura!' a voice cried from the house, and away the little princess skimmed. But what was happening at the back door? Why, the florist had arrived and just look at the pots and pots of canna lilies — so radiant and frighteningly alive on their bright crimson stems! And then, from the drawing room, was that Meg on the piano? Pom! Ta-ta-ta Tee-ta! Oh dear, was Jose really going to embarrass herself by singing at the garden-party? There she was, warming up — 'This Life is *Wee*-ary, A Tear — a Sigh — ' Oh dear, dear, dear. But now look! Someone else had arrived at the back door. Surely it was the Godber van, cluttering into the yard, bringing lovely cream puffs! And there was the man from Godber's talking to Cook, and —

Suddenly the sky was filled with a soft radiance and it was almost like — like a shooting star, in the daytime though, going UP into the sky — and Celia felt such sweet pain that she wanted to weep. Her heart was so full, so overflowing, so brimming over, and in that same instant she thought of her Dadda.

Strange really, but for a while after that the house fell into silence. Laura's voice could be heard piping and alarmed. 'What is happening now?' Margaret asked. 'I'm not sure,' Celia said. 'Perhaps it is lunchtime already.' Indeed it was — hadn't time passed quickly? So Margaret opened the hamper, Celia laid the food out, and Thomas said, 'Lady Margaret, would you care for some wine?' Margaret clapped her hands together and, 'Thank you, Sir Thomas,' she said as Thomas poured some cordial into her glass. 'And you, Princess Celia?' Celia inclined her head. Oh, it was so much fun to be sitting there sipping wine on the perfect day.

Lunch in *The Big House* was over by half past one. The green-coated bandsmen arrived and established themselves right next to the children near the tennis court. The man on the tuba saw them and gave a cheery wave. Would he tell? No — he was too jolly to do that. Soon after, the guests began coming in streams — one carriage after the other — the women so lovely, oh so *lovely*. The band struck up. The hired waiters ran from the house to the marquee. Wherever the children looked there were couples strolling, bending to the flowers, greeting, and gliding across the lawn. The children were enchanted, transported, transformed — in Heaven — by it all. There in the shadows they imitated the movements of the guests, and sometimes when the band played, Sir Thomas first asked Lady Margaret and then Princess Celia to dance with him, on and on and on. The man on the tuba smiled when he saw them dancing and, oh goodness, when the waiters came to offer the band refreshments he must have pointed out the children! Over came one of the waiters with a tray of delicious cakes and cream puffs, and he bowed gravely, saying, 'Mesdames? Monsieur?' And always, far away in the sunlight was dear, darling Laura. Something was bothering her, but she was so gracious, wasn't she? 'Oh, I must sketch her,' Celia cried. The perfect afternoon slowly ripened, slowly faded, slowly its petals closed. Soon it was all over.

The children were in ever such an excited state as they waited for their Dadda to pick them up. They had stayed beneath the trees until the very end when the last bandsman had packed his instrument and left. The man with the tuba had given a very cheery wave. By the time the children reached the gateway it was almost dark. 'Wasn't it wonderful when — ' the children would reminisce to one another. They wanted to savour every minute of the garden-party and, 'Oh, write that one down, Celia,' Margaret would cry. 'We forgot about that moment.' For a while they sat scribbling away in the gathering darkness. 'Weren't the guests all so lovely?' Margaret whispered. On and on the children chattered.

The darkness deepened. The children couldn't wait for Dadda to arrive so that they could get home quickly and tell him and Mam about the garden-party. When the night fell like a cloak, Celia said, 'Dadda must be delayed. Come along, let's go on home. Like as not we'll meet him coming up the hill.' Thomas was so happy that he didn't even think to be embarrassed should they meet any swarming children. Down, down, down into the sordid lanes the children descended. The lights were on in some of the houses. People were like silent wraiths slipping into and out of the light. All of a sudden someone came running from behind the children, passing them and turning the corner. When the children rounded the corner themselves, they saw a young man with a girl. The girl was pressed against him and she looked

136

as if she was crying. Celia overheard the young man say, 'Was it awful?' The girl shook her head — and there was something terribly familiar in the motion — but it was so dark, so dark.

Then the children were in sight of their own house and they started to run towards it. But what was this? Lamps were shining in the front parlour. A dark knot of people stood outside. Women in shawls and men in tweed caps were gathered there. Without knowing why, Celia felt an awful feeling inside her heart. She saw Gran, Mam's mother, sitting in a chair beside the gate. As the children approached, Gran gave a cry. The knot loosened and voices came out of the darkness at the children. 'Oh, the poor wee children.' Gran kissed the children and held them tight. 'What's wrong, Gran?' Celia asked. 'There's been an accident, Celia dear,' Gran answered. 'Your father — ' Celia pulled Margaret and Thomas quickly through the crowd and into the house. Auntie May was there in the passageway, but Celia didn't want *her*.

'Mam? Dadda?' Celia called. 'Mam?' Then another woman was there. Her face was all puffed up and red, with swollen eyes and swollen lips. 'Mam?' Celia whispered, because it was indeed her mother. But she looked so — so — *awful*.

'Your Dadda's gone,' Mam said. 'He's gone.'

Margaret started to wail and Thomas bit his lip and screwed up his eyes. The two children ran to the comfort of their mother's arms. But Celia just stood there. *Oh, Dadda, was that you, that soft radiance? Was that your soul coming to say goodbye before going to Heaven?* In the corner, Celia noticed a basket of fruit — the fruit looked so lovely, oh so very lovely — and she remembered the garden-party. *I must tell Dadda*, Celia thought. Her heart was breaking into a thousand pieces. 'Where's Dadda?' she asked. Mam motioned toward the bedroom.

For a moment Celia was too frightened to go in. She didn't want to *know*. She didn't want to *see*. All of a sudden, she felt a fleeting sense of unfairness that *The Big House*, with its gilded life, should be so impervious to all the ills of the world. But no, she shouldn't think like that. Dadda wouldn't want her to think like that, would he? 'Dadda?' she called from the doorway. 'Dadda?' She took a step and, why, there he was in his bed, and she had caught him asleep! There he was, glowing in the light of the smoky lamp, her handsome laughing Dadda. Fast asleep he was, sleeping so soundly that he didn't even stir when she knelt beside him. Curly headed Dadda, deeply, peacefully sleeping.

'Oh Dadda,' Celia whispered. She put her head against his, and the first glowing tear dropped down her cheek like a golden sun. 'It was a lovely garden-party, Dadda, just *lovely*,' she said.

THE AFFECTIONATE KIDNAPPERS

The two kuia began to weep when their rangatira came in. They wept not because they were frightened but because they were ashamed that their big chief should see them like this, in the whareherehere. For a long time they sat there, not looking at him, faces downcast, grieving with one another, and the tears were like wet stones splashing in the dust at their feet.

'Hei aha,' the chief said after a while. He turned to the sergeant standing behind him and said, 'Can I speak to my women alone, boss?' The sergeant knew that Hasbrick, the Maori guide, was a good and trustworthy fellow, but the law was the law and the two women might still be capable of some treachery — still waters ran deep among the Maoris. Nevertheless, while putting on a stern appearance, for at Police School he was always told that Appearances Must Always Be Maintained, he responded, 'Well, just this once, Hasbrick. But no funny business, mind.' As he left he closed the door to the cell and with an obvious gesture, all the more melodramatic because it was so ludicrously lofty, turned the key in the lock.

The rangatira sighed as he sat down beside the two women. 'You two are old enough to have more sense,' he said. At his rebuke the kuia redoubled their crying, turned away and tried to press themselves into the corner. 'Well,' the chief said, insistently, 'it's your own fault, ne?' The kuia were silent, their lips quivering. 'Kati,' the chief relented, 'enough. You two are just like the two birds making your roimata toroa on the ground.' The women smiled at their chief's remarks. He proffered a handkerchief but, shaking their heads, the women used their own scarves to dab at their eyes. Hesitantly they reached out for their chief to hold his hand tightly. 'You should leave us in the jailhouse,' they said. 'You should tell them to shut us away forever.' 'Kei te pai, Kuini,' the chief soothed the kuia in the red dress. 'Kei te pai, Puti,' he said to the old lady in the yellow and green. 'I know you two didn't mean to do wrong.'

'She was such a pretty little blonde girl,' Kuini said. 'She was swinging on a gate, all by herself, you know, down there by the hotera. As soon as I saw her I knew she was the Button's little girl. They come every summer to the Sounds and me and Puti, we did some work for Mrs Button last summer, cleaning and that. Eh, Puti?'

'Ae,' Puti agreed. 'Kua mahi maua mo te wahine Pakeha. A strict lady that lady.'

'Oh, and Pearl had grown,' Kuini said. 'The year before she only came up to here and *this* year — ' Kuini's eyes softened with tenderness. 'And her teeth were so white. But it made us sad to see her all alone. A tamariki all alone — no good. Especially near a hotel with all those boozers around. So I said to her, "You want to come with us, Pearl Button? Haere mai koe ki te marae?" And she nodded. And I saw Mrs Button in the window — '

'Ae. We waved and waved at her,' Puti said.

'When she saw us she waved back. So we made signs that we would take Pearl with us to be our mate. We pointed to the marae. Mrs Button waved her apron at us as if to say, "Go right ahead!" So we did.'

'We told the pirihimana this,' Puti said. 'We told him loud but he didn't want to hear us, I reckon. What did we do wrong?' Her face screwed up as if she had tasted a lemon, and she started to quiver. The tears started again, as if she was a bottle of aerated water that had been shaken too hard.

The rangatira kept a calm face. This was a no-good business this. 'Didn't you stop to think that this was a Pakeha little girl?' he asked gently, 'a white girl?' Kuini was offended. Her eyes opened wide. 'Kaore,' she said. 'This was a tamariki. Pearl.' Hasbrick's eyelids flickered, betraying his incredulity. Not only was this a white girl but this was also a pretty as a picture blondie girl. Pakehas didn't like their girls being messed around by Maoris. The idea of a pretty curly-headed white girl being taken away by Maoris brought all sorts of pictures to their minds — of sacrifices to idols, cannibalism, of white girls being captured and scalped by Red Indians — and *he* knew because these were the sorts of questions tourists asked him. 'Do you worship these wooden gods?' 'Are there still headhunters in New Zealand?' 'Do you have tomahawks?' No wonder the pirihamana had raised such a big posse.

'This was Pearl,' Kuini said again, emphatically. 'What's the fuss? Maori tamariki wouldn't have such a fuss made for them.'

At this, Puti smiled. 'Maybe because a Maori mother would be glad to get rid of her kids for the day,' she joked.

'So we took Pearl down to the marae,' Kuini continued, 'and she was as happy as anything. Everybody was helping to get kai ready for our hui today. Lots of people. They all made a fuss of Pearl. Old Joe, he said to me, "You're too ugly to be this kid's mother!" He made a pukana at her and gave her a peach to eat. "Kei te matekai koe?" he asked her. Boy, she was hungry all right. She started to hoe in and the juice ran down her front. It made us feel very happy, eh, Puti, to see that kid eat so much. Too skinny, the Pakeha children, but,' she sighed, 'that's the Pakeha way.'

'Didn't it ever pass through your minds,' Hasbrick asked, 'how her mother would feel about her daughter eating the Maori kai?'

Kuini looked startled. 'What's wrong with the Maori kai?'

Hasbrick knew they wouldn't understand the violence of the reaction of Pearl's mother. *Oh, Pearl, did you eat something from the floor? John, darling, did you hear what the Maoris did? They forced food on her. There's no telling what sorts of diseases she got down there. All those dogs they have. And no hygiene. The place should be burned down. Harbouring diseases and diseased people. Oh darling, she drank some water too. Some filthy Maori water. Oh. Oh.*

'Then all of a sudden,' Puti said, 'the koroua, Rangiora, came in, cracking his whip. "Haere mai koutou ki te ruku moana," he shouted. "Kia tere, kia tere." Before we knew it, old Joe had snatched Pearl up and put her in his green cart. He said, "You can drive the trap, tamariki," and Pearl just loved it. Kuini put her on her lap, and old Joe gave Pearl the reins, and we were off. You should have seen those ponies of Joe's. They knew they had a little Pakeha on board. The red pony trotted along with a high proud step and the black pony tossed its mane as if to say, "Anei! Titiro koutou ki ahau!" And Pearl played with Auntie's pounamu. She was very happy, and that made us happy.' Puti fingered her kete nervously. 'I suppose that is where the wrong lies,' she said in a small voice. 'We shouldn't have taken her to the sea.'

'What's done is done,' the rangatira said. But in his ears he could still hear the burning words of Pearl's mother. *How dare they. She could have drowned. Haven't they got any sense? Not only that, but they were all naked down there. And they unbuttoned Pearl's drawers. My little daughter, defenceless, in the midst of savages. It is too horrible for me to contemplate. Touching her rosy skin with their dirty hands.*

'She'd never seen the sea before,' Kuini said. 'Fancy a kid never seeing the sea! She was frightened at first. But we showed her that it wouldn't hurt her — not the Kingdom of Tangaroa. We took her over to Maggie's place and then across the paddock to the beach. There we started digging for the toheroa. Pearl started to dig too. Ka nui tana mahi! Oh it was such fun to have a Pakeha tamariki. A Pakeha moko. And *then*, when she felt how warm and tickly the sea was, she started to scream with delight. 'Oo, oo! Lovely! Lovely!' She was so excited that she threw herself into my arms, kicking and screaming, oh, the joy of it! Feeling that little body having such fun!'

That's not what the policeman saw, Hasbrick thought. He conjured the event up in his mind — a little naked girl, kicking and screaming, beating her fists against two black women, a Pakeha blondie girl, looking for all the world as if she was going to be drowned by two black women —

The sergeant reappeared, rattling his keys in the lock. The two women shrank into the shadows. Their eyes were like glowing paua. Then Kuini said, with dignity, to her rangatira, 'E koro, kei te pirangi maua ko Puti ki a hoki atu maua ki a maua whare. Puti and I wish to return to our homes.' The rangatira felt anguish in his heart. 'Kei te pirangi maua ko Puti ki a maua wharemoe,' Kuini said. 'We also wish to sleep in our own beds. Not here, in this place of shame.' Her voice trembled with the words.

'Aue, kui,' Hasbrick answered. And the two women realised by the tone of his voice that they would be lost — gone into the darkness, gone into the stomach of the Pakeha, gone into the realm of the night, eaten up by the white man. 'You are facing a serious charge,' Hasbrick continued. 'The Pakeha think you kidnapped the little girl.'

Puti cried out, and Kuini began to grieve, not because of the charge but because she had never slept anywhere else but in her own bed in her own house. Here, for the first time, she would have to lie down on a foreign mattress in a strange room which was noa and could not give her any protection. At that moment, something died inside her, something that had been her strength all her life. She felt it ebbing away, slipping away, leaving her a mere husk. Dimly, she heard Puti say, 'But Mrs Button knows. She knows us.' She heard her chief reply, 'No. Mrs Button doesn't remember either of you.' It came to Kuini, with blinding clarity, that Mrs Button was to be felt sorry for — it was not her fault that she couldn't tell one Maori apart from another. And Kuini reached for Puti's hands and face and pressed her face against Puti's saying, 'Never mind, kui. You and I will be mates for each other, just like the two birds.'

'I will be back in the morning,' the rangatira said. 'But you will not be alone. Some of the people have already gathered outside and will stay there to keep you company through the night.' Sure enough, as he was speaking, the two women

THE AFFECTIONATE KIDNAPPERS

heard soft singing drifting through the window. 'After all, you two are our kuia.'

Then the rangatira was gone. The two women sat in the gathering dark. Puti thought, *I will never forget. All those little men in blue coats. Little blue men. With their whistles. Running, running towards us. With their police batons raised. It was —*

Suddenly, she felt Kuini nudging her and pointing down to the floor. Kuini's voice was still and drained of life. 'Anei,' she whispered. Although the light was waning, the pattern in the dust could still be seen. 'Anei, te roimata toroa.' The soft sounds of waiata swelled in the darkness like currents of the wind holding up Kuini's words. 'E noho ra, Pearl Button,' Kuini said, 'taku moko Pakeha.' The syllables drifted like two birds beating heavily eastward into the night. Then the light went, everything went, life went.

THE WASHERWOMAN'S CHILDREN

Mrs Justice Fairfax-Lawson, sitting in the morning-room of her home at Calverley, Tunbridge Wells, received the morning post. Lying on the salver was a brown manila envelope from New Zealand bearing a crest that she had not seen for some fifty years. Despite her usual habit of opening the post before pouring her tea, this letter sat until Penny had cleared. Only then, with a self-directed criticism of 'Elspeth, you are being ridiculous,' did she lift her letter knife and open the envelope. Inside was a form letter, with blank spaces that had been filled in by hand, as follows:

45 Jackson Crescent
Wellington
New Zealand

Dear *Elspeth*,
Your name has been referred to the Karori Primary School Anniversary Committee by *your sister, Lilian Bates.*

   The Committee, which has been actively working towards the centennial celebrations of the school, would like to extend to you a warm invitation to attend an Anniversary Dinner in the school hall on 10 August this year, at 7.30 p.m. Roll Call, by year, will be taken at 5 p.m. A photographer will record the happy event. The Committee hopes you will be able to come along.

Yours sincerely
(Mrs) Lena Holmes

The letter was perforated with a tear-off portion bearing the address of the committee and, 'I will be able/unable to attend: I attended Karori Primary School from . . . to . . . My registration fee of $20 is/is not enclosed.'

Mrs Justice Fairfax-Lawson was somewhat nonplused. The use of her Christian name by a person whom she did not know, called Lena Holmes, irritated her. But most of all the letter brought memories of school days which she hoped had faded forever. Bearing in mind the time difference between England and New Zealand, she telephoned her sister in Wellington. 'Lilian, dear? *What* is going on?'

Given her initial reaction to the invitation, Mrs Justice Fairfax-Lawson was amused to find herself, three months later, sitting in the third row of the Business Class section of an Air New Zealand flight from Gatwick to Los Angeles en route for Auckland. Not only that, but no sooner had she seated herself than the purser, on the advice of the ground staff who had recognised her, invited her to take a seat in First Class. Her sense of gratification was only undercut by the fact that the passenger seated next to her, when told that she 'was in the judiciary', assumed she was a typist or else the wife of a judge (she was not the sort to be mistaken for a mistress); silly pompous little man. Luckily there was a window seat vacant three rows ahead and Mrs Justice Fairfax-Lawson firmly invited her neighbour to take it. Once that was achieved she took up her Dorothy Sayers, but only briefly, before setting it to one side and watching England sinking beneath her.

If anybody had been looking at Mrs Justice Fairfax-Lawson, they would have seen a slim and elegant woman of pleasant good looks and a fresh English rose complexion. They would certainly not have guessed from her appearance, or even any intonation of her voice or physical mannerism, that she had actually been born and raised in New Zealand. There was not a shred of the Antipodean about her, nor any of the hallmarks of the Antipodean Woman Abroad — the tightly curled perm, twinset and pearls and bright magpie look which characterised all New Zealanders south of Balmoral. Instead, what any other passenger would have seen was exactly what Mrs Justice Fairfax-Lawson had become — a romantic Englishwoman, in her prime, knowing exactly where she is because she can remember quite clearly exactly how far she has travelled — and Mrs Justice Fairfax-Lawson had travelled a very long way indeed. Home Counties style had always meant so much to her that being taken for English was quite a compliment and logical enough. All the same, there was a sense of fairness in Mrs Justice Fairfax-Lawson which allowed her to accept that her country of birth would want to claim her — as it was prone to do, given her successes — as one of its very own. As a judge, Mrs Justice Fairfax-

Lawson well knew that all *known* facts must be taken into account when any case came before the bench and, if she was trying herself for identification, she would have to weigh against the fact that although she was British by virtue of her marriage to the late Hon. Rupert Fairfax-Lawson, she had nevertheless maintained dual citizenship with the country of her birth. Much as she disliked the idea of balancing on both sides of the scales, Mrs Justice Fairfax-Lawson had to admit that giving up *anything* at all had always been difficult for her. Add to this that all her side of the family obstinately remained in New Zealand and that they were her *only* family (she and the Hon. Rupert Fairfax-Lawson being childless and not at all pleased with the Hon. Rupert Fairfax-Lawson's scurrilous nephews), and one realised the depth of her dilemma. She was as much a New Zealander because her family made her one. She could not escape them — and nor would she want to — because she loved them; yes, *loved* was not too strong a word. And she did so with familial pride and devotion, particularly her elder sister Lilian, who had become a grandmother again. So it was a *fait accompli* really, with the gavel confirming the decision and dismissing the court.

Mrs Justice Fairfax-Lawson was about to resume her Dorothy Sayers, but by that time champagne and caviar were being served. Not long after that, dinner — either roast duck or lamb — was offered. Bearing in mind the long journey ahead, Mrs Justice Fairfax-Lawson therefore decided to nap rather than to read. Eight hours later, after more champagne and more roast duck, her flight landed at Los Angeles. Shortly thereafter she was on her way again, with fourteen hours of flying time ahead and the vast expanse of the South Pacific below, bound for Auckland and thence Wellington, New Zealand.

Lilian Bates was waiting with her husband George at the Domestic Terminal. There was, at close inspection, a family resemblance to her younger sister Elspeth, but no one would ever have taken Lilian for anything but a New Zealander — at a pinch, an Australian perhaps — and that was where the likeness ended. Lilian's cheeks were ruddy, whereas her sister's were pallid, and Lilian's spontaneity expressed itself in its overeagerness and anxiousness, whereas Elspeth's was under control, *quite*. Apart from that, years of healthy living and appetite had turned Lilian's figure to pear-shaped, whereas Elspeth was still, as ever, a wishbone. Somewhere far back in their lives there had been a parting of the ways. In Elspeth's case it had been the winning of a major scholarship to Cambridge when she was nineteen. As for Lilian, her fate had been forever sealed when George Bates, then garage mechanic and now proprietor of Bates Towaway Trucks, admiring her lines, cast an eye over her, ran her round the block a couple of times, found her bodywork in good condition and pronounced, 'She'll do.'

'Now, George, don't forget,' Lilian told him. 'She likes to be called Elspeth. Not Elsie. Or Ellie. Or Else. Or anything but Elspeth.' She picked at his tie. 'The way you go on,' George replied, 'you'd think she was the bloody Queen of England.' Lilian grimaced as if she had never heard such words from his lips before. 'And keep your bloodys to your trucks, George — or save them up for when it's just us.' George rolled his eyes and Lilian tried to hug him around. 'Oh please, George, *do* behave. You know I haven't seen Elspeth for six years now. That's such a long time. She's my only sister after all and — Oh, there she is! Oh, George' — Lilian broke away from him and began to run toward the woman who had just come through the gate. George had always known that his wife was a real softie, but her abrupt emotional departure surprised him. *Why, they're as different as chalk to cheese*, he thought. He watched as Lilian flung her arms around her sister and wept on her shoulder — he hadn't realised that Lilian would be so affected. He felt a lump in his throat at the sight of these two middle-aged women embracing like this — Lilian, as always, so open with her emotions, and Elspeth as gracious as ever — you'd think she was waving from a bloody Rolls. He walked over to them. Elspeth said, 'Why, George!' in that cultured voice of hers and proffered a cheek for him to kiss. Lilian stepped aside, saying, 'It's really her, George, she's really here,' as if he couldn't see that for himself.

Mrs Justice Fairfax-Lawson had planned to stay in New Zealand for three weeks but had not expected that her sister would want to make the most of it. She should have realised when they arrived at the house and were greeted by Lilian's two daughters and their three children — plus the new baby — that she would be kept busy. It was understandable, she supposed, that Lilian would want to have dinner on the first evening for 'Just us and the family' — but when confronted with the cheery barbecue that evening and guests including the local mayor, she knew that life was not going to be that simple. Over that first week Lilian would alternate between expressions of 'Oh, you must still be jet-lagged, Elspeth. Why don't you go up to the bedroom and rest?' and frequent trips to answer the front doorbell with, 'Why, hello!' to yet more neighbours bearing yet more platefuls of lamingtons, pikelets or scones. Nor could the visits possibly be accidental, despite protestations that 'We just dropped by' — Oh no, these ladies in their cardies and pearls had just been to the local hairdressing salon, and once ensconced in Lilian's sitting-room with a cuppa, were there to *stay*. Even the innocent 'I'm just popping down to the shop, Elspeth. Why not come for a ride?' would turn into a virtual royal procession throughout the land. At each house the hostess would be ready and waiting with 'Why, Lilian, do come in! Is this your sister? Elspeth? Lilian has told us so much about you. You're just in time for a cuppa tea — ' before opening the door wider and turning to others gathered inside ' — isn't she, ladies!' These ladies knew that New Zealand hospitality was the best in the world, and they weren't going to let the side down — especially with such a famous person in their midst. And so the polite conversation would begin, with everybody minding their p's and q's and trying not to be too colonial — clinking the teacups ever so softly and not dropping one crumb of the lamingtons — until, with a little squeak of a cough, the hostess would turn to Mrs Justice Fairfax-Lawson and ask, 'So you live in England, do you?' Whereupon all tea-drinking would be suspended as Mrs Justice Fairfax-Lawson, as custom required, told them about life as it was lived by those whose Title and Reputation enabled an English Existence spread between an apartment in Westminster and a country home in Tunbridge Wells. On her part, Mrs Justice Fairfax-Lawson knew that *she*, too, couldn't let the side down — her side being her sister — and she rose to every occasion. For despite her caustic tongue, Mrs Justice Fairfax-Lawson would not have hurt her sister for anything in the world. And success was measured by the indrawn gasps of 'You don't *say*!', 'Listen to *that*, Millie!', 'How *interesting*!' and 'Do go on.' And if, near the end of the socialising, the hostess sighed, 'Oh, it sounds so different from life here,' then Mrs Justice Fairfax-Lawson knew also that form required her to offer generalities like 'But you are so lucky, New Zealand is such a paradise, it is so green, and your food is so delicious!' — even if she didn't really mean it herself. Then Lilian would drive her sister home, and Mrs Justice Fairfax-Lawson would go up to her bedroom and have a lie-down and listen to Lilian's happy voice downstairs as she responded to telephone calls from the friends just visited — 'Oh yes, I'll tell her! Yes, we are all very proud of her! No, *really*, do you really think that we are that alike?' Such things had always been important to Lilian.

However, when, at the beginning of the second week, Mrs Justice Fairfax-Lawson came across her photograph on page seven of the *Dominion* and read the accompanying article she became most displeased. It wasn't really the photograph, which was at the very *least* twenty years old — and while Mrs Justice Fairfax-Lawson was as vain as the next person, a photograph of that vintage could only draw unhappy comparisons with one's current state — nor was it the article itself, which was succinct and to the point:

Mrs Justice Elspeth Fairfax-Lawson, M.B.E., (pictured right) returned last week for a private visit to New Zealand, her first in six years. Mrs Fairfax-Lawson recently retired from the U.K. judiciary following the death of her husband, the late Hon. Rupert Fairfax-Lawson, M.P. Born in Wellington in 1910, Mrs Fairfax-Lawson will be well known to New Zealanders as the founder and first chairperson of the Wellington Women's Co-operative. Educated at Cambridge, England, Mrs Fairfax-Lawson served in British Intelligence during the Second World War, where she met her husband. Following the war she began a private legal practice in London, Fairfax and Madden, and was invited to join the U.K. judiciary in 1962. Her M.B.E. was awarded by H.R.H. Queen Elizabeth II in 1970.

The displeasure stemmed from the headline and last sentence of the text, to wit: FAMOUS NZER RETURNS FOR SCHOOL REUNION and 'Mrs Justice Fairfax-Lawson is a guest speaker at next week's Anniversary Dinner of the Karori Primary School, which she attended from 1915 to 1923.'

Mrs Justice Fairfax-Lawson was therefore *very* cross when she went down to breakfast that morning and, seeing this, Lilian said to George, 'You'd best leave us a minute, George dear.' To do her justice, Lilian was looking very contrite. She poured Elspeth a hot cuppa and, 'The photo's nice,' she said. But Elspeth could not be pacified so easily. 'How could you *do* this, Lilian. You *know* that my main reason for coming was to see you, and that I have only agreed to attend the school reunion because *you* want to go. I am going under sufferance, Lilian. You know how much I *hated* that school. The way the parents treated Mother and vilified Father was so unspeakable. Just because she had to take in washing and because father was a bankrupt.' Lilian bit her lip and, 'Yes, Elspeth,' she said. 'Can't you remember anything at all?' Elspeth continued. 'It wasn't Mother's fault that she had to send us to school in dresses made from bits given her by other people — other people's cast-offs and curtain material — but did the other children understand? No, they *didn't*.' Whenever Lilian was embarrassed, her face took on a silly shamefaced smile, and, 'You're quite right, Elspeth,' she said, her heart aching from the pain of the reprimand. *And a vivid picture flashed into her mind of Lena Logan sliding, gliding, dragging one foot, giggling behind her hand, shrilling, 'Is it true you're going to be a servant when you grow up, Lil Kelvey?' And taunting her again with 'Yah, yer father's in prison!' before running away giggling with the other girls.* 'We were *always* on the outside,' Elspeth said, 'They never invited us to play in any of their games, because we weren't good enough for them. And *now* I read in the newspaper that I am to be guest speaker — ' Lilian folded her hands in her lap and looked down and, 'They only want you to say a few words,' she said. 'A few words?' Elspeth cried. 'That's more than they deserve. There was only one girl, just *one*, who ever showed us a kindness and — '

Lilian couldn't take any more. Her silly smile opened too wide and let the tears through. She tried to say something to Elspeth, gulped and instead patted her on the hand and kissed her right cheek. Then she stood up and left the table. Elspeth, still furious, sat there in the grip of her own recollections and how, it seemed, she had only managed to survive by holding on with a piece of Lil's skirt screwed up in her hand, holding on all day, *every* day, holding on so tight, so *tight*. And not saying a word to anybody but wanting to scream, just *scream*, with the loneliness and pain and awfulness of it all. Then Elspeth heard George and looked up into his disapproving face. 'You were too hard on her, Elspeth,' he said. 'Lilian may be the elder of the two of you but she's the one who suffers more. You should have a care for your sister. She thinks the bloody world of you.' That only made Elspeth feel worse — about her petulance and, oh, at Lilian too for being such a *martyr* and running off like that! You'd think they were still children the way Lilian behaved — going off so bravely to sulk like that and make her feel so *mean*. Elspeth looked at George and sighed. He indicated the direction in which Lilian had gone.

'Lilian? Lilian,' Elspeth called. She heard Lilian reply, 'In here, dear,' and found her at a small card table in the lounge. Lilian had put on her reading glasses and was cutting the article about Elspeth out of the newspaper. 'What *are* you doing?' Elspeth asked. She came up behind Lilian and looked over Lilian's shoulder. On the card table was a large scrapbook. Elspeth recognised it instantly — it was the book their mother had begun when her daughters had both started school and filled year by year with school reports, handwritten memories, school magazine photographs, newspaper clippings: ELSPETH KELVEY IS DUX OF SCHOOL; LOCAL GIRL WINS CAMBRIDGE SCHOLARSHIP; MORE HONOURS FOR KELVEY; OUR ELSPETH TOPS CLASS AT CAMBRIDGE; ENGAGEMENT OF ELSPETH KELVEY TO SON OF LORD FAIRFAX-LAWSON — and other memorabilia. Elspeth gave a small cry and reached over to leaf through the pages: LOCAL PERSONALITY AWARDED M.B.E.; FAIRFAX-LAWSON RETIRES FROM U.K. JUDICIARY. 'It's mostly all about you,' Lilian said softly. 'I never did much myself except marry George and have my two girls. But oh, Mother was so proud of you, Else, love. You wouldn't believe the times she would go through this scrapbook, 'Look at our Else,' she used to say. 'All those brains, where'd they come from!' ' The mood sweetened between the two sisters, and Elspeth reached over and put her hand in Lilian's. 'Anyway,' Lilian said, 'when Mother died I kept the scrapbook going. I don't know why really. It would have been a shame to just let it go, don't you think?' Lilian started to weep again, saying, 'I'm so sorry, Else, I just didn't realise — ' And Elspeth replied, 'Come, come, Lilian. Oh, Lilian, *do* stop' — because she had begun to recall how difficult it had all been for mother and Lilian to keep her at school. 'Oh, *Lilian*!' she said, furious, because tears were so unseemly at their age.

Afterwards Elspeth told Lilian that she had better check with the Karori Centenary Committee how many words a 'few' constituted. They had a cuppa tea and laughed about the absurdity of two grown women losing control like that. 'There was never a jealous bone in your body, was there?' Elspeth asked her sister. 'A couple of times,' Lilian admitted. Elspeth smiled and turned away, intending to go up to her bedroom. Just as she went through the door, Lilian called to her. 'Oh, Elspeth,' she said. Elspeth turned and, 'Yes?' she asked. Lilian's attitude was resolute and firm. 'Although we may have been a washerwoman's children,' she said, 'we were never too proud' — which was just the sort of infuriating commonplace thing Lilian always liked to say.

And after all that, not to mention the effort that Elspeth had put into preparing a ten-minute address, Lilian came down with a bad flu on the very night of the dinner. 'You will get up this instant,' Elspeth ordered. 'Put on your pearls and come with me.' Her tone was similar to that she used when addressing felons from the Bench. Lilian nodded and tried but, 'Oh, Elsbed, I don'd thig I cad,' she said. 'You bedder go wib Geord. Geord? You go wib Elsbed to the didder.' Lilian reached for a handkerchief. George, taken by surprise, said, 'Go back to school? Not on your bloody life.' Elspeth interrupted him, saying, 'Lilian Kelvey, it is already after five. You are as strong as a horse and *never* get the flu. Get up at once.' But it was obvious that no command would work. 'Oh, by dose,' Lilian said, blowing on it. 'By hed,' she said, holding it. 'Elsbed, you should rig the cobbidee and ask theb to ged sobody to pig you ub.' And that was that — which explains how Mrs Justice Fairfax-Lawson was delivered, an hour late, by a nice but obviously awestruck Maori committee member called Mrs Maraki.

No sooner had Mrs Justice Fairfax-Lawson walked through the door of the crowded Assembly Hall than she saw a woman gasp and whisper behind her hand to her companion, and then *sliding, gliding, dragging one foot and shrilling* she came, calling, 'Elspeth! Yoo hoo, Elspeth!' Mrs Justice Fairfax-Lawson reeled backward as if she had been hit, and reached out for Lil's hand and to hold a piece of Lil's skirt. 'Elspeth?' the woman laughed. 'You *must* remember me! I'm Lena Holmes! See?' She pointed rather superfluously at a small tag on her dress with her name and CHAIRMAN ANNIVERSARY COMMITTEE written on it. 'I used to be Lena Logan. Remember? Lil and I were in the same class. But you were much younger of course. Come along with me.' Proudly, Lena Holmes took Mrs Justice Fairfax-Lawson's arm and began to steer her possessively in the direction of other committee members. *Yah, yer father's in prison.* 'Cora? May I introduce Elspeth to you? But you know her of course. Weren't you in Mrs Fredericks' class together? Oh, you will have some stories to tell! And this is Peggy, Elspeth. Peggy used to be the horrid little girl who did ballet — oh, we hated her, didn't we! And you can remember Annabelle? Her aunt was the postmistress. Oh, you *must* remember Miss Leckey and that terrible hat she used to wear! *Oh yes, I remember. When Miss Leckey had no further use for it, she gave it to Mother. Lilian used to wear it.* 'We are so sorry, Elspeth, to hear that Lilian won't be able to come. What a shame. Never mind, you are in good hands now. We'll look after you, won't we ladies!' *Yes, you'll all run after me and make fun of me and sneer and laugh and wrinkle your noses as I pass and —*

'Are you all right, Elspeth?' The voice sounded so loud in her ear that Mrs Justice Fairfax-Lawson was startled. Lena Holmes was looking at her, concernedly. 'Oh. Yes,' Mrs Justice Fairfax-Lawson said. 'The trip. The strain.' Lena Holmes nodded. 'I do hope you aren't catching your sister's flu. There's a lot of it going around,' she said. 'But come along, we must get you tagged!' She laughed as she took Mrs Justice Fairfax-Lawson's hand. *Yah, yah, your mother washes clothes and your father's a jailbird.* 'There!' Lena Holmes cried as she branded Mrs Justice Fairfax-Lawson with a label, ELSIE KELVEY, so that everybody — *everybody* — could remember that awful little girl with cropped hair, remember ladies? That's her, over there.

A hand bell began to ring. A middle-aged man who could *never* have been young was standing in the centre of the hall, swinging the bell to and fro. His face was red with mirth as the bell clanged and boomed and shattered the conversation. Lena Holmes put her hands to her ears and said, 'Oh, that Johnny Johnston! Isn't he a one?' One of the other men ran out to wrestle with 'Johnny' and the crowd watched and grinned with amusement — Wasn't this fun? That Johnny, he *never* changed, good old Johnny. And all of a sudden Johnny was running between people, trying to escape his friend, and the women gave little screams and the men pretended to scrimmage and then he was heading for Mrs Justice Fairfax-Lawson and the shock of recognition spread over his face as, pointing at her, he said, 'I know you! You're you're — ' *Yes. My name is Elsie. My sister is Lil. My mother washes your mother's clothes. You are a horrid boy.* But before he could say anything more he was tackled and down he went. Lena Holmes, pretending to be a little girl, went over to the two men lying on the floor, wagged a little finger and said in a squeaky voice, 'Bad boys. Bad *boys*. I'm going to tell Mrs Fredericks on you!' What a laugh that caused — that Lena Holmes, the same as ever. Then she laughed herself and clapped her hands, clap, clap, CLAP. 'Roll call, everybody! Roll call! Everybodeeee,' and she led the way to the English Room, where the group photograph was to be taken.

Mrs Justice Fairfax-Lawson closed her eyes and took a deep breath. *Pull yourself together*, she said to herself. The shock, the crowd, the smell of chalk, the bonhomie, all these people acting like children, pretending that school had been such fun and they were all friends. Whereas she had only had one friendly gesture made toward her. *Stop it, Elspeth.* For who was she to make such assumptions? STOP IT. Feeling better, Mrs Justice Fairfax-Lawson joined the others. She smiled at everybody and was as charming as they expected her to be. She laughed just like everybody else at the photographer's frantic attempts to arrange the 'children' according to height, and when she had to say CHEEEESE she did so as long as the rest did until the flash-bulb popped. But deep inside her the little girl she once was still cringed and sought for a piece of dress to hold on to.

The bell rang again to announce that dinner would soon be served. Well-wishers approached Mrs Justice Fairfax-Lawson to say, 'We are so looking forward to hearing you speak,' or, 'We are so delighted that you will be speaking on our behalf as fellow pupils of the school,' and she was so surprised, absolutely *overwhelmed*, by the warmth of it all. She realised that the address she was going to give would be too pompous and too serious, for these returned pupils wished only for companionship and good memories and wonderful tributes to friends and school. And she heard Lilian's voice in her mind saying, *We were never too proud, Elspeth, never too proud.*

So that when, following the dinner in the hall, it was time for Mrs Justice Fairfax-Lawson to rise and speak, she had to pause and reconsider her words. The hall looked so gay and colourful, with streamers hanging from the ceiling and flowers arranged on the trestles and food — jellies, pavlovas, salads, lamingtons — sparkling on the tables. And there were all those ridiculous elderly people, sitting on forms, faces gazing up at hers in expectation. And it came to her just what she should say. 'Ladies and gentlemen,' she began. 'Boys and girls,' and everybody laughed. 'Like you all, I attended this school with my sister. There was once a little girl and her sisters who came to school one day and told us all about a wonderful gift — a doll's house.' To one side Elspeth heard Lena Holmes gasp with pleasure. 'Inside was a little lamp.' Mrs Justice Fairfax-Lawson paused at the memory. *You can come and see our doll's house if you want to, said Kezia. Come on. Nobody's looking.* 'I think that girl died some years ago but what she did stands as a shining symbol to all of us. Certainly it became a symbol for me.' The silence was such that a dropped pin could have been heard. 'Although my sister and I were the children of a washerwoman' — *There, it was out* — 'that girl showed us the little lamp. I have never forgotten that lamp, ever. Its flame has been a constant inspiration to me to always reach out — like that girl did — to others. To extend myself, become a better person and perhaps make the world a better place to live in. Were it not for that kindness, or similar kindnesses which I'm sure you all remember being done to you at this school, none of us would have become the people we are today. I would not have become the person I have.'

Mrs Justice Fairfax-Lawson had to pause again. *I seen the little lamp, she said softly.* She went to resume but somebody had begun to clap and very soon that person was followed by another and another, until the whole hall was on its feet and clapping at the memory of a school-friend, now gone, who had been so important in all their lives. And as they clapped, Mrs Justice Fairfax-Lawson smiled a rare smile and thought to herself that what she had said was just the silly commonplace sort of thing that Lilian would have liked.

WIWI

SHORT FEATURES

**WHO ARE YOU TAKING
TO THE SCHOOL DANCE, DARLING?**

**A HISTORY OF NEW ZEALAND
THROUGH SELECTED TEXTS**

LIFE AS IT REALLY IS

FALLING

Throughout my life I've always had what people call a *real* job. Like a lot of creative artists in New Zealand, therefore, my work is shaped by the fact that I do it intermittently between one thing and another and tie it all together with No 8 wire. I take my hat off to all artists in New Zealand because this is our reality. I am proud to belong to such a distinguished group of alumni.

It's been a busy life but I've managed a decent output — some people call me prolific but basically I'm just a hard worker. I've concentrated on writing novels, plays, libretti, children's books, and editing books on New Zealand and Maori writing, arts and culture. My output of short stories has consequently declined and, most often, I now write short stories when friends ask or if I've got a few days up my sleeve while travelling overseas.

Three of the following stories are the closest I'll ever get to writing with a satirical quality. 'Wiwi' is a look at French testing in the Pacific — but what would happen if you turned that on its head and New Zealand was the metropolitan power testing its bombs in Paris? 'Short Features' is a response to the 1950s Hollywood view of the world and how Maori, Polynesian and other indigenous people were represented in movies. 'A History of New Zealand through Selected Texts' is similarly satirical, looking at New Zealand's literary history; it was written during moments spent beside the pool with Taban Lo Liong during a conference in Kuala Lumpur.

'Who Are You Taking to the School Dance, Darling?' was written at the request of Tessa Duder for young adolescents in Australia. Although I have written two novels with gay themes, *Nights in the Gardens of Spain* and *The Uncle's Story*, this is the only gay-oriented short story I've written.

'Life as it Really Is' also considers the power of mainstream movies, but it takes a much more cynical approach about how filmmaking influences the world view of black and indigenous peoples. While the balance is being restored by such filmmakers as Merata Mita and Barry Barclay, one must constantly prosecute or interrogate those processes which still privilege primary text and deny justice and equality.

'Falling' is a story I have been trying to write ever since I fell off a roof in 1975. I finally had the chance while on a plane coming back from Europe. It's absolutely true: when you are falling the past does flash before your eyes, and it takes ages to hit the ground.

WIWI

(or, If New Zealand Was the Centre of the World)

The Prime Minister of New Zealand's announcement today that New Zealand would resume nuclear testing on the remote island of Île de la Cité, Paris, has been roundly condemned by the local natives, known as the French, and by other governments in the European region.

'The tests are perfectly safe,' the Prime Minister said from her naval vessel at the test site, 'and although scientists have reported cracks in the substrate below the Île de la Cité from previous tests, there has been no leakage beyond the Seine lagoon.'

The Prime Minister was speaking in response to a report that there was evidence of cracks in Notre Dame Cathedral, which stands on the island.

'Nor,' the Prime Minister said, 'is there any evidence that nuclear emissions above ground have increased radiation counts to unacceptable levels. Prevailing winds have of course allowed any danger of such pollution to be taken over the isolated Atlantic Ocean, posing no hazard to anyone.'

The French natives have, however, appealed to the European Parliament, the equivalent of the South Pacific Forum, for support against New Zealand's action.

'This is an outrage,' the French Premier announced. 'The peoples of Europe strongly protest this action, which puts all our countries at risk.' He said that the governments of the atolls of Germany, Belgium, Switzerland, Italy, Monaco, Spain and Portugal were planning to meet urgently to discuss the situation.

'But what is the problem?' the New Zealand Prime Minister responded at the news conference, called just after she had taken a swim in the Seine. 'As you can see, the water is not contaminated and I intend to swim every day while I am here observing the tests. What the natives of France do not realise is that the tests will add immeasurably to the sum of our scientific knowledge and understanding.'

The Prime Minister looked tanned and healthy as she posed for our cameras. She noted that the natives of France had long been known as Wiwi to New Zealanders (after their quaint linguistic custom of saying *Oui, oui* — or Yes) and she was sad that a small group of international dissidents had inflamed them.

'After years of happiness and smiling agreement,' the Prime Minister said, 'it is so sad to see the great change in the native populations from Wiwi to Nono. I do not blame the natives at all but, rather, reactionary governments that are taking this action not because of the tests but because they really want to oust us from Europe.'

The German Vice Chancellor has, however, disagreed with this claim. 'It is not that we want them out. It is, rather, that we wish them to respect our cultures and our European environment.'

'What cultures?' the New Zealand Prime Minister asked. 'Anthropologists have made too much of the so-called treasures of the European cultures. Too much mysticism surrounds their customs of ballet, opera and theatre — and everybody knows that the smile on the Mona Lisa is because she has just discovered she is pregnant. As for the European environment, may we point out that the former Soviet Union maintained a nuclear test schedule until quite recently and nobody protested against them. New Zealand is being singled out.'

The European countries are planning to take their case to the High Court of Australia A flotilla of protest ships is at this moment rounding the Atlantic Ocean, intent on entering the test zone. They include representatives from all the governments of Europe. The Pope has also sent a yacht to represent the Holy See.

'If the tests are so safe,' protestors asked, 'why doesn't New Zealand detonate its bombs in Auckland?'

The New Zealand Prime Minister smiled. She had one last comment before racing back into the Seine for another swim.

'I am perfectly happy for governments of the region to send observers and scientific teams to the Île de la Cité test zone to monitor the tests. They are perfectly safe. I give my word as a New Zealander to all the people of Wiwi.'

'Perfectly.'

'Safe.'

SHORT FEATURES

1
Imitation of life

My cousin Georgina always hated her looks. Our grandmother, Nani Miro, would growl at her and say: 'What's the matter with the way you look! You are so beautiful! What you want to make your hair straight for! And no amount of biting your lips is going to make them any thinner! With all that makeup on you look like a pukeko. You are a beautiful Maori girl.'

'But I'm supposed to look like this,' Georgina wailed. She jabbed a finger at Lana Turner in a movie magazine. 'Instead I look like *this*.'

The movie magazine had a still from *Imitation of Life*. Lana Turner was in the foreground, in all her blonde beauty. In the background was black actress Juanita Moore, Lana Turner's kindly black friend, dressed in a maid's uniform.

Nani Miro stared at the picture and then back at my cousin, Georgina. 'God you're dopey,' she said.

2
Nobody wanted to be Indians

Of all the movies that came to our town my mate Willie Boy and I loved westerns the most. The local theatre would put on a matinee of two features and, if we were lucky, both were westerns. If we were unlucky, we had to suffer through one of those boring romance films full of kissing. Our husky cowboy idols were laughing

Burt Lancaster, Kirk Douglas, Alan Ladd and Audie Murphy. Willie Boy and I would toss each other for who would play the hero and who would play the villain like Jack Palance or Richard Widmark. Being the hero was best because then you would be rewarded with the beautiful heroine like Arlene Dahl, Joanne Dru or ravishing Rhonda Fleming. Trouble was that our cousin Georgina always wanted to play the heroine parts and she wasn't exactly what we had in mind.

Willie Boy and I always had our hardest battles over who would play whom when we wanted to re-enact those westerns in which the cavalry fought the Red Indians. How we would cheer and yell and throw peanuts when, at the last reel, the cavalry would appear to save the fort! You could always tell when the moment was coming. John Wayne would be down to his last bullet and all those people in the wagon train would start looking soulful as if it was time to go to Heaven. There might be a heavenly chorus singing along on the soundtrack. Then, just before the last attack by those varmint injuns, you'd hear a bugle and on they would come, the cavalry.

The white man was always right in the westerns and only in a very few were the Indians anything other than wrong. The Indians smoked peace pipes but you knew they were mean as snakes. Not only that, but they were an illiterate lot. All they could say was 'How' or 'Heap big medicine' and they communicated by smoke signals instead of by telephone. They were mean sons of a bitch. Even when they were played sympathetically, they weren't really Indians at all but simply Rock Hudson all browned up as Taza, Son of Cochise, or Jeff Chandler as Cochise himself, or Burt Lancaster as Apache. The women were either Jean Peters, Linda Darnell or other unlikely blue-eyed Indian squaws.

When we came out of the theatre Willie Boy and I saw ourselves as white, aligning to our heroes and heroines of the Technicolor screen. Although we were really brown, we would beat up on each other just to play the hero. Neither of us wanted to be an Indian.

3
Sacrifice to the volcano god

Not long ago I walked into a bar in this Polynesian city and saw a beautiful young Maori girl dancing with a white boy. In the background was a huge papier mâché volcano which, every now and then, erupted dry ice and showered laser beams.

My thoughts went back to the South Sea island movies I had seen. Burt Lancaster was in *His Majesty O'Keefe*, Gary Cooper was in *Return to Paradise*, Yvonne De Carlo was the halfcaste Luana in *Hurricane Smith*, Esther Williams was an American Tahitian in *Pagan Love Song* and, down in New Zealand, we had a little number called *The Seekers*. In this one, Jack Hawkins and Glynis Johns fought the Maori, and Indonesian actress Laya Raki played a Maori princess and did a dance with no clothes on. Willie Boy and I went to see *The Seekers* three times. Most of the movies were of the kind in which the local girl falls in love with the white hero. It's a pattern as old as Fletcher Christian himself and comes out of all those fantasies white men have that brown-skinned babes just love those hairy blond chests.

Then I remembered *Bird of Paradise* set in Hawaii, which was typical of the formula. Handsome white man Louis Jourdan comes to the islands where he falls in love with beautiful Polynesian girl Debra Paget who is loved by local Hawaiian boy Jeff Chandler. No Polynesian girl I ever knew looked like Debra Paget, which was another reason for my cousin Georgina to get all hysterical and for Nani Miro to mutter about her dopeyness. It was just as bad for us Polynesian guys who felt we could in no way match up to the handsome white stereotype that our girls were falling for.

In the movie, Debra Paget walks on hot coals and, for some reason I still can't fathom, sacrifices herself to the volcano god. Wouldn't you just know it, but the volcano accepts the sacrifice of her life, and her sad but sorrowing white lover is able to go on with his life and sail off over the horizon to the arms of, presumably, the white woman back at home.

All this came to me, watching the Maori girl scattering the light in a bar one night not long ago.

Surely the volcano god has had his fill by now.

4

Merle Oberon was a Maori

Nani Miro has been dead a long time now but Georgina and I still talk on the telephone. One night I rang her up.

'Hey, Georgina, you remember Merle Oberon?'

American audiences won't know as much about Merle Oberon as British audiences do but she was, and is still regarded as being, one of the most beautiful women on the screen. She had a fabulous almond-shaped face with slanting eyes set into a complexion of flawless whiteness. She played Cathy to Laurence Olivier's Heathcliff in *Wuthering Heights* and George Sand to Cornel Wilde's Chopin in *A Song to Remember*. People thought she had discovered the fountain of youth. As she aged, she seemed to get more beautiful.

Georgina and I had been too young to see Merle Oberon in her prime but we had always known of her perfect loveliness. And the reason why I was ringing Georgina? Nobody knew until Merle Oberon's death that the Indian woman who met visitors at the door had been her mother. Neither woman had, throughout Merle Oberon's long career, ever given any sign of family affection. To have done so would have destroyed the white image of Merle Oberon's distinguished career.

All her life Merle Oberon lived a lie. She told the press that she had been born in Hobart, Tasmania, Australia. She made a supposed pilgrimage to Hobart but fainted.

When she died it all came out including the fact that Merle Oberon's mother had Maori blood.

'God, I hope it's true!' Georgina said.

'Why?' I asked.

'Because in all those years of seeing all that stuff up there on the screen,' Georgina answered, 'at least I can now feel that there was somebody there for me, for us, after all.'

I put down the telephone and started to grin at the subversiveness of somebody playing white and getting away with it, who had a mother who was one of us. Since then I've gotten a photograph of Merle Oberon and drawn a moko on her chin. And you know what? It looks right.

Hey, Merle, right on, babe.

WHO ARE YOU TAKING
TO THE SCHOOL DANCE, DARLING?

The sixth form end-of-year dance was only a week away but Maryann realised that, as usual, her mother was too busy rushing around being the female executive at her company — not to mention visiting Grandma in hospital — to pay much attention to it. Then, one morning, between the muesli and the toast, Mum found time to devote some attention to her family. She looked across at Maryann, Dad and Maryann's two brothers Andrew and Luke as if she hadn't seen them before in her life. Recognition dawned and she asked brightly:

'So how is everyone?'

Four pairs of eyes stared at her and four spoons of cereal hovered midway between plates and mouths. Mum had arrived back on the planet.

'I'll see you tonight, dear,' Dad said as he left for the office, patting Mum sympathetically as if he hoped she would get well soon. Maryann and her brothers also tried to make a run for it but:

'And who are you taking to the school dance?' Mum asked Andrew.

'Gina,' Andrew replied, referring to the long-time girlfriend who had managed to squeeze herself between him and his surfboard.

'Paul, I guess,' said Maryann, non-committal. She was holding out for an invitation from the local hunk, the one to die for, Stephen.

'What are you wearing?' Mum asked. 'Don't forget it's formal. You boys, tuxedo and bowtie.' She paused. 'We'd better go into town,' she said to Maryann, 'and buy you a new dress.'

'I've already been,' Maryann said darkly. 'With Aunt Maggie.'

'Oh,' Mum answered. She sounded disappointed. Then Mum turned to Luke, her sixteen-year-old. Her voice tapped like a woodpecker. 'And you, darling? Who are you taking to the dance?'

Luke's grey-green eyes stared from beneath a shower of golden curls. Mum didn't see the hot blush storming into Andrew's face or the warning look that Maryann shot at her eldest brother.

'I'm thinking of asking Robin,' Luke said.

The next morning, Maryann was visiting Grandma in hospital.

'Has Luke told your mother about Robin yet?' Grandma asked Maryann.

'No,' Maryann answered. Mum had dropped off the planet again and, because she was trying to win a new client contract, was absolutely out of communication. Dad had taken over the supermarket shopping; it was either that or have the entire family die of starvation. Maryann supervised the washing, waving vaguely in the direction of the drier whenever Andrew and Luke complained about not having a clean jockstrap or underpants. God, brothers were so hopeless, and washing their underpants was starting to put her off men for life.

'Well, somebody better tell her,' Grandma said, looking meaningfully at Maryann.

'Why don't you!' Maryann responded. 'After all, you know more about this than I do.'

Luke was Grandma's favourite. He always told her things he never told anybody else.

All Grandma said to that was:

'There's a good girl.'

Then Grandma patted Maryann's hands and switched off her hearing aid.

Three days later Mum still had not been told.

'I don't see why I should do it,' Maryann hissed to her eldest brother Andrew. 'You tell Mum and Dad.'

Maryann and her brothers were having a party at their place to celebrate the end of school. They'd negotiated with Mum and Dad who were, of course, going out.

Andrew glared at Maryann. He was fiddling with the sound system. As usual everyone was half dressed, Maryann in a slip and Andrew in underpants. 'It's not my day to be responsible,' Andrew declared. 'Let Luke do his own dirty work.'

Andrew jerked his head in the direction of the bathroom where Luke had just finished applying masses of egg white to his hair, teasing it out into long punk-like spikes, and was now standing on his head until they dried.

Setting her lips, Maryann went to the bathroom and pounded on the door. 'Luke? Luke! Will you hurry up in there!'

The trouble was that before Maryann got a chance to talk to Luke, Mum arrived. She too was only half dressed. 'Luke?' Mum called. 'If you want your father and I out of here you'd better let me in to finish dressing.'

The door opened in a trice and there was Luke, totally naked. Maryann sighed. This was what happened when your parents were your typical liberated New Age couple who'd met at a nudist colony.

Mum sighed in desperation. Luke looked like a strange skinny hedgehog. 'Oh Luke,' Mum sighed. 'Why do you have to do that to your hair?' Mum went to the bathroom mirror and started to do her face, issuing instructions as she brushed, applied, pouted, powdered, pursed, brightened, gilded and glossed. 'Your father and I are going to dinner at Vinnie's. Then we are having after-dinner cocktails at the Regent. For some ungodly reason he wants to take me on a moonlight drive to Saint Leonard's. Which reminds me —' Mum fumbled in her purse and brought out two packets of condoms. 'You boys seem to be out,' she said to Andrew and Luke.

Andrew picked up the packets and inspected them. 'Oh great,' Andrew said to Maryann and Luke. 'Mum's done the shopping, guys. I wish Dad wouldn't buy us those cheap Knight Riders. Thanks Mum.'

'Now,' Mum continued. 'We'll be back at one-thirty on the dot.'

'Two,' Luke bargained.

'One-fifteen, and you do the lawn,' Mum responded.

'One-thirty, I'll do the lawn and cook on Friday,' Luke said.

'Done,' Mum answered. 'By that time I want everybody out of the house, nobody is to sleep over, all the beer bottles are to be put in the rubbish and the lounge tidied up. There is to be no dope smoked in the house and —' Mum turned to Luke, waving her hairbrush at him. 'Darling,' she said to her younger son. 'Your father and I are liberal, but we have to draw the line somewhere. I realise that the last party was your sister's birthday but even your father was shocked to find the male stripper on the kitchen table and all of you yelling out, Take it off, take it off. So no male strippers tonight, OK?'

A memory of Luke flashed in Maryann's mind. His flushed face as he laughed and encouraged the male stripper to go further than his G-string. The way the male stripper winked.

Mum primped her hair. She smiled, satisfied at her reflection. Then she turned to Luke and asked brightly:

'So when are we going to meet your new girlfriend?'

Two days later, on the eve of the sixth form dance, Maryann knew the shit had truly hit the fan when, that morning, Grandma rang Maryann. 'I'm very cross with you,' Grandma said. 'Your mother is terribly upset about Robin. Why did you drop me into it?'

'But I didn't tell her!'

'Well whoever did it,' Grandma said, 'will be cut out of my will.' She turned off her hearing aid.

Maryann turned to Andrew, who was standing nearby. 'Mum knows,' Maryann said.

Andrew nodded.

'How did she find out?' Maryann asked. 'Did you tell her?'

Andrew sighed. Then:

'Robin telephoned. Mum answered the phone. Robin wanted to check on the time Luke was coming to pick him up for the dance. Mum's on her way home right now to talk to us about it. Before Luke gets back from band practice.'

'I'm out of here,' Maryann said.

'So am I,' Andrew added.

But Dad was there. 'I'm not taking the blame,' Dad said. 'Your mother has already screamed down the telephone that this is all my fault. None of her side has ever been — er — different.'

'Let's all make a dash for it,' Dad suggested.

It was too late. With a hiss of tyres and a screech of brakes Mum arrived. The slam as she shut the car door could be heard all down the street. When she came into the living room she was looking tragic. Like Lady Macbeth. Or Cleopatra who had been bitten by an asp. She went to the liquor cabinet, pulled out a bottle of whisky, drank half the bottle and then:

'All I want to know is how did this happen!' she screamed.

'Look, Mum,' Andrew answered. 'Robin is a really nice guy.'

Mum took another swig at the bottle. She fixed Maryann with a glittering eye. 'Maryann, is your brother gay?' she asked.

The question teetered in the air. Then, before Maryann could answer it, there was a twang as the back door opened. Luke was back.

OhmyGod, Maryann thought.

'Look, Mum,' Maryann said quickly. 'I don't think that's a question you should ask Luke. If you do, he might have to make a decision about whether he is or not and I don't think he knows if he is or isn't yet.'

Then Luke was there. Smoky eyes. Wonderful grin. 'Hi, Mum,' Luke said. 'You're home early.'

Of course Mum couldn't resist. 'Darling,' she asked, 'why have you invited Robin to be your partner to the dance?'

Luke looked at her blankly as if she was stupid.

'Mum, Robin's the best dancer I know,' he answered.

A HISTORY OF NEW ZEALAND
THROUGH SELECTED TEXTS

(An abstract for a paper to be presented at the LALALAND Conference)

My paper will explore the various texts of identity, representation and construction as presented in eighteen selected New Zealand novels, films and poetic works. In so doing it will try to engage with the semiotics of contact and the various diasporic, immigrant, exilic and expatriate notions of this country, alternately known as the Land of the Wrong White Crowd. The alternative realities, asymmetries and linguistic aesthetics of Pakeha New Zealand and their textual collisions with the Maori race will also be explored, much as Shashi Tharoor has done for India in his seminal revisionist, eclectic and postmodernist work, *The Ingrate's Indian Novel*. My paper is offered in homage from one subversive to another. The selected New Zealand texts are:

Nohwere

This great New Zealand title belongs to an ancestral Pakeha settler society text, elevated to canonical heights by people who have, actually, never read it. The paper will examine the reasons for the deplorable level of English transported to this virgin country from Great Britain, especially the bad spelling.

Sold New Zealand

Another canonical text in New Zealand literature, *Sold New Zealand* considers the truths about the Pakeha settler society from the perspective of a so-called Pakeha-

167

Maori. Ostensibly a tract defending Maori, *Sold New Zealand* turns out to provide not the mediation between two binaries but rather the rationale for Pakeha to take over Maori New Zealand. Maori should never have signed the Treaty of Waitangi or in any way trusted the buggers.

The Greenstone Flaw

The paper will offer a critique on this rip-roaring yarn, a prototype of the romantic heroic settler novels of the mid to late-nineteenth century. It is typical of those constructs of white hegemony, involving such characters as the white hero, friendly Maori sidekick, Maori princess who saves the white hero from the usual volcanic eruption or earthquake presumably so he can go back home to marry the (white) woman who has been waiting for him all along. Freire, Said, Chandi, Spivak, Marx, Foucault, the Spice Girls and aspects of the film *Titanic* will be invoked in the paper to provide an utterly useless (con)text to text.

The Pardon Garty

Acknowledgement is made of one of New Zealand's greatest short story writers in the paper and the curious dichotomous ambivalent position she holds in New Zealand letters. The author disliked New Zealand, left it to its own devices, never came back and wrote all her major stories about New Zealand while living in France. The paper will propose this trailing of skirts through colonial space as being a metaphor for the meta-schizophrenic nature of the New Zealand psyche.

Land Brawl in Unknown Trees

One of the great verse sequences of New Zealand literature, *Land Brawl in Unknown Trees* lends itself to questions of power, resistance, indigenous essence, Fatal Contact, antipodean vision and the mapping out of Maori and Pakeha dialogical space. If you can understand what all this gobbledegook means please email the author of this paper: w.ihimaera@wellington.ac.nz.

Children of the Whore & Once Were Worriers

The paper will posit Britannia as prostitute and consider the sorry plight of her children, seeking diasporical haven in the new colonial space of New Zealand. The bifurcated problematics of the two books listed above will be compared and contrasted in one of those stupid and futile intellectual exercises beloved of academics to find contrasts and commonalities that don't exist.

Bowels do Dry

A Bakhtinian Perspective will explore the Architectonic Self implicit in the main character, Daphne Withers, of this brilliant New Zealand novel. Random and totally inappropriate parallels with Arundhati Roy, Margaret Forster, classical Tamil poetry, Caribbean hybrid literature and Hindu sacred cow beliefs will reveal that when bowels do dry you can always rely on Janet Frame to provide the excuse for superb but utterly inappropriate discourse.

All Visitors Aboard & Dumb

These two novels from the white, male and realist tradition reveal that the Pakeha male writer is still very much alive and kicking — is he *what*. The paper will explore how men have been empowered and disempowered and include discussion on the sexual politics implicit in other such seminal male gender texts as *Man Can Do It Alone*, *The Odd Boy*, *The Good Keen Ram* and so on. When the time comes would the last white (straight) male realist writer still standing in New Zealand please close the door before he leaves?

A Creed for Women

Just when Pakeha male writers thought they were home and scot free along came the feminist revolution to stop them in their hobnail boot tracks and Swanndris. The paper will explore the feminist imperative in New Zealand literature, the whinges and whines of women and why it is that this imperative has resulted in

169

some really awful first-person present narratives by the New Zealand sisterhood. This part of the paper could otherwise be titled *Save the Males/Whales*.

No Ordinary Son & The Clone People

By comparison, really excellent writing of a quality only matched by the Kalyani tribe of the Hindu Kush Mountains, a tribe only slightly lower than the Maori are to Heaven, is to be obtained in the texts written by Maori authors. Descended from the Gods, the poet of *No Ordinary Son* and the great Wordweaver of the West Coast, really do show that the Empire has indeed Struck Back. The paper will consider the negative aspects of global English on the sacred Sanskrit-Maori language and how the sterling battle has been waged by Kerewin Holmes and her Maori literary warriors to combat further marginalisation, invisibilisation, appropriation of text (cf *Seasons in the Stew* and *The Stinking Pukkah-Papa*) and demonising of the Maori people by the villainous Pakeha. Discussion will also focus on essentialism vs synthesis, post-nativism and indigenous essence, and the upturning of notions of Centre and Rim in other (r)evolutionary Polynesian texts such as *Cuzzies* and *Leave Us The Banyan Trees*.

The paper will also disclose the great literary secret, actually known to Maori all along but only confirmed by the recent discovery of gold tablets on sacred Hikurangi Mountain, that Shakespeare's mother was a Maori. The implications that post-Shakespearian literature in English is a long-lost branch of the Ngati Porou oral tradition (Shakespeare's appropriation is being contested in an action currently before the Waitangi Tribunal which seeks to reclaim him as a taonga) will be particularly highlighted in the paper.

Na reira, kia kaha, kia manawanui, kia toa ki a tatou mahi tuhituhi a te Ao, ka mate ka mate ka ora ka ora, etc, etc.

(Author's Note: This magical and spiritual ritualistic karakia or prayer must remain untranslated to preserve the very sacred nature of Maori textuality, all praise be to Allah, and to recognise the primacy of the reo.)

Good Fry Pork Pie, The Abrogator & The Piano Finger

These three texts exist in New Zealand film. The filmic intersections with literary equivalents show that postmodernism, postcolonialism and neocolonialism are structures which are perpetuated in films as well as literature. The first film indicates that New Zealanders are able to laugh at themselves — as long as the film involves a Mini — but the other two show that Pakeha unease and dis-ease still intersect with Pakeha New Zealand Lit. Questions of anxiety, uncertainty, evasion, ambiguity, ambivalence, deceptions, disclosures and the slipperiness evident in the Pakeha sense of self indicate that the postsettler identity of the New Zealand Pakeha is still in a whole heap of trouble. This is evidenced in the sidelining of Maori characters to the margins of discourse and, in particular, the metaphoric cutting off of the finger in the award-winning film, *The Piano*. Thus, the paper will also discuss dismemberment as a Pakeha response to having no culture, genital mutilation, pornographic culture, the conflicting discourses of homoerotic and heteroerotic narratives in the film concerned — and the crucial question of what happened to the finger? It was not, so far as the author of this paper is aware, thrown out of a plane.

Faking Peoples & The Fake-triarch

Finally, these last two texts, one historical and the other creative, confirm the rhyzomic nature of mythmaking (and, incidentally, the continued invisibilising of gay, lesbian, transgender, and bisexual people in New Zealand history indicative in the failure in 1997 of the Auckland City Council to recognise the liberating effects of the Hero Parade).

Primarily, the paper will propose that all history is lies and all lies can be made into suspect novels or histories. The paper considers these two texts as both salvation of and destruction of mythmaking. In New Zealand, it doesn't matter what the myth, demolish it (especially if it's Maori) and you may end up with a knighthood.

The novel under discussion is the last of all the texts to be considered in the paper and should not in fact be included. To be frank, why critics have considered *The Fake-triarch*, aka *Kiss of the Spider Woman Part 2* aka *Magic Realism's Last Gasp* as an impossible and unbelievable cybertext is beyond its author's comprehension. Many beautiful Maori grandmothers existed who once lived in Italy, sang arias by Verdi while fighting the Pakeha, and were pursued by vengeful mothers who could swim through the universe.

The paper, as above, will be presented in the Atrium of the Peking Cluck Hotel

171

at 5.30 pm on Thursday. Those students wishing to get A+ in the author's Masters Papers at Victoria University of Wellington, and other members of the public lucky enough to find a seat in the packed hall, should attend. Please note that the paper is programmed to deconstruct five minutes after presentation.

The author exerts his moral rights and, to pre-empt those who wish to take out a fatwa against his pure and innocent intentions, asserts that any resemblance to any New Zealand writer or to the proceedings of the 11th Triennial ACLALS Conference, December 1–6, Kuala Lumpur, 1998, is entirely coincidental.

LIFE AS IT REALLY IS

1
Going Hollywood

It will help if you are white, blue-eyed, blond and cute with a nice butt. If you're a woman, you will need to be, similarly, white, blue-eyed, blonde, what is known as a 'babe' and under twenty-five. Because the camera photographs you heavier than you actually are, girls will need to be as anorexic as possible. The more you look like Barbie the better. Don't worry about any physical imperfections as these can be fixed. Be prepared to have your teeth straightened, nose bobbed, jaw wired, boobs siliconed, waist scalpeled and any individuality you might have possessed botoxed or plastic-surgeoned out altogether. The object is not to look different but to look the same as the other boys and dolls who inhabit the world.

Should you not fit the physical criteria above, *viz* you are bald, fat and plain, don't worry. You still have a part to play. However, it will not be as the main actor or actress in life's drama. This does not necessarily mean that you cannot make it. Barbra Streisand is surely one of the world's oddest looking women — but she can sing. The fantasy of the ugly duckling who becomes a swan is for most of us a drama that is ironically only purveyed by a society obsessed, in fact, with beauty. Once an ugly duckling, always an ugly duckling. So best to resign yourself to being the Friend of the Star, or the Comic Relief or the Mother of the Star.

If you are a person of colour, you need not apply unless you're tall, black and stupid enough to think you matter. Otherwise, forget it. Remember your pride and let those white folks go ahead and pick a white actor to play the villain.

173

2
There's no business like show business

You may have to sleep with the director or the producer or the associate producer or the casting director, no matter how foul-breathed or cocaine-smashed he (or she) might be. Don't bother with the scriptwriter as he has no power as far as casting is concerned. If you're a young girl, try to remember that it's all over in five minutes and, after all, what's five minutes if you are guaranteed stardom? If you're a boy, grit your teeth and just remember that some of life's great stars played their first starring roles with their jeans around their ankles. Whoever you are, four pieces of advice: try not to chew gum, do not under any circumstances make any reference to his toupee, make him believe his is the biggest you've ever seen and don't forget to have the bastard sign your contract before you let him in.

If you are a person of colour, the above route also applies if you are really desperate to get that job as a maid, Mexican bandit, the girl who gets shot so that the white hero can go back to marry the white woman in the last reel.

Should you have been stupid enough to be saddled with your childhood sweetheart, or married him (or her) or have had a teenage pregnancy, don't worry. That's what your publicity agent is for. Your agent will evaluate all the stupid things you did before you got into the business and either fix it (i.e., love doesn't go with the business, so out goes the teenage sweetheart) or put a positive spin on it (i.e., your teenage spouse couldn't take your new career so you both agreed that, for his sake and yours, you both have to part). Having been pregnant is okay, as long as it was illegitimate. This helps give you a reputation. However, under no circumstances will you be allowed to be photographed with your child as this will only detract from your image and reveal that you are older than you look.

None of the above applies if you are a person of colour.

3
Lights! Camera! Action!

When you report for work, do not expect a set which at all resembles reality. Life is a movie, for God's sake, didn't your Momma tell you? But don't worry. At every script meeting before you are shot (on film and by the camera, that is) your friendly coke-supplier will be on hand to give you a fix that will get you through the day.

When you walk onto the set the lights that are blazing don't come from the sun. Get used to the light as it is the only kind you'll see for the rest of your life. Everything around you will be artificial. The mountains, rivers, houses are all fake and most of the time they're only frontages. None of the doorways or roads lead to anywhere. There's nothing behind the façades you work in.

The costumes you wear will have been worn by others who have appeared in similar life stories. Sometimes, when you put them on you can catch a whiff of the scent of the person who has worn the costume before you. None of the jewellery is real.

Sometimes your script might lead you to believe you will be going to Italy or filming in Tibet. Most times, however, all the filming will take place on the backlot of Hollywood USA. Don't look too closely at anything around you. It will not be what you think it is but, rather, a phantom construct, something without any substance.

At other times you will find yourself acting in front of a blue screen delivering dialogue in a setting that isn't really there to people who are not able to be on the set on the day. They do incredible things with computerised special effects these days. The most amazing simulacrums have been developed and you will be surprised, when you see the rushes, to see yourself delivering your dialogue to Ben Affleck or Gwyneth Paltrow or any other ghosts who are appearing in your film. Nothing is real. Nobody is real. Ben Affleck and Gwyneth Paltrow don't, in fact, exist.

Do not expect any intelligence in the script. Above all, do not question the script or the way the director wants you to deliver your lines. The director is God and he knows better than you do how you should portray your life. His idea of great dialogue is for you to say 'Wow!' or 'Great!' or 'Oh, wow!' for maximum emotional effect. Be prepared to spout the most inane, stupid, incredibly unbelievable load of shit you've ever read.

If you are a person of colour you are lucky. You are not given lines as such but, rather, your part will consist of reaction shots, grunts and body poses. Thus, if you are dumb, no problem.

4

A star is born

You will not need to know how to act. There are basically only four facial expressions to master. The first is the 'I love you' expression. For this you widen your eyes, let your lips go slack, run your fingers through your hair and look yearningly at the camera. The second is the 'I hate you' expression. In this one you widen your eyes even wider, let your lips go slack, run your fingers through your hair (you must have *lots* of hair if you want to be successful in life) and look yearningly at the camera so that everybody knows you want to escape the jerk playing opposite you. The third expression is the 'I'm in danger' expression. This is the same expression as the 'I love you' expression. The fourth expression is the 'Now we can go home' expression, which you save for the end of the picture. In this one you really have the opportunity to emote. The best way to obtain this expression is to think of yourself as Lassie waiting to be given a bone. You widen your eyes, let your lips go slack, run your fingers through your hair — if you have any left — and look yearningly at the camera. Why they ever need humans I'll never know. Computer images do the job just as well these days.

Have you thought of other positions in the industry? For those prepared to kill themselves there's always stunt work. For those interested in design, all stars need somebody to make them look good. If you are the kind of musician who doesn't mind composing with Novocaine, this industry is made for you.

Be prepared for nude scenes. For those with a perfect set of boobs or the perfect (white) penis but with unfortunate looks in every other department, you will be able to find work as a body part.

If you are a person of colour take note that while equality was achieved years ago very few directors will allow you to actually be seen in bed with a white partner.

You have three choices of scenario. The first is the romantic drama which may be in costume or contemporary dress or, if X-rated, no costume or dress at all. The main actors will get the best lines and the best costumes. The rest of you will be colour coded according to the designer's idea of what will best accessorise the main actors. Nobody needs to worry about acting. All the men need to do is to strike heroic poses. The women need only heave their bosoms and scream while waiting for the hero to rescue you. If you are appearing in an X-rated movie, you have no lines at all. If you are a person of colour you die.

The second is the action drama, which may be period, western, thriller, horror or kung-fu. The action drama is a lot of fun. Again you don't need to know about acting. The gadgets and special effects take this role over. All the men need to know is how to jump through windows, escape blazing aeroplanes, stop the bomb from going off and fight the villain. The women need only heave their bosoms, scream for help and, in the horror movie, it's pretty inevitable that you will be the victim in the gory slash sequences. There's nothing better than to see a young girl being cut up by a killer. If you are a person of colour — and if you're not Will Smith — you are the villain and you die.

The third is the fantasy drama, including animation (the new word for cartoons) or space opera. In this one, the main actor must look like Harrison Ford or a handsome(r) American president than George Bush because, as we all know, all space operas are really about America saving the planet from an evil intergalactic force. Be prepared to make lofty statements, delivered deadpan and to soaring music as you face almost insurmountable odds. The women need only heave their bosoms if they are playing the wicked part or act the virgin if they are playing the princess part. Interestingly, the person of colour, like Hiawatha or Jafar or Moses, has actually become a hero, but only if he or she appears in a cartoon. Failing that, he or she is cast to type — as an animal like the Lion King or, as happened to Whoopi Goldberg, a hyena.

However, in a live action drama we're back to basics. This type of drama is best avoided if you want to live a long life. They are usually written to a very bad formula in which you have a few words of dialogue, a chase sequence and a great explosion at the end of it. An incredible number of cars are disposed of in such movies. So are a *lot* of people who just happen to be flying on the plane that gets hijacked or the train that goes off the rails or the ship that sinks. Still, it's fun for the spectators.

If you are a person of colour you are the sidekick in the detective thriller, the second lead in the space opera, you don't get the princess, you live long enough to congratulate the hero for saving the world and then you die.

5

Sunset Boulevard

If you are lucky enough your first picture will be a hit. Should this occur you must let your publicity agent run your career. He (or she) will tell you what to do, where to go and what kind of image you are supposed to present to an adoring public. The problem will be that this image will stay with you for life. Only a few manage to escape the typecasting but not everyone is a Meryl Streep or Dustin Hoffmann. The rest will remain trapped either as eternal blonde-headed virgin — or worse,

Meg Ryan, still so very young at forty — or as the eternal golden boy like Robert Redford (Brad Pitt, beware).

You will be asked to pose for front covers where every blemish of face and body has been digitally removed and you become somebody you do not recognise saying things you never recognise as coming out of your sweet little mouth. This is when you start reading about yourself, the fun you're having with people you've never met and the affairs you've started with people you don't know. If at all possible avoid believing in the stories about yourself. Do what the others do — begin wearing dark glasses and try to avoid photographers and your public. Otherwise they will ask questions about a life you are not leading which you won't be able to answer. Not only that, but do you really want to be associated with the crap you are supposed to have said?

By this stage, you may well be advised to get married — preferably to your leading man (or woman) or to the director. This is called life imitating the movies and your public will love the idea that two people who met while filming, say, *Titanic* may have been drowned on the screen but found true lurve while doing it.

Marrying your director is second best — but okay. Such marriages only confirm, anyway, that you got the part not because of any talent you have but because the director fell in lust with your picture in a magazine or wanted to play Svengali with you. The golden rule is to accept a director's proposal. If you don't, he can spread the word around that you are difficult and, honey, if that happens you won't get another job in this town. After a few years you can ditch the bastard anyway with a quickie divorce in Las Vegas and do him for as much alimony as you can get.

Marriage will also help your career at this stage because it will prove that you are not gay or lesbian and, rather, a regular guy or gal. While life says it's okay to be sexually ambivalent best not to Come Out. Nobody wants to see a faggot kissing a sex goddess like Nicole Kidman on the screen. It's not Nicole's fault when the audience starts to snicker. They all know that the guy who's kissing her would rather be kissing the hunky gardener.

Persons of colour don't need a publicity agent. Nor will they appear on a front cover unless it's *Ebony* magazine. Kissing Nicole? Get real.

If you should still have aspirations to be the main actor in any of the above but have been relegated to the sidelines, never fear. Television may be just the right place for you, especially as a news presenter where, because you are always photographed front on, you need no torso or profile. If there's no room in TV-land, tough. Life wasn't meant to be easy.

Five years later you will be thirty and in mid-career. If you're lucky you will still be on the big screen. If not, you'll be on a series like 'The Young and the Brainless' or, by now, have faded into the back row of the extras or else become the adoring public at premieres at the Mann Chinese Theatre.

You will now be onto your second marriage (there are another two or three to go) and your body, while still okay, may be looking the worse for wear and tear. Little things may need to be fixed or adjusted, so if you are still a star, be prepared for a mid-career nip and tuck. Some men that I know have their lives so tied up with their ego that they go further and have penile implants or extensions. The problem is that plastic surgery goes only so far. Surgeons can fix the face but from the neck down the prognosis isn't good. However, full body transplants are just around the corner and, very soon, you'll be able to get your head attached to some fresh new body recently harvested out of Eastern Europe. When the technology is available have no remorse about receiving your new body. You'll probably make better use of it than its previous owner anyway.

Be prepared for your first visit (wearing dark glasses so that the news photographers won't know it's you) to the Betty Ford Clinic for drug or alcohol addiction. Don't let this get you down. After all, better people than you have trodden the same path — and Elizabeth Taylor met a garage mechanic at Betty's

To help your flagging career, widen your interests so that people realise that you have the world's future at heart. Support a charity. AIDS work has already gone and so has raising money to save the starving children of Africa. Make sure that whatever you choose is politically acceptable. Something like 'Save the Rabbits of the World' will do just fine.

6
End credits

By the time you're forty you will have become a veteran of your world. You will start playing older parts. You will also be watching younger men and women of little talent taking your place. Although you might want to poison their drinks at the next cocktail party try to desist. They will get everything they deserve.

Some very few actually manage to survive life with some distinction. Listen to the tale of ravishing red-headed actress Rhonda Fleming. She played the typical American dream. She was born in Hollywood, made some good films and bad films, married four times and in her last marriage achieved apotheosis — as the wife of the late Ten Mann, owner of the Mann Chinese Theatre on Sunset Boulevard.

Not everybody can marry a movie house owner, however. For most of you, remember that after you turn fifty (I'm being charitable here) you are not supposed to exist. The best idea, therefore, is to kill yourself in a car accident like James Dean, take sleeping pills like Marilyn Monroe or die of an overdose like River Phoenix. It worked for them. After all, they are better known in death than they were in life.

But if you're a coward and still around, clear the set willya?

And if you're a person of colour don't worry.

Nobody notices the cleaner.

FALLING

He was on the roof of the house repairing the tiles when his left foot slipped. Before he knew it, he was tumbling down the steep pitch. The guttering, at the edge of the roof, was like a cliff. He thought, 'You stupid bastard,' cursed the slippery soles of his shoes, tried to grab for a hold —

Missed.

A precipice of startling blue opened beneath him.

And he was falling.

He thought of Hannah that morning. After the kids had left for school, they'd had a screaming, vicious row. Their accusations spiralled out of control.

'Twenty-three years I've invested in you,' she said, 'and you still trail the smell of other lovers.'

Her blazing eyes filled the sky, became a single iris. Blinked. He thought he'd be caught in her lashes but he passed through. The iris widened out, allowing him to enter.

It was twenty-three years earlier. White bed. Hannah's white skin. Her face white. He was still pumping. There was blood on the sheets. He knew he loved her.

And he was falling.

He had an erection. It stormed out of his phallic sheath. He remembered the night when he was a boy in the bathroom, looking in the mirror, in awe and admiration of himself. His mother had entered, seen, turned and walked away through the mirror. She'd loved him once.

There was a flash of sun as he pinwheeled down.

He was three years old. He was sitting in his father's lap on a white wooden horse, going up and down, round and round on a circus merry-go-round. His mother was standing on the ground, her arms held out. She was laughing as he went round and round.

'Catch me, Mummy!'

And he was falling.

'Why should I remember that?' he wondered.

The rush of fear and exhilaration exploded, his semen like dew, and he saw that Hannah, having heard him tumbling down the roof, had come out to see what was happening. She had a fist to her mouth. She was wordlessly screaming.

He knew he was going to die and, with a terrible certainty, that Hannah would marry again. An extraordinary prescience came to him about his daughters, too, and the men they'd marry.

He saw that his youngest daughter, Fay, was calling to him across the expanse of the airport on his return from a business trip to Australia. She came toddling through the crowd, her arms outstretched to him. He'd been unfaithful in Sydney.

'God, I'm so sorry,' he said, as he swept her up.

He watched as Fay grew big and bloated with his sin over all those years.

And he was falling.

They say you never forget your first love.

The sky was blue and golden fields ran right through the middle of it. He saw his love waving to him from the edge of the sky. Then he was running and running. As he approached, his love turned from him and started to walk away. No matter how fast he ran he could never catch up. Exhausted, he stopped. He called —

'Did I ever tell you that I never knew my father?'

The concrete slabs of the driveway came up like jagged mountains. His skull cracked apart. An eggshell. Bacon and eggs sizzling in a pan. A millisecond of terrifying pain. Someone screaming.

He remembered reading somewhere that your life flashes before you at the moment of —

He was alone in a huge white waiting room.

The minutes ticked by.

He was dressed in his best suit.

There was a mirror on the wall.

He looked into it. Took out a comb.

Combed his hair.

Adjusted his tie.

Saw, in the mirror, a door.

Looked at his watch.

Saw it was time.

Turned the doorknob.

Opened the door.

A 60 SECOND STORY

LIFE AND DEATH IN CALCUTTA

SOMEONE IS LOOKING AT ME

A KISS BEFORE DYING

I always like to think of myself as being a witness of my times, and my primary witness is as a Maori writer who belongs to the iwi. I'm not the only one. There's a whole academy of Maori writers including Api Taylor, Renee, Keri Hulme, Roma Potiki, Alan Duff, Robert Sullivan, Briar Grace-Smith, Hone Kouka, koutou katoa.

I am, of course, also a witness of other peoples, other places and other issues. Once upon a time I was just a young boy from Waituhi who used to sit on the side of the road and watch the cars go past. Now I travel the world and my view is bigger and connects me to international concerns.

Roger Robinson is to blame for 'A 60 Second Story'. In 1999 he edited *Writing Wellington*, a collection of writing by twenty Victoria University writing fellows — and invited all of us to the launch. Obviously, it was going to be a long night so, to make sure we wouldn't overstay our welcome at the microphone he wrote that '30 seconds would suffice'. I decided to take him up on his challenge, wrote something 30 seconds long, and have now expanded it to 60 seconds. At the time my thoughts were much taken by Elizabeth Knox's *Vintner's Luck* so I thought I would have angels in it. As well, the whole world was watching in horror what was happening in Kosovo, so that had to go into the story too. And it had to be epic.

'Life and Death in Calcutta' was the second of two stories I wrote beside the pool while escaping from the ACLALS Conference in Kuala Lumpur. The story is informed by discussions that were just beginning internationally about globalisation and the inequitable distribution of the world's food supplies and wealth, discussions which still fuel huge international protests.

I've been a committed fan of science fiction ever since I was a boy, and 'Someone Is Looking at Me' was written for a New Zealand science fiction anthology — but I never finished it on time. It's a fable, an updated biblical story, and its themes will be familiar to anyone who knows Fritz Lang's *Metropolis* or Andrew Niccol's *Gattaca*. I decided to complete it for this collection. It's about biotechnology and genetic engineering. It's also about my mother. If I was ever lost on a dark sea at midnight and there was one person I would call to rescue me, it would be my mother.

Sometimes I write 'unlisted stories'. 'A Kiss Before Dying' is one of these. It's the kind you can't access through the telephone directory.

A 60 SECOND STORY

They were twin brothers. They had been at war with each other all their lives. It was incredible that brothers from the same womb should be so different. That one would hate the other so much, would want power so much, as to cause war between them.

The war had consumed a thousand years. By the end of it, the landscape had been totally destroyed, the population decimated. But one twin had managed to defeat his brother. On the eve of the peace talks, reports were still coming in of the atrocities discovered. Rape. Murder. Mass executions.

Even so, the victorious brother wanted to be kind. To be forgiving to his twin. While the smoke of burning cities still singed the sky with insanity, and the wind brought the sharp taste of rotting flesh, he said to his defeated brother:

'If you will agree to my terms and bow down to me, I will allow you and your armies to stay. But if you will not, because you are my beloved brother, I will not have you executed. Rather, you will be banished.'

His twin brother paused thoughtfully. He lifted his head to the light. He was beautiful to look upon.

'No, brother, I will not bow down to you.'

He began to lead his troops from the battleground. Their dark wings started to unfold from their backs.

'I give you one last chance,' his victorious brother said.

His twin laughed and shook his head. As his own wings unfolded they were seen to be crimson red, jagged as a bat's and veined with a thousand sparkling rivers.

'I would rather rule in Hell,' he said, 'than serve you in Heaven.'

The sky shrilled and crackled as he departed.

LIFE AND DEATH IN CALCUTTA

Two friends had invited a third to have drinks with them beside the pool of the exclusive hotel where they were guests. The pool was on the roof of the hotel, which was not in Calcutta but in a city far removed from the Indian continent. When, on his arrival, the third friend expressed his amazement at the pool's rooftop location, an engineering feat that must have cost much more than had the pool been placed on the ground floor, his two friends exchanged smiles of understanding. After all, their friend had not been successful in industry as they were and, therefore, his lack of understanding of the appurtenances of five-star living needed to be indulged. They watched as he stripped to his shorts and dived into the pool. They had yet to wet themselves in the water, preferring to sip their cocktails and watch, shaded by an umbrella from the sun.

The third friend was a teacher in Calcutta and, after he had finished his swim and was towelling himself beside the pool, his two friends began to ask him questions about his life in India. They did this more out of politeness than interest. Noting his surroundings, and surmising that his friends would never ever set foot in a Third World country, the invited friend responded gently that there were hotels in Calcutta similar to the one they were in and that if they wished to visit India in the five-star manner, they would find life exactly as it was anywhere else. However, if they wished to see the real Calcutta, all they would need to do was venture a few steps into an alley off the main street and, there, they would find twenty beggars within hands' reach. His two friends expressed sympathy at the poverty of life their third friend conveyed, and one made a chance remark of the kind we all do that he always kept some change in his pocket just in case he was confronted with a beggar on a city street. At this point the invited friend closed his eyes and posed the following parable to his friends.

'There was once a man in a white suit,' he began, 'who, in his hurry to return to his hotel, took a detour and found himself in a street full of beggars. At once surrounded, the man brushed the outreaching hands aside but, failing to escape, put a silver coin in one of the hands and proceeded on. As he departed he heard a commotion and realised that the other beggars were trying to wrest the silver coin from the one who had been given it. As well, a second group were now in his pursuit. Luckily, the man in the white suit was quick on his feet and was able to elude his pursuers, all, that is, except one who caught up with him as he rounded the corner and touched his sleeve to detain him. "Kind sir," the beggar said, "you have given a silver coin to my colleague. It was my hand that was uppermost and should have received the coin. However, in a moment of jostling my hand was pushed to one side and, in that split second, the coin span away and into the hand which received it." '

The friends to whom the parable was being told looked at each other. 'The second beggar was unlucky,' one of them shrugged. 'He was in the right place at the right time but his was not the right palm. This is life. There are winners and there are losers.'

The invited friend nodded in agreement. 'Yes, and the second beggar was aware of this. He had been prepared to accept the whim of Fate. However, when he saw his colleague in possession of the coin his first thought was, "Why him? Why not me?" '

'For that matter,' one of the friends interjected, 'Why not any of the other twenty beggars in the street? The man in the white suit should not be blamed for an act of charity which albeit privileged one beggar over the others.'

'Indeed,' the invited guest agreed. 'Why not any of the other beggars? It was random chance that had dropped that silver coin in one palm and not another — and the second beggar realised this. But acting in hope he had run after the man in the white suit and, upon catching up with him, now wished to offer him the great gift of dispensing his bounty by choice as he had earlier done by chance. "Sir," the beggar said, "I wonder if you would also consider a silver coin to me. You see, sir, I have a wife who is ill and four children who have not eaten for five days whereas the man to whom you have given the silver coin does not have a wife or children and has only his own mouth to feed." '

'But how does one know,' one of the friends interrupted, 'that any story told by a beggar is true?'

'Yes,' his companion nodded. 'Simply because a person says it is so does not mean that it is so. Not only that but one cannot give silver coins to every beggar that one meets. Justice is blind, the world is a random place, these things happen.'

'You are being too defensive,' the invited guest said. 'My point is not to criticise the man in the white suit but to engage a story of his moral dilemma and questions of responsibility. Previously the man in the white suit had given his silver coin unthinkingly and, now, he was being asked to give another silver coin on trust, on faith, on the presumption of truth. The beggar pressed on, "I am pleading with you, kind sir, to honour me with your bounty," and, as it happened, the man in the white suit did have a second silver coin in his pocket which he could easily have given. Indeed, he was on the point of reaching in to give it to the beggar until he thought he saw something in the beggar's eyes. A glint of triumph, perhaps, a touch of contempt that the man in the white suit had believed his story — or was it merely that sunlight reflected in a second-storey window had lodged in the beggar's eyes and made them seem to be those of thief, a liar, a dissembler? It was simply a moment, as ephemeral as that same moment when the man in the white suit had dropped his first silver coin into that lucky hand, but it was enough to make the man in the white suit revert not to trust but to distrust. There is nothing more contemptuous to a man than to think he is being made a fool of. Thus it was that he made his choice and thereby his second decision —'

'What was his first?'

'Agreed, his first was perhaps unconsciously applied when he gave a silver coin to a beggar, possibly the wrong beggar at that. But this second was consciously applied when he decided not to believe the beggar's story. The man in the white suit pushed the second beggar aside, passed on and entered his hotel.'

The storyteller lapsed into silence. His two friends signalled a waiter and ordered him to refresh their drinks. But their invited friend had no intention of letting them escape the narrative he was telling them.

'When the man in the white suit entered the hotel that was the end of the story, insofar as it applied to him, but it wasn't the end of the story for the beggar. As it happened he did indeed have a wife who was dying and four starving children. Life and death in Calcutta does often turn on who is given a silver coin and who is not. Should the man in the white suit be expected to take responsibility for the one who does not receive a silver coin as well as the one who does? Even if the man in the white suit had given him a silver coin that might not have prevented the death of the wife though it may well have prolonged the life of his children.'

'What are you trying to say?' one of the storyteller's friends asked with some impatience. 'First you imply that the second beggar should have been given a silver coin and now you indicate that, even if he had been given one, it would have made no difference?'

The invited guest nodded. 'Although at that level of existence the choice of prolonging life or not is equally deplorable, the possibility of maintaining life is so precious that it must surely be sought over the terminality of death — but that's not what I am trying to say.'

The storyteller's friends waited for him to elaborate.

'This is not a story about a beggar,' he explained. 'It is about the man in the white suit.'

The two friends of the storyteller were fortunate to be in a country where afternoon showers were common because, at that moment, they noted that such a shower was about to begin. They decided it would be best to adjourn to an inside bar, thanked their invited friend for coming, quickly collected their clothes and left.

The invited friend stayed by the pool. He had not meant to offend his friends but had merely wanted to respond to a chance remark about keeping change in your pocket for beggars in the street. He decided to have one last dip before leaving. He stepped to the edge of the pool and dived in. When he resurfaced the water was dimpled with raindrops.

SOMEONE IS LOOKING AT ME

1

Once upon a time there was a woman living on World 1. She was a breeder, married to a worker, and together they had bred a family unit of three daughters. The sex of children depended on gender demographics and, at the time, females were required to balance the over-supply of males.

One day, the woman's husband arrived home with the news that the family were to be shipped as workers to World 16. After many years of climate engineering, this once hostile planet in the Nebula Quadrant had now been rendered fit for human habitation. Workers were being sent to erect City 1 of World 16, in preparation for subsequent colonisation.

Before departure, however, the woman was required to breed again. Her husband introduced his genetic material into her and, when she became pregnant, she duly presented herself to her medical clinician. Once he ascertained that her egg was viable, he manipulated its chromosomatic structure so that she would have a son and, like his father, that he would be a worker of the requisite submission and obedience. The family then departed for World 16.

In those days, generations of wise patriarchs had managed to solve all the problems of the times before when the petty political hierarchy of nation states had ruled World 1. It was the patriarchs who, at the beginning of the Second Millennium, had brought humankind back from the brink of extinction. They managed to bring a sense of sanity to the growing nationalism and racism which had beset their world. They then began to establish a new world order based on the notion that if all people were equal and if all resources were shared, they could minimise man's ancient biblical enmities. At the same time, with the technocrats they ordered an all-out onslaught on atmospheric pollution and tried to mitigate the catastrophic disruption to world weather patterns. They entered into partnerships with scientists and environmentalists to control unsustainable development and increase international food supplies.

It took another thousand years for the turnaround to be achieved but, by the Third Millennium, the wise patriarchs had stabilised the world. However, World 1 by itself could not sustain the population growth that ensued under international peaceful conditions, so they began explorations of outer space that led to the discoveries of Worlds 2, 3 and 4. Extrapolating into the future, they set about offsetting requirements for growth, expansion and building for the future survival of the human race, by colonising the stars. When each new habitable world was discovered, workers were sent out to bring them to harvest.

Did I say workers? Ah, there was the rub. During the latter part of the Third Millennium the wise patriarchs realised that computer technology and the peaceful conditions brought about by a united world had created the potential for human equality but workers were still required to operate the computer technology. The wise patriarchs decided to go to the next step. They developed, instead, biotechnology, as the science by which man could expand his possibilities. By genetic engineering, they created two classes of humankind: rulers and workers. It was upon this framework that the patriarchs built their new vision of life and ensured that their order was maintained, supported and kept operational. Eventually, the worker replaced the computer. He became the computer. From the very beginning of a worker's life, the worker's genetic material was formatted to include a computer circuit.

World 16 came into harvest at the end of the Fourth Millennium. There, seven months after her arrival, the woman gave birth to her son. Because he was destined to be a worker, the woman was not given the preferential treatment of carrying him in an artificial womb. Instead, she carried him to term within herself and he was delivered in the gruesome, old-fashioned way. The birth was excruciatingly painful and the woman thought she would die. When she saw him, slipping bloodied and squealing from between her legs, she realised why: his head was hideously deformed, being extraordinarily large and hydroencephalic. But his eyes were wide open and beseeching when he looked at her, and they bespoke an unusual intelligence. When he reached for her and curled his webbed fingers into her hair, she realised she didn't care about his appearance. Although she was just a breeder whose design specifications had not included maternal affection and ownership, she was stabbed with dagger thrusts that she knew was love for her child.

The woman hid her son from the medical clinicians on World 16. She took him home and, abandoning the normal protocols, nursed him with her own milk. Her husband and daughters could not understand her passionate involvement with such a hideous child but accepted her aberrant behaviour.

However, it was only a matter of time before the boy's existence became known. He was almost a year old when the clinicians discovered him. They were shocked. They took him from his mother. She did not see him again. When she asked about him they upbraided her for hiding him from them. They told her that because his genetic material was of such deformed condition he had been terminated.

2

Now I must tell you a story which runs parallel to the woman's story. I swear to you that this second story is true. It hasn't happened yet, but it will happen in the near future. That very future, itself, is already at hand. Already, scientists have the power to insert genetic material into a woman's egg.

In that future, which was the same future as that inhabited by the woman, her husband and three daughters, there arose a young prince of remarkable powers. The rumour was that he had been created according to the specifications of the wise patriarchs. They had asked the scientists to use their genetic technology to create a super being who would take humanity to the next level of advancement.

From his creation, therefore, the young prince was marked for greatness. Through his leadership it was predicted that he would begin a new *galactic* order based on a profound new logic. The patriarchs also planned that he would provide their new paternal governance which would enable the complex administration of sixteen outer worlds with another three coming on stream.

And how would he do it?

This is how:

The young prince, it was said, was creating a new communications system based on the telepathic abilities that he, and he only, possessed. He would be its matrix.

The very idea of telepathic communication simply took people's breath away. It would mean the death of the individual consciousness and, with it, any return to tribal, divisional thinking. Humanity would truly become universal. The young prince stood at the opening of a portal to a future of infinite transformation. No longer would man need to rely on technology to expand his horizons. Those mechanisms lay at hand *within* himself.

But there was a mystery. The young prince was kept isolated from view. Only a few people ever visited him. Nobody saw him. The wise patriarchs told everyone that this was to protect the young prince from contamination. They said it was also to protect everyone who lived from the development of the young prince's extraordinary powers. So it was that he grew up, through infancy to adolescence, in an atmosphere within which he was spoken of with awe and reverence.

And, of course, because the young prince remained unseen, many fanciful stories were related about him. Some people said he was painfully beautiful. By that, they meant that even to look upon him was to feel tears at his physical and intellectual perfection. Others said he was so glorious of aspect that he was like a star child. By that, they meant that he had been fathered by the universe itself. There was about him, people said, an extraordinary sweetness. An extraordinary innocence.

One thing, however, was troubling. He never showed emotion. Not a smile or a tear.

3

The woman's story and the story of the young prince now intersect. As I have said before, it is a true story and it will happen soon.

Fourteen years later the woman was old, had reached the end of her capacity as a breeder and therefore the end of her productive life. The notification came that officers of a termination unit would come to collect her at the end of the summer. As she was programmed to this acceptance, she had no emotional response to this decision. Her husband, a worker, had already preceded her the year before. The city he had helped build was completed and awaiting colonists. Her three daughters, however, were still living and had agreed to accompany her to her termination.

One day, the old woman heard the news that the young prince was to visit World 16 to officially open City 1. His visit would also mark the first time the young prince had been seen in public. His arrival would occur an hour before her attendance at the termination unit, and she was pleased that she would be able to be part of the celebrations. She asked the officers of the termination unit if they could take her and her daughters by way of the public plaza where the festivities were to take place. After that, they could escort her to the unit.

By the time the officers, woman and her daughters reached the plaza, it was already crowded. The old woman could only watch from a balcony on the outskirts of the crowd. She saw the young prince's craft arrive and heard the moan of horror when he appeared. The people, so long expectant of a handsome young man, were unprepared for the hideous *thing* that appeared before them. His head was deformed, being extraordinarily large and hydroencephalic. It was of such weight and size that it had to be supported by a collar which acted as a brace to keep it up.

To the old woman, however, the young prince was beautiful. His eyes were so wide open and beseeching. She realised that years ago someone had lied to her. She gave a cry.

The young prince was about to enter the main complex of City 1. He approached the doors. He was about to go through. All of a sudden he paused. Came back. His voice curled across the crowd.

'Someone is looking at me.'

The crowd murmured, astonished. After all, they had *all* been looking at him.

The young prince called again.

'Someone is *looking* at me,' he repeated.

He moved down the steps and immediately everyone in the plaza fell to their knees. The young prince walked this way and that, trying to divine something. He moved further and further from the centre and found himself on the perimeter of the crowd. He saw steps leading to balconies overlooking the plaza. As he ascended, officers of the termination unit came down with an old woman. He stopped them. Like everyone else, the officers and three younger women fell to their knees. The officers forced the old woman down with them.

The young prince knelt beside the old woman and cupped her chin in his hands.

'Someone was looking at me,' he said.

'Yes,' the old woman answered.

She lifted her face to the light. He looked into her eyes and saw that she was just a breeder. The young prince curled his webbed fingers into her hair. A tear dropped silver on his cheek and then, for the first time ever, he smiled. The wise patriarchs, seeing that smile, realised that the breakthrough had been made. What they did not understand — and this is why we will date that encounter as our day of liberation — was that the division they had devised between ruler and worker so many years before, and had sought to perpetuate through the young prince, was over.

'Mother,' the young prince said.

Everywhere, in all the old worlds and new, wherever there was anyone listening, everyone heard his voice.

A KISS BEFORE DYING

Our lovemaking, wife, is disjunctive.

My desire for you is quickened by Empire's ghosts, a postcolonial quest to subvert your orthodoxies. I am Polynesia & I take your lips, an inverted construct. Uncanonical, my tongue probes your imperialistic centre and finds it there in the moist recesses of your mouth.

When I hold you, Desdemona, my arms usurp your space. I seek decolonisation in your embrace, decoding and dismantling of your hegemony. I touch your neck, breastplate & the unprotected whiteness of your thighs. I tattoo you with arabesques, crosshatchings, letterings of spice. Intensely spectral, you cry *ah* to my inscribement black on white, my intent to disempower, deny the main discourse and reconstruct my own prose form. I seek in you to reterritorialise and to dominate.

I am Africa too, wife. Slick with sweat, the White man is my burden. When we kiss I divest myself of him. In the penetrative wounding of sex, I repay with revenge killing and open the way to my own mythic origin. Through you my body is able to seek narrative momentum. The blood, spit, sweat and mucus of our coupling recall his murders, oppression, rape and violation. No virtual reality, no synthesis, can sanitise these memories of destroyed histories.

Desdemona, I am also the Indies. Rage has a prosthetic effect. It turns our lovemaking into vivisection, an impaling, a semiotic rupture & an arrival at the apocryphal moment. At my command you shift, tilt, settle, *yes*.

Wife, our lovemaking is the intersection of body with history. Through it we negotiate headlong issues of race, gender & language.

But within the seductions of closure is also our complicit entanglement.

Desdemona, one kiss, and now another before dying.

197

BEGINNING OF THE TOURNAMENT

GOING TO THE HEIGHTS OF ABRAHAM

Te torino haere whakamuri, whakamua.
At the same time as the spiral is going forward, it is going back.

The Maori people always say we walk backwards into the future. I guess it's another way of saying that wherever we go, we take our past with us. So I want to return to my past again with 'Beginning of the Tournament' and 'Going to the Heights of Abraham'. The past is not behind us. It is before us, a long line of ancestors to whom we are accountable and with whom we have an implicit contract. It's where I draw the line.

Although thirty years separate the two stories, both are a homage to my Dad. As a writer, I am fully aware that if it wasn't for a family to write about or a people to love, I would have nothing to say. So I acknowledge with deep gratitude all those who I belong to — and, in particular, my father. It was he who taught me how to work and the great excitement of pulling the throttle and, just when you thought you couldn't go any faster or do any more, to hit the override button on yourself and go into free fall.

I've written about Dad in my novel *Bulibasha, King of the Gypsies*. He is older now, but he and Mum still farm family land at Waituhi; he centres me and I love spending time with him, moving his cattle and filling his troughs at Waituhi. Dad is the one who taught me to say 'Yes' to life. He honours the past, lives in the present and is so excited about visions of the future which he knows he will never see — but which is the rightful legacy of all his mokopuna to come. I hope when I am his age that I will have his same qualities of generosity, love, unselfishness, mentorship and forgiveness.

Although an international reality may have claimed us all, I return at the end of this collection to where it all began, at Waituhi and with Te Haa o Ruhia Ihimaera Smiler, whom some call Czar. 'Beginning of the Tournament' is another of those stories that people think of as quintessential Ihimaera ('Really liked that story about the hockey match'); it's the kind of Witi-Boy Walton story I used to write when I began my writing career. 'Going to the Heights of Abraham' confirms that the longest relationship I have ever had is with my Dad. At the end of this collection I want to pay tribute to him with these two stories.

After all he was there at the beginning.

BEGINNING OF THE TOURNAMENT

The phone rang just as I got back to the flat. It was Dad, ringing from Waituhi.
'Hello, son,' Dad said. 'Are you coming home for Easter?'

'I'm not sure,' I answered but, even as I said the words, I could sense Dad's
disappointment. 'It's just that I'm broke at the moment,' I continued, floundering
for a reason. 'If you give me a loan, I'll give you the time.'

'A loan?' Dad laughed. 'I'd rather put the money on a horse; at least that way
I'll have a chance of getting my money back.'

'So what's on in Waituhi?'

'The Maori hockey tournament,' Dad explained, offended. 'Surely you haven't
forgotten that it's Waituhi's turn to host. I want you to come home and to help out.
Not only that, but the Waituhi men's team is short.'

'Okay,' I answered.

'Can you bring a mate?' Dad asked. 'When I say our team is short, I mean it's
really short.'

'Don't you worry, Dad. I'll see what I can do.'

Later that day I asked Jerry Simmons if he'd like to come home with me at
Easter. Jerry was a Pakeha mate of mine who was a good hockey player. Actually,
we were university students and had made plans to go with the university ski club
at Easter to Mount Ruapehu. Jerry had visions of pulling a few women.

'Every year the East Coast has a hockey tournament with a dance afterwards,'
I told him. 'The teams come from all over the Bay.'

I could tell Jerry was disappointed at this change in plan. 'I didn't know you
blokes had separate tournaments,' he said.

'For tennis, rugby and golf too,' I answered. 'As far as my family is concerned, though, the hockey tournament is the most important. The supreme trophy in the men's competition is for my grandmother's shield.'

'How big a tournament is it?'

'Well . . . ,' I began, uncomfortably, 'once upon a time the tournament used to attract over fifty teams, but big Maori events have been declining in our area for some time. As more and more people leave for the cities there's less and less people at home. We don't always go back. We're probably down to around twenty-five teams that still arrive for the hockey though. I guess that makes the tournament more important than it ever was. Anyway, you'll see when you get there.'

'I haven't said I'm coming yet! Don't rush me, don't rush me.'

'I've got a terrific looking sister,' I said, giving Jerry a wink. That did the trick. I had told Jerry a lot about Mere and how pretty she was. Anyone would know by just looking at me, that any sister of mine would be pretty: I'm quite a handsome fella myself. But I hoped Jerry wouldn't be too wild with me when he met Mere.

Easter came and, although Jerry moaned about not going to Mount Ruapehu, we started off in the car for Waituhi. It was a long journey and, as I'd been out rather late the night before, I wasn't in the best of moods when Jerry began pestering me about Mere.

'Is she really pretty? Is she really pretty?' he kept asking.

I got so sick of it I couldn't resist teasing him. 'She's terrific,' I answered. 'She's tall for her age, but not as tall as you. Good figure, long legs, eyes that smile right at you, and a mouth that's just waiting to be kissed.'

As I was describing Mere, however, I began to realise, hey, Jerry was a bit of an animal. No *way* would I ever want any woman I knew, no matter what age she was, to even be in the same room with him.

'She hasn't got a boyfriend already, has she?'

'Come to think of it,' I answered, backing off, 'I think there might be somebody who's got his eye on her.'

Did Jerry get the joke? Nah. When he met Mere he gave me a dirty look. She was seven, and Jerry saw her playing with her dolls when Dad opened the door.

'So you came,' Dad said, as if he hadn't been too sure I would. 'I thought you might have been studying too hard or having too good a time down there in Wellington.' My father was like the sky above me, wide open, embracing, filling my life with sunlight. There's so much love between us, and I regretted the earlier hesitation about coming. *Yes, Dad, I was studying hard and having a good time. But you called and I came.*

I forgot all about Jerry until he pounced on me after dinner. 'I should have known better than to trust you! Good figure, huh! Long legs, long hair, a mouth just waiting to be kissed!'

'Easy on! Take it easy, Jerry! I was only joking. Wait. Where will violence get you? Wait! Listen, Jerry! I've got this fantastic looking cousin and . . .'

But Jerry wasn't going to be taken twice. He was really sorry though when he discovered that this time I was actually telling the truth.

The next morning I woke at dawn and went up to the family graveyard to pay my respects to my kuia, Nani Miro. She had died at the end of winter. Somebody had stuck an Ace of Hearts onto her grave, and small windmills whirred brightly with the wind. Then I saw Dad waving from the homestead and went to join him.

'Miro would have been pleased that you came home to help out,' Dad said. 'I've had to take on a lot of the responsibilities she had for Waituhi. And somebody —' he nudged me hard, to make sure I took the hint — 'will have to take it on when I go. Never forget your obligations to your family and to your iwi.'

We had breakfast, I helped Dad sort out the programme for the day and, because Jerry was still sleeping, we left him to get breakfast started for the visitors at Takitimu Hall. Dad stayed there while I went to finish marking up the grounds where the hockey games would be played. By the time Jerry arrived, quite a few of bystanders had joined me and some of the teams were practising. Jerry had polished his boots and put on his socks and shorts. When he saw the hockey grounds he was horrified.

'Is this it?'

'Yes, Jerry.'

'You mean this . . . this paddock?'

'Yes, Jerry.'

An hour later, Jerry was still wandering around, dazed. I'd begun introducing him to the multitude of my relatives and there was not a white one in sight. The buses had started to arrive from Takitimu Hall and the tournament was gradually gaining some semblance of order. A tent had been put up in the paddock, and my Auntie Annie was doing great business selling soft drinks and lollies to the local kids.

'You should have warned me,' Jerry said. He cast a gloomy eye over the crowd. They all seemed to be wearing gumboots or old dresses, balaclava hats, holey jerseys and baggy pants. He knew he looked oh so clean.

Indeed, as one of the men's teams walked past one of them said, 'Ace, man, somebody's brought me a Pakeha to make really *dirty*.'

'Don't take any notice of them,' I said to Jerry as he went even whiter. 'Anyway, you'll be a sure hit with the girls.'

'I can just see it,' he said sarcastically, glancing at the group of little kids who were following him, pointing at him and giggling. But before he could brood any more, the tournament began.

Nani Kepa wandered onto the field, shooed away a couple of cows, and shouted into a megaphone. 'People, would you please remember to close the gate when you come onto the paddock?' he asked. 'Otherwise you're all going to put your feet into some rather embarrassing substances.' He announced that it was time for the Grand Parade.

'What's *that*?' Jerry asked.

'Before the games begin,' I told him, 'all the teams parade around the field and the best-dressed team wins a cup.'

'You've got to be joking.'

'No,' I answered. 'Come on!'

I pulled Jerry over to where the Waituhi men's team was standing. All four of them: Dad, Uncle Hepa, Boy Boy and Hone. Now we were six. We needed five more.

'Mo-Crack will be here any minute,' Dad said. 'He's coming from the pub. Then Frank'll be here after he's dropped Bub at her work. That makes eight, enough for the parade. Come on, boys.'

We followed Dad onto the field where all the other teams were milling: eight other men's teams and sixteen women's teams from the Coast. The women, naturally, were dressed in uniform. One of the men's teams was too. But the rest . . . well . . .

'I feel so con-*spicuous*,' Jerry muttered as we were marching around the field. I couldn't help but agree. Apart from being a head taller than anybody else, Jerry was also the only one with red hair and freckles. Not only that but he was spotless as.

'Hey, Pakeha,' somebody laughed. 'See that cowpat? It's got your name on it.'

Dad consoled Jerry. 'We'll protect you,' he said. Dad turned to me. 'That was a great idea for you to bring such a well-dressed friend with you. With him on our side we're bound to win the parade.'

We all laughed and, by the time the parade had lined up to be judged, Jerry was feeling more at ease.

Nani Kepa and a woman from an East Coast team were the judges. They wandered along the ranks of the women's teams, inspecting the dressage, uniforms and overall appearance as if the women were on military parade. Nani Kepa's eagle eyes darted here and there, making sure that socks had been pulled up to the right length, shirts were tucked in and boots polished and laced properly. Competition for the parade was always a more serious business for the women than the men — and, after all, there was more at stake than just a hockey match. You think these girls had taken hours to glam themselves up just for a walk around a *cow* paddock? Get real. They were here to find boyfriends too or, at the very least, a date for the dance — *and* get that cup and their brief shining moment of stardom.

Nani Kepa and the woman from the East Coast team went into a huddle. They announced the winner. Unfortunately, that winner happened to be the team of which the woman judge was captain. There was great applause from their followers and catcalls from their rivals. 'Favouritism! Favouritism!'

'I must say that *that's* a bit unfair,' Jerry said.

'Actually,' I explained, 'it's a good decision. That team hasn't won for a few years and it's their time this year.'

The judges took less time over the men's teams. The woman judge took a shuddering look at the motley lot and hastened quickly over to the only men's team which was wearing uniforms. However, on the way the clouds opened and the sun blazed down on Jerry in all his flawless glory. That did it. The woman judge came staggering over to our team to make sure that she wasn't having a vision and then pointed a finger at him.

'Oh yes,' she said, taking a closer look. '*You* are most definitely the winner.'

The crowd clapped and cheered. The few derisive hoots were soon booed out of existence.

'But that other team should have won!' Jerry said.

'They always win,' I answered. 'It's about time they lost.'

'No, it's not that,' Dad said, winking at Jerry. 'Didn't you see the way that lady judge was looking at you, boy? You better watch out. She's a man-eater!'

Then Nani Kepa rang the cowbell again, which meant that the games were to start. He announced the first round: a game between two of the women's teams. The fun began. The women began yelling to one another.

'We got enough sticks?'

'Who's worrying about sticks! Worry about whether we got enough players first!'

'Hey, Huria! Put the baby down and come and be our left wing, eh?'

'Which side is left!'

'What about Nani Marama? What about asking her to play for us? She used to be a good player.'

'Yeah, fifty years ago maybe, when she was twenty.'

'Well, she can still stand on her legs and walking stick, can't she? She can be our goalie. So how do you play this game again? I've forgotten.'

'So have I! Hey, Cissie, what's the rules!'

'Don't you girls worry. Look, you hold the stick this way and you try to hit the ball over into the other side's goal. Not that one, that's ours. The other one. See? It's only easy.'

All this time Jerry was just standing there, stunned.

'I don't believe it,' he said, as he saw the women taking the field. About half were dressed in uniforms, so one could assume they knew what they were doing. As for the others, well, Huria was hitching her skirt into her pants, Nani Marama was borrowing Nani Kepa's glasses so she could see where the goal was, and Cissie was still yelling to other girls to come and help out. Among them was my cousin Moana, who was actually supposed to be playing for another team.

'Be a cuz, Moana!'

'But I've left my stick in the bus!' Moana answered.

Jerry came to the rescue. 'You can borrow mine,' he said.

Moana was the fantastic looking cousin I had actually tried to tell Jerry about. Not that I needed to. I saw the way she and Jerry looked at each other and, even though it was a sunny day, I had the uneasy feeling that both had been struck by lightning. It was one thing to introduce Jerry but did I actually want it to go any further?

'What a babe,' Jerry said.

No, no, three times no. 'Don't even think about it,' I warned him.

The game began. It was a match showing all the expertise of military manoeuvres, and the women played it superbly.

If you couldn't reach the ball and a rival player could, you threw your stick at it or her.

If you swung at the ball and missed, you swung again. Whatever you hit, player or ball, it was all the same. If you missed the ball and hit the player, too bad for her. She shouldn't have been in the road anyway.

If you hadn't played the game before and you didn't know what to do when the ball came your way, don't worry about it: just sit on it. Then the referee would blow the whistle and the game would start again.

Not to worry if you got hit yourself. Just remember who it was who hit you and, some time later in the game, hit her back.

See? It was an easy game.

'This isn't hockey,' Jerry said. 'Look at that girl! She's standing way off side.'

'Oh, that's all right,' I answered. 'She's from Waituhi. Nani Kepa is refereeing this game. He's from Waituhi too.'

'But that's favouritism!'

'No it isn't. That other team won last year. It wouldn't be fair . . .'

'I know,' Jerry sighed, '. . . if they win again this year!'

'There's another reason,' I added. 'Nani Kepa actually can't see without his glasses. Wasn't that clever of Nani Marama? I tell you, Waituhi people are cunning as.' I laughed and patted Jerry on the shoulder. 'It's always like this at the beginning, Jerry. After the first rounds are over only the good teams are left, the ones who have really come here to play hockey. As for the rest, well, they've come not just because the game's important but because coming is important. Coming, meeting together, laughing together, having fun together, remembering our family ties, that's what the tournaments are all about. We have to make the most of these few days we have because, afterwards, it's back to work, back to life. Back to —'

Yes, Dad, sometimes I do lose track of who I am and what I am. Pakeha life is so seductive.

At that moment there was a roar from the crowd. The opposing team were approaching the Waituhi goal. Alarmed, Nani Marama yelled out to Nani Kepa:

'Kepa? Hoi, Kepa! You better stop that girl, or else you're sleeping in the cowshed tonight.'

What else was Nani Kepa to do? After all, Nani Marama was his honeybun. He blew the whistle. 'Offside,' he said.

The Waituhi supporters cheered and laughed. The other side started to remonstrate. But Nani Kepa was unmoved. He ordered a penalty hit for Waituhi. Cissie slammed the ball and it sped down the field. Huria picked it up, saw Moana standing in the opposing team's circle, and lifted the ball to her. However, one of the fullbacks fell on it and wouldn't get up.

'Oh, Auntie, please get off the ball,' Moana yelled.

'Nope,' the woman answered. 'And if you hit me, Moana, I'll tell your mother.'

Other women crowded around. Nani Kepa tried to get through to see what was going on. One of the Waituhi women tripped him up — and while he was otherwise occupied, Moana reached under her auntie, picked up the ball with her hands and threw it into the goal.

'Goal!' Cissie cried.

Nani Kepa got up. What was that? Where was the ball? Oh, was that it in the other side's goal? How did it get there!

'Goal,' Nani Kepa confirmed.

This time, a really huge argument began. The coach for the other side came running onto the field to eyeball Nani Kepa. Laughing, Moana and the Waituhi team came back to the middle of the field to wait out the commotion. She looked at Jerry. He looked at her.

'Great goal,' he said.

'Thank you for letting me use your hockey stick,' Moana answered.

'You might even win,' Jerry smiled.

Moana's eyes twinkled. 'Does that really matter?' she asked.

Then Dad was there. 'Well, son, we've made it through to another year,' he said.

I thought of my kuia, Miro, and how she had begun the tournament as a way of keeping up our tribal links, one village with the others. You know: the family that plays together stays together. *And what's going to happen when it's Dad's turn to go and the sky falls down?*

Even so, I smiled at Dad.

'Yes, Dad,' I answered.

GOING TO THE HEIGHTS OF ABRAHAM

My father's voice whispers out of the stomach of the night. *Are you there, son? Are you there?* Although spiders have spun me tightly into my dreams I tear the webs apart to reach for him. *Did I wake you, son?* It's three o'clock in the morning and, yes, he has woken me up but I lie, 'No, you didn't wake me Dad.'

The telephone calls have been coming for over four years now. They come from the family farm just outside Gisborne, far from where I live in Auckland. When they come I look out the window at the moon and I realise that this same moon is also sliding low across our mountain, Maungahaumia, skipping the light like glowing stones into Mum and Dad's bedroom. Mum is asleep but Dad has crept from her side. He has been awake for hours and has gone into the study to telephone me. *I wouldn't have rung you son, but I'm so afraid. Can you help me?*

My father is eighty-seven. How could he have become so old? None of us, my sisters, brothers and I, even noticed when it happened. One minute we were teenagers going to high school and our father had dug a sandpit so we could practise the long jump for our school Sports Day. On that same day he taught us to run in hobnail boots because, according to him, when we took the boots off our feet, we would feel so light that we'd run on the wings of eagles. Somehow or other, between the time when he called a practice run, Ready, steady, go, and the time we ran back to him, laughing and arguing about who had come first, something happened to our God of a father, our laughing, muscled, carelessly handsome Daddy. Somebody took him away and put this other, older, person in his place. Who did this to him? Who turned his hair white, who trapped him in a different body with its musk smells, failing eyes, dry rasping breath and replacement hip? Who gave him all his fearful words, his querulous and frightened imaginings? *I don't want to bother your mother about any of this, son. She's got enough on her own plate as it is.* I grasp for words with which to reply. 'What is it, Dad? Why are you afraid?' *I'm frightened to close my eyes, son. If I close my eyes and go to sleep I mightn't wake up. I've got to stay awake. Will you help me? Will you?*

This is why he rings me, this father whom I love. He doesn't want to close his eyes because if he does Death's dark angel might sneak up on him and grab him unawares. He doesn't want to go because he's afraid to die. So he rings me up and we talk until dawn. He doesn't mind going to sleep in the day because he thinks that Death doesn't come in the daylight. He has old-fashioned attitudes, my Dad. For instance, my sisters and I were often puzzled when we began to have boyfriends and girlfriends that Dad would always insist we were home before midnight. It was my sister Kararaina who guessed the secret. 'Dad thinks that you don't do it, you know, *it*, before midnight.' When I had Dad up about it and suggested to him that you did, or could if you wanted to, he was absolutely disgusted.

My first inklings of Dad's fears about dying came seven years ago, just before he turned eighty. That's when he began to call. In those early days I simply humoured him, telling him he was stupid to have such thoughts, to go back to bed and go to sleep. Then, one early morning, Dad said something which slammed me in the heart. *Did I ever tell you, son, that I've always wanted to see the Heights of Abraham?* His words really broke through my defences and, shivering, I said to Karl, 'I think this is really serious. I think my father's giving up. He wants to die.' Karl calmed me down. 'You've got it wrong,' Karl said. 'Your father wants to go to Canada. He wants to go to Quebec.' I was puzzled and asked, 'Why Quebec?' Karl answered, 'That's where Britain's Major-General Wolfe fought the French during Canada's Anglo-French wars. The battle took place on the Heights of Abraham.'

In a subsequent telephone conversation with Dad I asked him, 'Why didn't you tell me that you wanted to go to Canada!' He answered, *I thought you knew. I've always wanted to go, ever since I learnt about the battle at school when I was a boy.* However, his own words triggered his fears again, reminding him how far ago his school days had been. Where did this capacity to frighten himself come from? He never used to be like this. What first reminded him that the moon was lowering onto the horizon, the tide was turning and ebbing out? Was it my Aunt Helen's tangi? Or three years ago when he buried another younger brother? At every death in the family it has always been Dad who has said, *Oh well*, loaded up the truck with his shovels and gone up to the family graveyard to dig another hole. *Better me to bury my brothers and sisters and cousins, uncles and aunties, than some stranger.* My

Dad has always been the one who digs the graves. What happens when the digger dies? The thought is inconceivable.

So what do you say to a father who is so old and frightened? Four years ago, I had tried laughing it off. Then three years ago I thought being angry with him might do the trick. 'Dad,' I would say, 'I'm tired, I have to go to work tomorrow and I won't talk to you about this. Of course you're not going to die.' I tried diversionary tactics like, 'Why don't you wake Mum up and bother her instead of ringing me up and being such a nuisance.' Or I would say, 'Go and have a cup of tea and watch television.' But there were times when he began to chip away at my resistance and make me afraid and, forgive me, but I let the telephone ring and ring and ring. Then I would get angry with myself for not answering the only telephone in the world that was ringing and I would take the handset off the cradle and say, 'Yes, Dad, I'm here.'

The trouble is I have always thought my Dad was indestructible. This was the father who, no matter his ageing body, I regarded as invincible. Even at fifty he had still been playing rugby. For God's sake, he was still shearing at sixty. I had always been good at playing the game of Let's Pretend as far as my father was concerned. 'Look,' Kararaina scolded me, 'this is your wake up call. Is anybody home? Your father's been growing old for years now. The trouble is that you've been stuck up there in Auckland and never been around to notice it.' True, when you're living somewhere else you think that time only ticks by where you are and not everywhere else.

To complicate matters, Mum rang. 'I think your father is seeing another woman,' she said. 'He gets out of bed in the middle of the night and he goes to telephone her. He thinks I don't know what he's up to. I'm sure it's Mabel,' Mum continued, referring to one of Dad's old girlfriends who must be at least eighty-one, 'Mabel was always after him.'

I reassured Mum. 'It's me that Dad's been ringing.' My mother paused and then her voice came down the line, 'Are you two jacking up some story behind my back?' I answered, 'No, Mum, it's true. Dad rings me up.' Mum was still suspicious, 'What about?' she asked. I answered, somewhat ridiculously, because Dad was the one who should be telling Mum what it was all about, not me, 'It's a male bonding thing.' There was another long silence, then, 'I'll never understand about you and your father,' Mum said.

Son, I'm so frightened, so frightened. It is so difficult to listen to a father calling across the night and to listen to the panic in his voice. *What will happen to your mother when I go? Who will look after the farm?* With surprise I have realised that once upon a time I was the one who used to run to Dad but now he's the one — and he's running to me. I the son have become the father. He the father has become the son. Surely this is not the way it's supposed to be! The father who was always there for me is now the child wanting me to hold him in my arms. The man who hugged me when I won my races is now the boy who needs to be embraced. *See? Wasn't I right about the hobnail boots? You had the wings of eagles, son, the wings of eagles.*

So, two years ago, I tried another tactic. I told him, 'Dad, we all die sometime,' and then, to get his mind off death, I began to tell him how much he is loved in his life because isn't that what people really want to know when they are fearful? I told him he was the greatest father that anybody could possibly have and that he was my best friend. I reminded Dad that his own father had a long life and the likelihood was that he would have the same.

However, any small thing, any newspaper report, any incidental occurrence has surrounded him with darkness and taken him away again into the dread stomach of the night. For instance, the frogs stopped croaking in the dam on the farm. He hadn't heard a weka calling for many nights. Worst was when he read a report that the Department of Conservation had closed Ninety Mile Beach and now you had to have a permit to transit the Beach. *How am I going to get to Te Reinga, son? Will I need a permit so that my soul can fly across Ninety Mile Beach?* He began to rail against DoC and the Maori people of the Far North. *Don't those people up there know they're the kaitiaki, the guardians, and that they're supposed to keep the airways clear for us? You better get me a permit just in case I need it.*

The telephone rings. The sticky threads of the webs are not sufficient to restrain me in sleep, not strong enough to keep me from answering. 'Yes, Dad, I'm here, I'm here.' He begins to talk and I can hear his heart beating in his voice and his lungs breathing air through his words. *So afraid, son, so afraid.*

With a great sense of awe I have come to realise that loving my father in his autumn years has become my greatest gift to him as a son. I never thought it would be like this and that I would have the privilege of being so strong for him. A year ago, listening to my father spinning his fears across the night, I realised with shock, 'I think Dad wants me to save him somehow. But how can I do this? Can anybody combat Death himself?'

But I have figured out a way of at least stalling those dark angel wings.

'But you won't die, anyway, Dad, because we have to go to see the Heights of Abraham.'

And so the questions that my father asks have changed. *When are we going, son? When are we going?* And I have begun to answer, 'Next year, Dad, next year.' At first I made this promise for him. Now I realise, however, that whenever the telephone rings and I hear his voice once again, *Are you there, son? Are you there?*, that I am also making the promise for me as much as for him. Why? Because I need my Dad to keep on holding onto his last breath. As old as I am now, I cannot bear the thought of running back to him on my wings of eagles and not finding him waiting with all his masculine pride and fatherly admiration. God-like, I have found a way of keeping my father alive.

When are we going, son? When are you going to take me to see the Heights of Abraham?

My father's voice reaches through the spider's webs of my dreams. The filaments shiver and are suddenly drenched with dew.

'Soon, Dad. Next year. Yes, let's make it next year.'

ACKNOWLEDGEMENTS

'A Game of Cards' and 'Beginning of the Tournament' first published in *Pounamu Pounamu*, Heinemann Educational Books (NZ) Ltd, 1972.

'The Halcyon Summer' (originally 'Halcyon', *Te Ao Hou*, Maori Affairs), 'The Boy with the Camera', 'This Life Is Weary', 'The Affectionate Kidnappers' and 'The Washerwoman's Children' first published in *Dear Miss Mansfield*, Viking, 1989, reproduced courtesy of Penguin Books (NZ) Ltd.

'The Seahorse and the Reef' (originally 'The Pupu Pool', School Publications), 'Tent on the Home Ground', 'Masques and Roses', 'Big Brother, Little Sister' and 'Truth of the Matter' first published in *The New Net Goes Fishing*, Heinemann (NZ) Ltd, 1977.

'Dustbins' and 'Short Features' first published in *Kingfisher Come Home*, Secker & Warburg, 1995.

'Wiwi' first published in *Below the Surface*, Vintage, 1995.

'A History of New Zealand through Selected Texts' first published in *Writing Wellington*, Victoria University Press, 1999.

'Who Are You Taking to the School Dance, Darling?' first appeared in *crossing: Australian and New Zealand Short Stories*, Reed for Kids/Mammoth, 1995.

'Life and Death in Calcutta' first appeared in Richard Corballis & André Viola (eds) *Postcolonial Knitting: The Art of Jacqueline Bardolph*, Massey University, 2000.

'Life As It Really Is' first appeared in *skins: international indigenous writing*, published by Kegendonce Press and Jukurrpa Books, Canada, 2000.

'Going to the Heights of Abraham' reproduced courtesy of the *Sunday Star-Times 2000 AD Millennium: The Anthology*.

'A New Year's Story', 'A 60 Second Story', 'Someone Is Looking at Me' and 'Falling' first published in this anthology, 2003.